Within These Walls

By

Maaya Brooker

Also by Maaya Brooker

Children's Horror Series:

*The Danger Kids: The Haunted House and Other
Stories*

Dedication

For Nin.

The day was perfect for a wedding. There was barely a cloud in the sky and the breeze was just right; cool enough to stop you from feeling sticky, but not so much that you felt the need to wear a coat. The heat from the sun was ideal too, beams caressing the skin with gentle kisses shining brightly over the olive-green grass which was mowed down so short it could have been green dust. Standing proudly on the lawn like an oracle, was a willow tree, its large frame like a mother's embrace; warm, comforting and full of love. Everything about this scene was perfect. Everything that Anita wanted for her perfect day.

The willow tree was one of the things that had attracted her to the venue. Standing beside it, Anita felt insignificant, unworthy of being in its presence, yet it was welcoming. She knew this was the place; this was where she was going to get married, right under this immense tree that seemed to radiate happiness and joy.

The windows of the building were large, allowing plenty of light to shine through and warm the many rooms inside. The stone and brick walls were kept pristine and stood strong, complimenting the delicacy of the garden surrounding the manor. The steps that led down to the garden were grand, and on either side at the top stood beautifully crafted statues of angels in flight. Just walking down those steps made her feel like a princess. Yes. This was the start of a happy life; Anita felt it in her bones.

She first met Khush the stereotypical Indian way, what she and her sister, Henna, jokingly called the Indian Marriage Directory. A place where somehow Indian parents would 'sign up' to and search for the right match for their child. Anita and Henna would spend hours laughing at the way their parents tried to match them with other 'good Indian boys' based on their jobs, education and of course, family money. But to the sisters, it was just a joke. Until one day, whilst laughing and sifting through the eligible bachelors in Milton Keynes and the surrounding areas, they came across Khush's profile. Anita's laugh caught in her throat, her eyes widened.

"Khush Govind," she giggled as she scanned his profile image, "well hello there."

Khush was handsome. Almost too handsome for words; his skin was what her mother would say, the perfect tone of brown; his eyes were wide and shining with mischief; and his body was something Anita couldn't tear her eyes away from. His shoulders broad, his hair wavy but not long, and he was tall. A perfect man, and perfect husband material.

"Look at him," whispered Henna in Anita's ear as she craned her neck over her sister's shoulder in order to see the profile better, "we have a winner."

"Stop," giggled Anita swiping at her older sister's shoulder as Henna ducked quickly away, "How's he a winner? I'm not even looking and we've only seen his photo."

"That's enough sometimes," said Henna dancing about the childhood bedroom they once shared as teenagers. Draping the light green curtain over her shoulder like a sari and swaying her hips seductively she added, "I see an old-fashioned wedding, grand, bright, full of gold, flowers and goats."

"Goats?" laughed Anita almost falling off her chair watching her sister dance about, "what year are we in? 1890? Marriages don't work like that anymore."

The sisters laughed together. Even though there were a few years between them, they were close. The kind of sisters that spent nights whispering under their covers telling each other their secrets, who they fancied, and which celebrity they'd like to meet and kiss. Anita looked at her sister through scrunched up eyes and smiled. Henna was your traditionally beautiful Indian woman; she was slim, had long beautiful hair and big brown eyes. She spoke fluently in Gujarati with the elders of the community, she was religious (most of the time), she was a mother-in-law's dream. But she was also kind-hearted, clever and very independent. She was perfect, and if she wasn't already married to a brilliant man, her husband of three years, she would probably have suited Khush Govind pretty well. Anita loved her sister to bits. They had their moments when they were younger where they screamed at each other, scratched at each other, and spat venomous insults at one another, but those times were always short lived. No matter how much they fought and bickered, one person always kept them in check and on the same side; their grandmother.

Their grandmother, or 'aajima' as they called her, was a stern and serious lady. She had moved to the UK with Anita's mother and father in the 1970s when there was a major migration of Indians from Africa and India. Anita's aajima, mum and dad had moved to Milton Keynes, buying a three-bedroom house and had been there ever since. Anita's dad had found work as a Civil Servant, he worked for the 'taxman' and took the train into London every day. Anita's mum wasn't educated like her husband, she moved to the UK with only a few high school qualifications and at a very young age, freshly married she needed a job so chose the first one available. She worked tirelessly in a factory, picking and packing for minimum wage, her hours were long and the work hard on her feet, but she never complained. Not once. Anita's aajima stayed at home and looked after the girls when their parents were still at work. As it happened, every other week, Anita's mum worked late, so it was a chance for aajima to teach the girls the Indian way.

For the two sisters, this was hell. Of course, they were proud of being Indian and having an Indian heritage, but aajima always forced it on them and made it sound like it was their duty to behave as she had years ago, first when she lived as a young girl in India, then as a married woman and mother in Kenya.

"You must grow up to be good housewives and mothers," she would say, "and as aajima it will be my honour show you how."

This is how she started all of her 'lessons' with the girls, and each time she uttered these words, the girls would roll their eyes, glance at each other sideways and begin to giggle. Aajima would tut, shake her head, mutter something in her native tongue about 'ungrateful girls these days' and begin her lessons. To her credit, Anita's aajima was a great teacher. The only problem was, she still taught the 'old' way and when the girls complained about this, she would say proudly and with severity, "that's the way I was taught, that's the way I taught very well for years, and that's the way I will teach for the rest of my life."

"Aaji," Henna would add in smiling, "don't talk like that."

"I have to," she would reply looking serious, "I'm old, and won't be around for long, but I will keep teaching you girls. And I will teach your children too."

"Our children?" Anita would add in giggling, "what if I don't want any kids?"

"I don't want any," Henna would say knowing this would wind up their grandmother.

"Me either, no great grandchildren for you aaji," Anita would tease.

Their grandmother would hold her hand to her heart, eyes wide and shake her head, muttering about what would they do if they didn't have children. Henna and Anita would laugh some more and tease their grandmother until she told them off and began the lessons.

Anita's relationship with her family was a good one; built on love, trust and honesty. It was a strong bond, and as much as she always dreamed of getting away from the expectations of Indian tradition, she knew she would never turn her back on her family. Her mum, dad, sister, and even aajima, were everything to her. Her dad taught her how to be independent, strong and challenge the world around her, and her mother taught her kindness, generosity, and compassion. Even her aajima taught Anita so much more than how to fold the perfect samosa.

"What you staring at me all gooey eyed for?"

Anita blinked, her sister's voice invading her thoughts. She giggled turning back to her computer, back to Khush Govind.

"Nothing," said Anita smiling at his broad grin. In his picture he was sipping a beer at some sunny beached holiday.

Henna wandered over the room back to looking at the computer over her sister's shoulder, "So, this one interests you then? When's the wedding?"

Chapter 2.

Eight months before the wedding

Anita sat in the kitchen looking at her phone, her finger hovering over the send button. She'd been here before, about to send a text, thinking and rethinking all the different scenarios that could come from her pressing send; only to move her thumb and delete the message.

Sighing heavily and closing her eyes, Anita placed her phone back on the kitchen counter. She needed a drink. She walked over to the cabinet and picked out her favourite wine glass- a little bigger than the rest- and poured herself a glass of crisp white wine. It wasn't exactly her favourite, but it was the only one she had left in the fridge. The past few weeks had seen her devour more than she normally did. Planning a wedding and dealing with Khush and his random mood swings hadn't been easy, and Anita needed something to help numb the nights. Wine helped. It soothed her, and if she drank enough, it made her feel warm and fuzzy inside too.

Taking a long drink as she closed the fridge door, Anita enjoyed the cool bubbles rejuvenating her mouth and dance down her throat. Swallowing, she sighed and smiled. Turning to her seat, Anita nearly dropped her glass. Standing there was Khush. Watching her. Arms crossed and face furrowed in disappointment. She opened her mouth to say something but nothing came out. Khush shook his head, grabbed a bottle of water from the side and stomped out of the room.

Placing her glass next to her phone Anita sat down. She looked at the message that she had yet to send: *need some advice on Khush, can I come over?*

"Just do it," she muttered to herself as her thumb hovered again over the send icon, "what's the worst that could happen?"

Gulping down the rest of the wine in her glass for courage, she pressed send.

"Done," she said as the message disappeared.

For the next few minutes Anita watched her phone like a hawk. Time crawled on and her nerves began to get the better of her. Maybe she's upset with me for texting? She thought as her fingers tapped on the edge of the counter, a habit that had caused a massive row between her and Khush only a few months into their relationship. She looked at the fridge, itching to have another glass of wine, maybe even finish the bottle. But then Khush's disappointed face appeared in her thoughts. Next time she thought her shoulders sagging.

A shrill ring made her jump. Her phone was ringing. She looked at her screen and panicked: Payal, Khush's sister-in-law, and sometimes Anita's only reprieve in a house of misogynistic men.

"Hello?"

"Hi Anita," Payal's soft singsong voice felt like a much needed hug.

"Hiya, how are you?"

"I'm ok, I got your text about wanting to talk," Payal paused. Anita held her breath. "Well I'm free to chat Saturday morning if you want?"

"Saturday? Yeah thanks," said Anita disappointed that she would have to wait a couple of days, "will you be alone?"

"Yeah, the boys have football and Pritesh will take them."

"Great," said Anita relieved. Having Khush's brother, Pritesh, around was the one thing that had put Anita off from reaching out to Payal before. Pritesh didn't like her, and he made that very clear. He said she was too modern and too 'white' for his brother.

"Say 10 in the morning?" asked Payal.

"Perfect, see you then," said Anita picking at her nails, another habit Khush despised.

"Is everything ok?"

But before Anita could answer she heard a muffled voice on the other side of the phone. A deep voice.

"Ah, nothing," she heard Payal say.

Another muffled sound.

"Ok," said Payal this time louder, "look Anita I need to get going, see you Saturday ok?"

"Yeah, thanks," said Anita, "I'll see-"

But Payal had already hung up.

**   **   **

Saturday arrived and the wait had been hell. The atmosphere with Khush was horrid, no matter what Anita said, or didn't say, did, or didn't do, Khush found a way of making her feel like she was in the wrong. Even when she had spent the whole evening talking to caterers, florists and trying to solve all the issues that came with planning a wedding, Khush had found a way of making Anita feel like she was the cause of all this stress.

As she walked up the pathway to Payal's house she thought about the what she was going to say, and how she would talk to Payal about her brother-in-law. She stood at the front door and knocked. She heard Payal moving around inside and then the sound of the front door unlocking. The smile on Anita's face froze as she looked up at the looming frame in front of her. Pritesh.

"Oh," she whispered.

"Expecting my wife?" Pritesh asked a sneer spread across his face.

"Yeah," said Anita pausing to control her voice, "we were just meeting to have a catch up. Where is she?"

"Football with the boys," he said. Then turning and walking into the house he added, "come in, you can catch up with me."

She followed Pritesh in silence through to the kitchen where she watched him rummage through the cupboards. *Like you know where anything in this kitchen is* Anita thought to herself, allowing a small smile to escape her lips.

"Wine?" he asked glancing over to where Anita was sitting.

"What?"

"I asked if you wanted wine."

"Oh, it's 10am."

"So?" said Pritesh turning to face Anita, "Khush said you liked wine."

The comment hung in the air clinging to Anita's skin and making her uncomfortable. Anita stared, unable to form words. Something about being around Pritesh always made her uneasy. They had never gotten along and he intimidated her and seemed to enjoy doing it.

"So? Wine?" he asked again waving an empty wine glass at her.

"No thanks," said Anita, "nothing for me."

"No tea or coffee either?"

"No thanks, Pritesh."

"You know it's insulting to come to my house and then refuse a drink," he said his smile all gone.

"Oh, sorry," said Anita, her face flushed, "just some water then please."

Anita sat in silence as she watched Pritesh pour her a glass of water. His movements were deliberately slow, as if he was waiting for a reaction from her. Or for her to start the conversation. She tried to keep calm and controlled. Said nothing.

"There," said Pritesh placing the beverage in front of Anita, a forced smile on his face.

He watched intently as she took a sip. The air became thick and heavy. Pritesh revelled in how uncomfortable he was making Anita. Finally, he spoke.

"Payal said you were coming," he said his voice gravelly and serious.

"Oh, yeah, we were just going to catch up, really," mumbled Anita.

"I think," he said leaning in close, "I think you came here to bitch about my brother,"

"No," said Anita meekly, "just girl talk."

"Liar," his voice was hard, "you came to my house to talk to my wife about my brother."

"No, I didn't-"

"Don't lie," he barked making Anita flinch, "so what's the problem with my brother?"

"Nothing, we just argued about something for the wedding," said Anita scrambling for something to say to Pritesh that wasn't going to get him angry again.

"Clearly it wasn't nothing if you decided to come to my house and bitch to my wife."

"No, I just needed someone to talk to," said Anita tears welling up in her eyes.

"And you thought my wife was the right choice?"

"I didn't mean to-"

"I think you'd better leave," said Pritesh standing suddenly and taking the glass of water from Anita's hand. "Go home, stop bitching about my brother over nothing, and carry on planning the wedding the way you should. Be a better fiancée for my brother and stop talking to everyone about silly arguments. Especially when you paint my brother as in the wrong when you clearly are."

Anita sat there gobsmacked and confused.

"Please leave," said Pritesh menacingly, "now."

Anita grabbed her bag and stumbled out of the kitchen. Her confusion mirrored in her inability to open the front door. Pritesh leaned over her, his breath hot against her now tear stained cheek.

"You're not good enough for my brother or my family," he whispered in her ear as she bolted out of the house.

Chapter 3. Wedding Day

Anita looked nervously across the manor garden and the guests all waiting for the wedding ceremony to start, then back at her sister who was applying lipstick to her perfectly shaped lips. Henna looked stunning as usual, in a deep plum sari glittered with silver embroidery that flickered and shone with every movement. Her slim figure was accentuated by the way the sari was draped over her shoulder and across her torso, and her bangles lightly tinkled as she moved her hands. There was something about a sari, bangles and the traditional Indian jewels that could make any plain looking girl look like a movie star, and Anita was stunned at how magnificent her sister looked; like she had just walked out of a fashion shoot.

"What?" her sister said as she looked at Anita in the mirror reflection. She smiled and pouted, dabbing at her her lips, "too much?"

"God no," said Anita moving away from the window and towards her sister, "you just look, wow. Ash is a very lucky man."

"Yes he is," smiled Henna, taking Anita's shoulders and gently moving her to the full length mirror in front of her, "but he knew that when he married me. Today's not about me. It's about you. How are you doing sis?"

Anita nodded as she looked at herself in the mirror. Instead of her usual straightforward simple self, a look the 24 year old had cultivated, there was this glamorous woman looking right back at her wearing a nervous expression she knew as her own. Even with all the arguments and mocking about traditional 'good' girls Anita shared with her friends and sister over the years, looking at herself there and then, it was obvious she had made the right decision to have an Indian wedding. The elaborate and expensive pageantry wasn't what she desired the most from the ceremony, it was the spiritual feeling and the deep meaning behind the stages of the wedding ceremony that had lured her into going against her rebellious ways and succumbing to the rituals.

Her eyes flickered down to her hands; they were elaborately patterned with mendhi, not too much like the pictures she had looked at of her mother's very conventional wedding, but subtle and delicate so that she wouldn't eventually look like she had drawn on her own hands with an orange felt tip pen. Her nails, usually short and void of any colour, were deep red with tiny golden gems on. On her wrists hung dozens of gold and red bangles, all neatly patterned and glittering. She moved her hands and they jingled melodically making her smile. She was wearing a deep red, almost maroon coloured sari with heavy gold embroidery; a statement- *she* was the bride today. The sari draped around her shoulders and her waist, for once making them seem more feminine and delicate than usual; it was amazing to see how something so simple as wearing a sari could transform her whole look.

Casting her eyes back at her face in the mirror, Anita confessed to herself that everything about her today was typical. Even her make-up was typical; usually she would wear minimal make up, the odd eyeliner and mascara with some light blusher and natural eyeshadow, her lips, barely touched other than some rose coloured lip balm. But today, it was full on. Her lips matched her nails, a deep red with a touch of golden shimmer, her eyes coloured with gold and maroon eyeshadow that swept across her eyelids dramatically, and mascara and eyeliner accentuating her deep dark irises. Anita had on the most intricate bhindi that she had ever seen, and it was just as heavily decorated and pretty, as her sari was. She looked beautiful. For once, Anita saw someone that was worthy of her life partner, and hoped that Khush would approve.

Today she was ready to get married.

A knock pulled Anita out of her own thoughts, it was her mum peering her head around the door, "Ready my girls?" she asked with a big wide grin.

Stepping into the room she gazed lovingly at her two daughters standing side by side in front of her. Anita's mum looked just as beautiful as her daughters did; matching Henna's colour scheme, she wore a silver-grey sari with deep purple embroidery and gems, her hair was up in a messy bun with further glittery embellishments placed in to make her look just the perfect part of Mother of the Bride. Her face glowed with peachy cheeks, purple eyes and her signature red lips. The three of them smiled at one another and then carefully embraced.

"Oh, watch the hair," said Anita as she almost tangled herself up against her mum, "don't want to have to sit for another hour while it gets fixed."

"Yes," said her mum grinning and shaking her head, "I wouldn't want to watch you squirm and fidget like a two-year-old again. That was painful."

Anita giggled, "It took so long though."

"Typical," said Henna rolling her eyes and laughing, "Right, how long do we have to wait now mum?"

"Not a minute more," said a deep voice from the doorway. It was Anita's dad, and just like the women in his life, he looked handsome and breath-taking today. "They are ready for your entrance m'lady."

As the family left the room, Anita saw her uncle standing there with his hand out towards her and smiling proudly. As in most traditional Indian wedding ceremonies, it was customary for the maternal uncle or uncles to walk the bride down the aisle, not the father. But as was the way with Anita, she made a slight change. There was no way that she wasn't going to be holding on to her father's arm as she walked down to the wedding canopy; even with arguing with her aajima and mum, and disappointment and annoyance from her future father in law and Khush, she had decided that she wanted both her dad and her uncle to walk her down the aisle. She got her way, as usual. She took her uncle's arm in one hand and her dad's in the other, she looked at her sister and mum as they began to walk away to take their places.

"Wait," she called to them. They turned around and looking worryingly at her, "how am I supposed to hold my sari up whilst walking so I don't fall over?"

Her mother and sister began laughing at this ridiculous dilemma, and as they turned and walked away again, her sister replied in a mock accent, "Like a lady, Anita, just like a good Indian lady."

Chapter 4. Wedding Day

Her father and the owners of the venue had decorated and set up the canopy exactly as Anita had hoped and drawn out on her detailed sketches. The four pillars were sturdy and wrapped with golden material that shimmered as the sun shone on them, and cascading from one pillar to the next were small crystal-like spheres that would reflect light in a way that would make the scene magical. In the centre of these four pillars in where the rituals would take place, stood two grand, red and gold chairs where the bride and groom would eventually sit. Beside the stone pit in the middle, where a fire would be lit and the ceremonial prayers would take place, was a spot for the priest; a younger than expected man who would deliver the sermon, translate for all of the non-Gujarati speaking guests, and wed the couple, all in Anita's pre-planned directed time of one hour.

Anita's mother had argued that it wasn't enough time for the full ceremony but once they had taken out all the unnecessary hymns, games that were played by the two joining families throughout the ceremony, and the pomp, she had managed to persuade her mum that the actual wedding, would be done perfectly in one hour. Anita had made it clear she wanted everyone to be quiet and to be listening to the vows and the rituals, having a priest who could translate it all so everyone understood what was happening, made it much easier to win this argument.

The doors opened at Anita's feet, her nerves soothed somewhat by her uncle and dad squeezing her arms. Her dad leaned in, whispering "you look beautiful. I am so proud of you Anita."

"Thanks dad."

"I love you so much, you are perfect."

"Dad, stop or you'll make me cry," whispered back Anita blinking away tears that already formed.

"Just keep smiling beta, you're the centre of attention today."

Anita looked at her dad and they shared a loving smile. Everyone there was watching her, she wasn't prepared for all the eyes, all the smiles and all the attention directed towards her at that moment. She smiled at the faces but couldn't quite make out who everyone was, they all looked like blurs shimmering as she walked on by.

Anita stole a glance towards the man who would be changing her life forever and found that a golden blanket had been held up blocking him from view. She looked at Henna and her sister had clocked this stolen glance and smiled. It was also part of Indian wedding rituals that the groom and bride were not able to see each other until their hands had been joined by the priest. Anita always joked with her family that this was done 'back in the day' so that one of the parties wouldn't be able to run away if they didn't like the way their betrothed looked. But now, as it was happening to her, she realised it also added to the romance, to the excitement, and to the butterflies she was already feeling fluttering inside of her.

Carefully sitting her down in her chair, her father and uncle both kissed her forehead softly and muttered a blessing for her. Anita closed her eyes to try and hold back her tears, she was so happy and couldn't believe this was happening. Keeping her head facing forward, she avoided looking at her family all sat beside her as she knew if she looked at any one of them, she was going to either laugh uncontrollably, or begin to cry. Something she knew everyone from Khush's side would tut about. *Be more composed* she thought to herself.

She vaguely listened to the instructions and what the priest was saying as she stared intently at the blanket still held up in front of her, obscuring her view. The only thing she could see were his hands clasped together on his knees; knees that gently knocked together in the nervous twitch she had grown to love.

The priest gently took her hand from her lap and brought it to the base of the sheet, with his other hand he brought over his hand. Anita held her breath and watched with wide eyes as the priest placed her hand in his. It felt like the first time they had touched, sparks and a tingling sensation at her fingertips. At once Anita realised that her palms were very sweaty, all her nerves and anxiety about the day seemed to manifest itself into her hands, making her palms clammy and hot. Her hands were also shaking, or was that because his hands were shaking as he held on to hers? Anita couldn't tell but it felt like the moment of all the build-up and anticipation was about to come to a head and burst, she lifted her head up and from the corner of her eye she noted the priest asking for the cloth to be dropped. She held her breath. This was it. Her moment, her life, her decision to marry the man of her dreams. All very real now.

As the cloth dropped Anita blinked and in an instant there she was, face to face with the man who had changed her life forever, the man she had giggled with her sister only two years earlier- Khush Govind. His face was as perfect as it was the first time she'd spotted him. As their eyes met, for what felt like the first time, he smiled at her, his big wide grin showing off his perfect white teeth and his eyes twinkled. The crowd clapped and cheered, and Anita could hear herself laugh quietly as her sister's voice called to her to smile.

"Hey," he whispered rubbing his thumb gently on her hand.

"Hey back," she replied looking at him properly for the first time.

He was wearing the groom's suit, cream and gold trousers with a long matching tunic on top, gold embroidery; not as dazzling or as heavy as the bride's but still as elegant. On his head Khush had decided to wear a traditional headdress to finish off his look.

"You look amazing," said Anita her smile getting wider as she looked him over.

"You look…" he said his eyes casting over her face, sari and hands, "you look, just wow. So beautiful."

Anita smiled shyly, the way she always did whenever Khush gave her a compliment. He had a way of making her feel like she was the only person he could see, even if they were in a room full of people. It felt just like that now, in a serene garden, under a willow tree, next to a grand manor and surrounded by all their friends and family, one wink from Khush, and Anita felt like it was just the two of them, alone and in secret. She wanted that moment to last forever.

Chapter 5.

1 year before the wedding

Anita was nervous. She stood in the hallway feeling her clammy skin stick to her blouse and the taste of bile creeping into her mouth as she waited for her future mother-in-law and father-in-law to knock on the door. Licking her dry lips, Anita breathed deeply; she wasn't looking forward to this meeting of her parents with Khush's. Her nerves were getting the better of her and her mind was going into overdrive- what if they didn't like her parents? What if they didn't think they were good enough for their son? What if her parents didn't like her future in laws? So many things could go wrong; she could say something stupid, her sister could make an inappropriate joke, her aajima could reveal how old fashioned and backwards she could be. A flurry of different scenarios flashed through Anita's mind, and if she was being completely honest, all of the worrying scenarios involved her family embarrassing her in front of Khush's family.

"Hey," said Henna tapping her on the shoulder, making her squeal and jump.

"You scared me," said Anita rubbing her hands across her hot face.

"Sorry," said Henna grinning at how nervous her usually confident sister was, "you alright nervous nelly?"

Anita nodded and swallowed hard.

"Look, it'll be fine. Mum and dad have been through all this before with Ash's family. They know what they are doing. They'll be fine, you'll be fine."

Anita nodded, "I just want it to go smoothly, you know?"

Henna nodded as she and Anita walked into the kitchen where her mum was preparing snacks for their guests imminent arrival. She grinned as she popped a bhaji into her mouth, "So why did you invite me then?"

Their mother slapped Henna's hand and scowled, "those are not for you Henna, they are for our guests."

"Just doing the taste test mum," said Henna winking at Anita and making her smile.

"Let her have one, Bina," said Anita's aajima waving a hand at their mother.

"If you want to help," said Anita's mum ignoring the grinning old lady in the corner, "go and check the living room."

"I'll help you," said Anita turning to follow her sister.

"Wait," said her mother, "I want to speak to you."

Sighing, Anita turned to face her mother and aajima. Her mother was now wiping plates and the cutlery clean.

"Mum, I'm ok. I know this is important, don't worry, I won't mess this up," said Anita trying to prevent the 'good Indian girl' speech that she knew was coming.

"That's not what I wanted to say, beta," said her mother smiling softly.

Her grandmother's voice cut in, "I think you need to change into something more respectable, Anita. Maybe put on a sari or Punjabi suit or something…more Indian."

Both Anita and her mother turned to face her aajima who was looking at what Anita was dressed in.

"Mum," said Anita's mum.

"Bina, she should be wearing something better that jeans and a blouse," insisted her aajima.

"No," said Anita's mum putting a supportive hand on her daughter's shoulder, "she wears what she wants. She must be comfortable. And she looks great."

"Thanks mum," said Anita her voice small.

"Bina, I really think she should change."

"No more of that now mum," said Anita's mum giving her mother in-law a hard stare, "she is fine, she is nervous, we should be calming her."

Anita's grandmother tutted and walked out of the kitchen.

"What I wanted to say," said her mum turning to Anita, "is, be yourself. You don't have to be nervous. You and Khush love each other and respect each other. His family love you. Don't worry everything will be fine."

Anita smiled and closed her eyes and ignored the pang inside her at her mother's comment about Khush's family. Her mother's soft hand on her forehead calmed her instantly and quietened her mind.

"Thanks, mum."

"You're welcome, beta."

A knock on the door made the pair turn their heads.

"Go answer the door," said her mother taking off her apron and smoothing down her sari, "before your sister does."

"Come in," said Anita as Khush, his mum and dad stepped into the house, "make yourselves at home. Come into the living room."

Anita stood aside, smile plastered on her face, as her future in-laws walked down the corridor and into the living room, their eyes taking in their surroundings like an inspector looking for revealing clues. Watching Khush's dad 'accidentally' slide his fingers across the banisters and discreetly check his fingers for dust or dirt made her bristle.

She looked over at Khush who pretended not to see the exact same thing. She looked at his face, his smile always made her feel warm. She leaned in towards him to give him a kiss, but

Khush pulled away. Startled, Anita looked at Khush. His refusal to look at her or kiss her stung.

"Not with my parents around," he hissed as he brushed past her, "remember you need to make a good impression."

Feeling like she had been slapped in the face, she bit her lip and closed the front door. *This is going to be fun* she thought to herself. She followed the others into the living room and stood by her father as she had been instructed to do by Khush the day before and her aajima that morning.

"Chai? Pani? Coffee?" her aajima asked, and without waiting for a reply she looked at Anita and nodded.

Too nervous and still thrown by Khush's rejection, Anita looked blankly at her grandmother.

"I'll get it," said Henna quickly moving to the kitchen.

Anita caught the look that passed between her future mother and father in-law. Khush saw it too. He turned to Anita.

"Shouldn't you go in to help your sister?" he said forcing a smile with no warmth to it. His voice had an edge to it Anita feared to hear.

"What?"

"Your sister, help her," said Khush frowning and shaking his head in disbelief.

Still confused Anita frowned, "it's just water."

The sound of Khush's dad sucking in breath and tutting echoed throughout the shrinking living room, casting a chill in the room.

"Anita beta," said her dad softly touching her arm, "can you get the snacks please?"

Anita noted the pleading tone in his voice and realised she was the one embarrassing the family. She jumped into action and left the living room, her face hot and her eyes wet.

"Shit. Shit. Shit." Anita muttered as she walked into the kitchen and picked up the plates.

"Don't worry," said Henna sympathetically as she held a tray of drinks.

"I should've realised," said Anita shaking her head in frustration, "shit."

"It's ok, shhh," said Henna, "grab the food and plates and come into the living room now."

"I just didn't think," she said noticing her hands were shaking, "mum and dad never ask us to do the serving just because we're girls, I just didn't think. Shit!"

"Shh," said Henna more sternly now, "let's go in there and change the direction this visit is going ok?"

Anita nodded, took a deep breath and followed her sister out of the kitchen. As she neared the living room she heard her name.

"...Anita is allowed to use such language in front of her elders?"

Anita slowed and listened to the comments Khush's dad was making. Her sister slowed too.

"Oh, she doesn't normally," stammered her dad shooting a nervous look towards the kitchen, "I think she is just nervous."

"No way for a girl to speak," Khush's dad continued shaking his head, "she needs to be taught how to behave respectfully."

Anita's breath caught in her throat. Taught how to behave? Use such language? She felt her grip tighten and her panic was washed away and replaced with frustration. She straightened her shoulders and walked into the living room, stopping any further discussion instantly.

**   **   **

Awkward silences with strained conversation dragged out the next two hours. The sound of chewing and clinking of glasses against table tops and spoons against plates echoed throughout the room and Anita was certain everyone could hear her heart beating and heavy breathing.

"You have a lovely home Bina," said Khush's mum, breaking a wave of silence once everyone had finished eating.

"Thank you Lekha," said Anita's mum nodding and smiling proudly.

"Yes," added Khush's dad looking around, "it's small but charming don't you think? Suitable."

Anita shot Khush a look, but was only offered a small shrug in response. She looked at her mum who looked liked she had been punched in the stomach, her face pale and wide eyed. Henna bit her lower lip and frowned.

"I love it," said Anita forcing a lightness to her voice, "it's a perfect family home."

"Yes," said Henna through gritted teeth and picking up the plates to take into the kitchen, "it's been a home full of lots of love and respect." The last words were punctuated with a clash of plates being stacked.

"I like a smaller home," said Khush's mum trying to ease the tension, "easier to clean!"

"Very true Lekha," said Anita's mum smiling softly at the attempted joke.

Khush's mum placed a warm hand over Anita's mum's hand and laughed awkwardly. The two mother's shared a knowing look.

"Well," snapped Khush's dad, clearly unhappy his wife had contradicted him, "we should go now. Khush, Lekha, let's go."

"Let me help Bina clear all this up," said Lekha reaching to pick up a glass.

"She has two girls to do it. Let's go."

As Khush's dad rose and turned to leave the living room, Anita's dad stood up too.

"It was nice to meet you both, Lekha and Akash," he said opening his arms for a hug, "I'm looking forward to us all being one family."

"Yes, yes," said Khush's dad twisting his body so to avoid the hug and extended his arm for a handshake, "a family."

Anita watched in horror as her parents continued to smile and say their goodbyes to Khush, his dad and his mum as they left the room. Her blood boiled at the total disrespect Khush's dad had shown towards her family. She grabbed Khush's arm as he walked past her.

"Khush," she began.

"That was embarrassing," he said frowning at her and pulling his arm away, "you embarrassed me."

"What?" Anita stood open mouthed.

"You messed up, all you had to do was behave and be respectful, and you couldn't even do that. You embarrassed me."

"Wait, what?"

"We'll talk later," he said and stormed past.

Chapter 6.

The honeymoon period was over in a flash, and married life wasn't as blissful as Anita had been promised. Living with her in-laws until her and Khush found the 'perfect home' certainly didn't help. Being constantly around her now father-in-law, Anita was always walking on eggshells, making sure she said the right thing and did the right thing. She had to make sure she 'behaved respectfully' and was told on a few occasions to 'act like a good daughter-in-law should. All rules were dictated by her tyrannical father in-law, and Anita learned quickly that Khush was not going to support her at all. Every day she spent in the house, the more she became desperate to leave. She became determined to broach the subject of buying a home of their own with Khush, even though she knew it could upset him- depending on his mood at the time.

"It's not that bad," said Khush one evening after Anita had been asked to iron everyone's clothes following a long day.

"For you," Anita muttered massaging her sore neck.

"What are you saying?" said Khush facing her, his voice hardening.

Anita turned to look at Khush and suddenly her neck didn't feel sore. She shook her head and sat on their bed.

"Nothing."

"What's so wrong with living with my family?"

"Nothing, I just want a place for ourselves."

"We need to save first."

"I know," said Anita tiredness kicking in.

"It's not like you're helping."

Anita looked at Khush, his words a slap across her face.

"That's not fair, Khush. You know I'm saving as much as I can. I just don't earn as much as you do. Everything I can, I put into savings."

"And I'm not trying?"

"You are Khush, you're doing so much and I appreciate it all," said Anita trying to diffuse the tension building in the room.

"Back off then Anita," said Khush walking towards their bedroom door to leave, "it's still better than living with your family."

Anita bit her lip as the bedroom door slammed shut behind Khush. Her hands were in fists and her whole body was rigid. This is how a simple conversation with Khush could end up; Khush dismissive and walking away and Anita tense, angry and no way of expressing herself without a blow up.

"Fuck," she said to herself, "fuck you Khush. My family wouldn't treat anyone as a second class citizen just because they were female. I wish I was there instead."

**   **   **

Anita looked at the front door and sighed. The urge to stay in her car for longer was overwhelming but she knew her father in-law watched for her arrival home after work each day, so he could start giving her jobs to do around the house. The curtain twitched, he knew she was home. With heavy feet and a sadness in her heart she never thought she would experience with family, Anita made her way through the door.

"Anita is that you?" her father-in-law's voice boomed through the house.

You know I'm home. You watched me from the window, Anita thought bitterly, "yes papa-ji I'm home," she said wincing at having to call him papa- an affectionate name she only ever called her own loving father. It was another thing he insisted she do whilst living in their home.

"Good," he said appearing out of the living room, "it's time to make dinner."

"What would you like?" Anita slowly took off her coat and shoes still feeling a pressure on her shoulders.

"I don't care, I am not eating."

"Oh?" Anita turned to look at her father-in-law, "is everything ok?"

"Yes," he said turning to walk back into the living room, "I am not hungry."

Anita nodded. She looked at the kitchen where her mother in-law was sitting waiting for her. She walked past the living room holding her breath.

"Anita," his voice scratched at her nerves.

"Yes papa-ji?"

"Go get changed first."

Anita spun around and trudged up the stairs. As well as dictating what she did in the house, what she called everyone in the house, and what happened in the house, Anita's father-in-law also insisted that whilst she was under 'his roof' she needed to look the part of an Indian wife too. She was instructed to get changed out of her 'westernised' clothes after she finished work, and change straight into a simple punjabi suit. At first she had argued and tried to put her case forward but without any support from her mother-in-law or her husband, Anita's argument had fallen on deaf ears. Standing in front of the mirror looking at her thin face and the dark circles under her eyes, Anita held back tears. She pressed a stick-on bindhi on her forehead, tied her hair back into a plait and looked at the stranger in front of her.

Come on Anita, she thought to herself, *just a few more months of this and you and Khush can get out of here. No more backwards rules or misogynistic talk you have to put up with. You can do it.*

Anita walked into the kitchen and smiled at her mother-in-law; she had begun to soak the rice for their dinner.

"What would you like for dinner?" Anita asked her.

"Something simple, no hassle, please," her mother-in-law could tell Anita was tired and in no mood to cook a typical all the trimmings meal that her own husband expected on a daily basis, "papa-ji isn't eating, so we can all have some biriyani. Is that ok?"

"Sure, I can do that," said Anita moving to the cupboard.

"Lekha," called a voice from the living room, "let her do it. She needs to learn. You come in here with some chai, why else did we get a daughter in-law?"

Anita shook her head at the comment, one she was used to hearing now, and her mother in-law rolled her eyes.

"Coming Akash," she said as she wiped her hands on a towel and picked up two mugs of hot tea she had just made.

No tea for me then? Thought Anita feeling a scream build up inside her.

**   **   **

Her hands felt sore and her back ached, but Anita knew she needed to clean up the kitchen and the dinner dishes before she would be allowed to sit in the living room with her new family.

"Hey," said Khush as he passed her some dirty plates at the kitchen sink.

"Hey."

"Dinner was great."

"Thanks."

"Dad missed out."

"Yeah."

"What's wrong?" Khush pulled her towards him.

"Just tired," said Anita her eyes welling up and her body tensing at his touch.

"Are you sure?"

"Yeah…I'm sure, just tired. Glad you liked dinner."

"It was great."

"Fancy helping me clean up?"

Khush's eyes widened and he laughed awkwardly. He looked around the room and picked up a tea-towel.

"I'll help dry the dishes but that's all, I got stuff to do."

Stuff like sit around the living room with your dad and do nothing?

"That's fine, thanks," she said turning back to the dishes, "can you put them away too please?"

"I don't know where anything goes," said Khush his voice showing an edge of annoyance, "I'll dry up to help, but that's all. There's not a lot left for you to do anyway."

Anita continued with her work in silence. A few minutes later and Khush left the kitchen, he had dried the dishes, and left them on the counter for her to put away, the tea towel he used sat crumpled on the side. Anita shook her head and tidied everything up. She didn't want her father in-law to find anything to complain about…although she knew he always found something.

"Anita," his voice still made her stiffen with unease.

"Papa-ji, I've just finished cleaning," Anita said.

"Yes, I can see that," he said looking around the room, "Anita, I am hungry now."

"Oh," said Anita standing facing her father in-law, mouth dry, "I can warm up some biriyani, there is some leftover."

"I don't want that," he said folding his arms.

"Oh."

"I would like some paratha please."

Anita blinked. She wasn't sure she had heard him correctly. She looked down at her hands which were hanging limp by her sides.

"Sorry?"

"I would like some paratha please."

"We don't have any," whispered Anita her throat dry.

"Then make me some," he snapped, his eyes burning into hers, "you do know how to don't you?"

Anita nodded, her body trembling with fatigue and defeat, only muscle memory kept her legs from folding underneath her.

"Good," he nodded as he left the kitchen, "don't be too long."

Chapter 7.

Rising from her deep sleep, Anita could feel the heat of the morning already intruding into her bedroom. Outside the sun was shining brightly and she could hear the birds singing again. Just one morning. That's all she wanted, one morning without being woken up by the screeching sounds of the birds.

She screwed her eyes shut again and groaned. It was too early. She turned over in her bed kicking the duvet off her feet which felt like they had been soaking in a steam bath and reached out. Nothing there. She opened one eye and looked at the empty half of her bed.

"Khush," she called, her throat dry and scratchy from the heat, "hon, where you at?"

Nothing. No sound. No movement.

Anita lifted her head up and strained her ears to listen out for noises around their newly bought house, still nothing. That's strange she thought, where is he? She got up out of bed, tidied up the duvet just as Khush liked, and plodded into the bathroom.

"Khush," she called again, "Khush. Where are you?" As Anita walked out of the bathroom, she stepped on something sharp, "ouch, damn."

Suddenly more awake now that something was in her foot, she looked down at the carpet and what she had trodden on. Anita looked further down the hallway and smiled, a small trail of orange and yellow rose petals led a path down the stairs and into the kitchen. Shaking her head and calling out to her husband again, Anita followed the trail into the kitchen, making sure not to step on any stray thorns she saw along the way. This was the beauty of having a home to call her own.

Walking into their kitchen Anita saw a beautifully set out table, with two roses, one orange and one yellow, in the middle. On either side of the roses were two plates with knives and forks. A big steaming mug of sweet tea sat in what had become Anita's spot, and an equally big mug of coffee opposite. Smiling, Anita looked over to where her husband sat with a card and present in his hands.

"Happy anniversary," said Khush grinning from ear to ear, "Love you."

"Aw, love you too," said Anita walking over to him and giving him a long deep kiss on the lips, "all this for me?"

"Of course it is. I don't care much about anniversaries, do I?"

Anita's smile wavered, "and that?" she said pointing at a wrapped box in his hands.

"For you, beautiful wife of mine," he said handing her the gift as she sat down in her seat, "would madam like some waffles for her anniversary breakfast?"

"Mmm, please," she said unwrapping her gift.

"Chocolate sauce? Berries?" he added.

Anita looked over at him and nodded.

It had been two years since their fairy-tale wedding and Anita was happy. She was married to Khush who showered her with gifts and affection. They had a lovely home, albeit too close to her parents place according to Khush. They had jobs they loved; Anita a trainee psychologist, something she had wanted to do since she was a little girl and had worked very hard to achieve, and Khush, a well-established dentist in a private practice, in London. They had very few friends they spent time with, family they loved and saw often, and each other. Anita's life felt complete.

"Thank you for the flower trail," Anita mumbled through a mouthful of waffle.

"Oh Anita, manners," said Khush with a mix of playfulness and scolding which weighted heavily on the side of that telling off she used to get from her aajima.

He hated seeing her talk with her mouth full, a habit he had tried to nag out of her since day one.

"Sorry," Anita said, waiting to continue speaking until she had finished what was in her mouth, "I said, thank you for the flower trail, it was sweet of you. Although I did step on a thorn."

Anita winked at her husband who was eating his waffles and drinking his coffee. Looking at his reaction Anita realised she had instantly made a mistake in joking about the thorn.

"What?" he said frowning again.

"Oh nothing, don't worry, I was just joking." Anita said quickly, forcing a smile.

"No, what did you say? You found a thorn on the flower petals?"

"Yeah, but don't worry, it didn't hurt that much. Easy mistake to make when you are doing it all quietly and it's such a sweet gesture, don't worry. I shouldn't have said anything."

"But you did."

"I know, but I shouldn't have, sorry hon. Forget it."

"How can I forget it? I did all this for you because you like celebrating anniversaries, birthdays and all that stuff, and all I get in return is a complaint about one little thorn."

Anita could feel the tension building in the room, too often their conversations went from friendly to hostile so quickly. She needed to calm the situation down otherwise this day would be completely ruined.

"No, no, no complaint at all. Just a silly joke. Sorry shouldn't have mentioned it. Leave it, forget I said anything, let's enjoy the lush breakfast you've made. Thank you so much for all this, it's so romantic."

Khush looked at his wife in a way that made her squirm in her seat, like being reprimanded by a head teacher or her aajima, "fine. I just wanted to do something special for our two years together. To show you how much I love you. I thought you'd like it."

"I do, I do like it. I love it. So thoughtful honey, such a lovely thing to wake up to. Thank you."

"I just want to make you happy."

Khush's tone had bounced so quickly from loving, to angry to hurt it made Anita's head spin. He had a knack of being able to do this, and it always left Anita confused.

"You do make me happy hon," said Anita getting up and moving over to Khush, "I am sorry, it was a silly joke, I didn't mean to upset you."

"Ok, if you're happy then I am happy," said Khush slowly smiling as Anita kissed the top of his head.

"I am happy. You make me happy."

"No one else?"

"Nope, just you."

"And you're mine?"

"And I am yours, all yours Khush. Mostly because no one else would have me now."

This silly joke which Anita used all the time, always worked. Khush's shoulders relaxed and he finished off his waffles and coffee in a few short mouthfuls.

"What are we doing today?" he asked as he took his plate to the kitchen sink.

"Well, it's Saturday, neither of us have work, and it's too bloody hot to go outside, how about we stay indoors and spend the day celebrating two years as husband and wife?" said Anita winking at Khush. She added with raised eyebrows and a grin, "you know, celebrate a little and then fall back to sleep…?"

Khush smiled and winked back, "Love that idea, I'm going to go for a quick shower, why don't you finish your breakfast, tidy up a little and join me?"

"Already there," said Anita taking a big bite of her waffles as Khush walked out of the room.

Anita finished her breakfast relieved that she had just escaped a big argument over a tiny thorn. *Better get that picked up and cleaned up first* she thought as she stacked the dishwasher.

With only the two of them they could have a whole day without needing to reuse any dishes and then turn on the dishwasher in the evening. It was like a routine, Khush would empty the dishwasher in the morning, and Anita would fill it during the day.

Today however, the dishwasher wasn't empty. She smiled to herself as she quickly emptied the dishwasher, cleared up the waffle mess on the counter, and picked up the loose petals from the trail on her way upstairs. She could hear Khush already in the shower waiting for her. She needed to tread carefully today, one small slip up again could change his mood and ruin everything they had planned.

Chapter 8.

As a trainee psychologist Anita spent a lot of time reading, she read often to keep her mind sharp from current research and findings in her career to learn everything she could about different case studies that would eventually help her pass her exams. But mostly she read to keep her mind occupied. Anita tended to meander in her thoughts, and this was not helpful to her. She would revisit and re-enact conversations that she had with all the people around her; doctors, patients, tutors and friends; but what she revisited more than any of these, were her conversations with Khush. He had a way of building up her confidence and breaking it down almost simultaneously. She would go over these arguments again and again questioning what had started the disagreement and how it had ended, often coming to the conclusion that she had opened her big mouth yet again and the wrong thing had fallen out. Most of the conversations ended with Khush being upset and Anita apologising until she thought he had forgiven her. Just like today.

Since their anniversary a few months ago, Khush had become more and more obsessed in having conversations about having a baby. Khush was desperate to be a father which surprised Anita as she knew he never really wanted children or spent time with his young nephews. He always seemed like he wasn't prepared for a chat with them and didn't know what to say, often speaking to them as if they were adults like him. This, unsurprisingly, bored them and the boys would begin to say random things that were irrelevant and confusing in order to try and make their uncle Khush smile and laugh and be silly with them, without any success. Khush would try, but he never really bonded with them.

Khush's ways with the younger members of the family were never a surprise to Anita; especially considering what his family were like. His father was a large domineering man with a fierce looking face and an intimidating presence; his brother Pritesh was the same and if he had a beard like his father, they would be the same person. Both men had an intensity and the conversations Anita had attempted with them always felt strained. They had nothing to talk about. Khush's mother however, was delightful. She was, like Anita's own mother, a small Indian woman. She was traditional in her nature; always served her husband, never went against what he said when others were around, and she was always wearing traditional dress. No matter what the weather, or the occasion, Khush's mum would be impeccably dressed in a simple sari, bhindi, bangles and a sindoor (a red powder worn along the parting hairline); all the unchanging symbols of a married Indian woman. When she spoke, it was like a whisper, and everything she said sounded like she was asking a question, or for permission.

Pritesh's wife was very much the younger image of her mother-in-law. Small in height, slim in build and with thick wavy black hair spanning down to her lower back, and she had soft round brown eyes, she looked like she had walked out of the set of an Indian serial drama. Always dressed smartly and although she didn't wear saris like her mother-in-law, she did always wear the bangles and bhindi with any outfit.

Next to these two women, Anita felt like an imposter, like she shouldn't call herself Indian. On a few occasions she had heard her father-in-law gruffly tell Khush that his wife behaved like a white woman, she was more English than Indian. Those comments hurt but what had stung Anita more, was that her perfect husband had replied with, "Sorry dad, I am trying." That felt like tiny daggers in her heart.

Since then, Anita had tried to be more like Khush's mother whenever they went to visit his parents; she would wear a modest long top and jeans and bangles. To Khush's annoyance, she couldn't bring herself to wear a bhindi and during reoccurring quarrels on the subject, she had always come back to it just wasn't her. Anita hated to disappoint Khush, but sometimes, like today, it was inevitable.

Khush's day began with a phone call from his father. This never ended well for Anita. She knew whenever Khush went from jovial and loud on the phone to quiet and sombre, she knew one of his parents (usually his dad) were complaining about her. Anita watched Khush pass his phone from one ear to the other, his neck getting redder and redder with every passing minute. His back was straight as an arrow and he couldn't sit still. His knees knocked together as they had a habit of doing whenever he wasn't relaxed, and Anita was becoming equally unnerved. As she tried not to show she was listening, she pottered around the kitchen watching her husband through side glances putting dishes away, tidying up things Khush had left on the side from the night before, preparing things for lunch the next day and so on. Anything to ease the situation when he was off the phone.

Between Khush picking up the phone and hanging it up, it was less than thirty minutes, but to Anita, it felt like hours. Instantly his shoulders slumped, he exhaled and stood up stretching. Anita watched in silence, there were a few ways to play this situation, and today seemed to be the 'ignore it happened until Khush speaks about it' day. She was right. Khush came into the kitchen, still red faced and frowning. Shaking his head, he came over to Anita and rested his head on her shoulder.

"Want coffee?" Anita asked soothingly.

"Please," mumbled Khush nodding at the same time.

"Ok, sit down and I'll make you one."

As Anita turned to flick the kettle on Khush put his arms around her and squeezed. They stood like this for a few minutes and his breathing slowly went back to normal. Anita stayed where she was, feeling his heartbeat against hers. She thought about how much she loved him and how she would do almost anything to make his dad, her father-in-law, less of a pain. She felt him nuzzle at her neck and give a little kiss against the top of her collar bone, his hands slowly moving up and down her back, eventually stopping at her hips. She looked at him unsure what to say when he lifted his head, looked straight at her and embraced her in a deep and passionate kiss.

Coming up for air, Anita pulled slightly back and said, "All ok?"

"Mmm," said Khush still caressing her hips and leaning into the kiss, "just love you so much."

Anita smiled, "Love you too."

"I just..." her husband began taking a small step backwards but still holding Anita and facing her, "I just love you so much. I feel I have almost everything I need to make me happy."

"Almost?" joked Anita, and then she saw the look on his face and realised where this conversation was going, "Khush..."

"I just think it's time Anita. I love you so much and nothing would make me happier than to have a baby with you. Don't you want to have kids?"

No. Is what Anita wanted to say, she had always been clear with him from the beginning that kids were not really part of her plan. She loved them and had a few cousins who had kids whom she played with and enjoyed the company of, even Pritesh's boys were fun when they weren't being told off for something inane.

But her own? No thanks.

However, she couldn't say all this to Khush right now, it wasn't the time. So instead, she shrugged her shoulders.

"I'm not sure I'm ready."

"But we've been married for more than two years now, I think we would be amazing parents, and I think it's time...my parents think it's time."

And there it was.

The topic of the intense phone call Khush had just had with his father, was about them having, or not having, children. Anita and Khush had been through this conversation so many times; each time Khush leading back to what is expected of them as a young married couple, and each time Anita explaining that she wasn't ready and that they didn't need to have children in order to be happy. But looking at his face right now, Anita began to feel herself crumble under the weight of what was expected now that they had been married for a while.

It wasn't just his family that had begun to pile on the pressure with hints about having children, although they were hardly subtle, it was her family too. Her mum and dad had also begun to drop it into conversation, talking about how other people her age were having kids, and some were already on their second or third. Every time Anita told them she wasn't going to have any and her and Khush didn't really want them. They looked disappointed but grudgingly accepted it. She knew if they found out that Khush wanted them, the pressure would intensify, but Anita just didn't want kids and didn't want to fight. Henna and her husband Ash had been trying for a baby for years but they recently found out they were unable to have them. Anita felt that she couldn't speak to her sister about not wanting children at all, not when Henna was so desperate to have one of her own. No, that conversation would never happen.

"You're parents? Is that what that phone call was all about then?" asked Anita turning her back to Khush and fidgeting with the kettle.

"Kind of, but it's something I really want too. Don't you want to complete our family?" Khush moved beside Anita and using his hands, he turned to her shoulders to face him.

"Khush...you know I'm not sure, I don't think I really want-"

"You don't want kids with me?"

"Come on, that's not what I am saying. That's not fair."

"But we love each other so much, why not add the final piece. It's missing. I feel it is. I need to be a dad Anita. I need to be."

Anita felt guilt surround her as she looked at her husband. He was desperate to have a child, she was indifferent. He wanted their family unit to be complete with a child, Anita was happy just the two of them. Looking into his eyes, she began to soften.

"Khush, I love you and-"

"Love you too," he added kissing her lips softly.

"No, let me finish. I love you so much. You are perfect for me. I knew you wanted kids, and even though you knew I wasn't really fussed, you still married me. You are so loving and caring and I hate not being able to give you what you want."

"I want you, me and a diddy one too," Khush said smiling sweetly.

"And I want you to be happy with me." She took a deep breath, "so, if you really want to, then I guess we can try for a baby."

Anita watched as Khush's eyes widened and his face broke into a grin. He began hopping from one foot to the other and started giggling.

"Are you sure?" he asked kissing her lips over and over.

"Yes," giggled Anita at seeing her husband so animated, "stop that. Yes, ok, I guess I'm sure. Yeah, ok, we can start trying for a baby." *I don't want to disappoint you and get into another argument.*

Khush took Anita into his arms and kissed her, a long passionate kiss, and swung her around the kitchen, laughing and whooping constantly. Anita began to laugh too and although she wasn't as confident about a baby, she thought maybe it would be a good thing in the end.

Chapter 9.

Anita sat in her bathroom for what was the third time in that hour having another forced wee, listening to the music, and people laughing and chatting all coming from the garden. She looked down at her swollen belly, then at her ankles and back to her swollen belly, rubbing it gently and smiling to herself.

"Won't be long now munchkin," she said giving her tummy a little tickle, "then it'll be you, me and your dad. A family. Everything your dad wanted. This is going to be great isn't it? Everyone out there in the garden is looking forward to meeting you."

Struggling to pull up her leggings and cursing that she hadn't gone with loose comfortable dress she had wanted to wear today; instead listening to Khush who had said his family and her family would be at the baby shower, so really she should wear 'something suitable'. Anita had joked and said she didn't think there was enough material in a sari to cover this immense bump, and they'd just have to deal with it, but the laughter quickly became compliance once she saw the look of annoyance on his face.

"Joking," she said clearing her throat and turning back to her wardrobe of clothes that no longer fit her, "how about I wear leggings under the dress? A compromise?" but when she turned back, Khush had already left the room.

Now fighting with the back of the dress that was stuck inside her knickers, Anita wished she had stood her ground. She wished for the confidence from just a few years ago, when she would have fought her case for hours, and eventually get her own way.

The baby-shower her sister had put together for her was beautiful. It wasn't as big as Khush had wanted it to be, but then again, he wasn't the one organising it. He hadn't even thought about it until one evening a few weeks previous when Henna and Ash had visited, Henna had mentioned it. Khush and Anita were surprised, and when they showed no idea on how to organise one during the conversation, Henna had taken it upon herself to organise the event. A guest list was quickly drawn up and numbers given to her. Everything else, Henna said she would organise.

"Are you sure about this?" Anita had asked as they were saying their goodbyes at the front door.

Looking behind her sister into the house, Henna rolled her eyes and said, "Well if not me then who? Him? Anita, he's barely done anything tonight, you should get him to do more and you should be resting."

"Don't be silly Henna," Anita said looking down at her feet, "you know I love doing all the hostess stuff, and it's you and Ash, of course I'm going to do everything I can to make sure you have a good night."

"True, but you're the one who's pregnant, and he could've at least helped out a little." Henna insisted giving her sister a cuddle, "He needs to do more so you can relax. Want me to have a word?"

"No." Anita snapped regretting it straight away, she smiled at her sister, "Uh, I...no thanks. It's all good. He does stuff to help me don't worry, you just didn't see it tonight. Are you sure about this baby shower? We don't have to have one. Khush thinks it's a bit silly."

"Shut up," said Henna smiling, "I want to do it. I want to give my niece or nephew in there," she pointed at Anita's belly, "and my amazing sister, a party to celebrate."

"But, really, I feel bad because, well you...I feel bad..." Anita felt a flood of guilt wrap around her as she looked at her sister's eyes at that moment. A slight flicker of pain flashed across them before Henna smiled and waved away the comment.

"Don't be silly, just because Ash and I can't have a baby, doesn't mean we can't be happy for you. Don't let our issues stop you from being happy and enjoying your baby. I will enjoy the baby too when he or she arrives. You wait I'm gonna spoil that kid."

"Oh please don't," said Anita laughing as her sister turned to walk to the car where Ash was waiting patiently with the engine running, "no spoiling. They'll be spoilt enough by the grandparents too."

"No promises," called back Henna blowing a kiss as her sister, "I'll get on to this baby shower right away."

"Thanks," called back Anita waving, "love you."

"Ditto," said Henna as they drove off leaving Anita standing in the slightly chilly evening sun.

As she turned around Anita noticed Khush's shadow moving from the hallway into the living room. *Oh great* she thought shutting then locking the front door, *he heard that. This'll be a fun evening now.*

**   **   **   **   **   **

"Bloody leggings" she muttered as she made one last attempt at pulling the dress free. It worked. "Right munchkin," she said to her bump, "let's do this, I need some food."

"Ah here she comes," boomed Ash's voice as Anita stepped out from her kitchen into the garden and into the very hot afternoon, "Guest of honour to join the fun and games."

Anita laughed as she looked at all the people who had turned up to celebrate her and Khush's soon to be new arrival. They were all smiling, holding cold drinks in their hands, chatting and eating the food that her mother had provided for them. Anita was in awe of how much her sister had managed to do in such a short time; there were baby shower balloons, banners, music playing, a massive baby elephant themed cake, silly baby games set out and ready to be played by everyone and of course, plenty of food. No Indian party would be complete without enough food to feed an army. There would definitely be take out tubs being offered when people left.

The only thing missing for Anita, was the ability to drink alcohol, and as Anita couldn't drink alcohol, Henna had made the decision that no one else should be able to. Henna had orchestrated a bar full of all of Anita's favourite cocktails, without the alcohol. The only person who had complained about this was Khush himself.

Partial to the odd beer, Khush couldn't see why as the dad to be, he wasn't allowed one of his favourite drinks. After much whinging and arguing, Anita had given in and said that it was ok for him to drink, although it would be better if he waited until the party was over, so he could enjoy one in peace and quiet. At this outlandish idea, Khush stubbornly walked over the fridge, picked out a beer and happily guzzled half of it down in one go. By the look on her face, Henna wanted to snatch it out of his hands and tip it down the sink but before she could say anything Anita placed a hand on her shoulder.

"Leave him, he is the father to be after all. Let him have a beer," and then added whispering so only Henna could hear her, "he may even cheer up and smile."

The afternoon flew by in a blur of laughter, hugs and gifts. Anita didn't want the day to end. She felt so much love from her friends and family and wanted to stay in that safe moment for longer, after all the baby's arrival would change everything and she wouldn't be able to relax like she had done today.

As the final guest left and as Anita started to kiss goodbye to her parents, and aajima she felt an enormous kick in her stomach. Laughing and grabbing her tummy as she waddled over to the living room where Khush had spent the entire party (apart from when he was dragged over to cut the cake and feed

Anita a mouthful). She stood in front of him, "Khush. Hon. Feel this," she said excitedly, "the baby's kicking like mad!"

"So what?" said Khush, now on what was probably his fifth beer, "It's done it before. Anita, come on, you're in the way of the TV."

"But it's proper kicking, like more than it has ever Khush. Feel." Anita said pleading her husband to place his hand on her stomach.

"No, I'll do it later, I'm trying to watch the game." Khush snapped as he moved to the side to see what he had missed whilst Anita had stood in his way, "Come on Anita, move."

Anita's shoulders slumped as she turned away from her husband, tears welled in her eyes and all the excitement from the day celebrating her pregnancy dissolved into a nauseating feeling at the base of her throat. She moved back into the kitchen where her mum was standing looking confused.

"What's wrong?" she asked stroking her hand gently across Anita's cheek only the way a mother could do.

"Nothing," said Anita trying to sound upbeat, "I went to Khush when the baby kicked, but by the time I got to him and he put his hand on my tummy, the kicking had stopped."

Her mum didn't believe her.

"Are you sure you're ok?" said her mum looking deep into her eyes and making Anita feel like a child again.

"I'm fine, mum," Anita said smiling. Moving around her mum Anita began to busy herself with clearing up the food table, "I'm just gutted the baby stopped kicking, it's silly. By the way, thank you for the food, it was delicious, everyone loved it. I loved it."

"You don't have to thank me," her mum said picking up a plate and handing it to her daughter, "It's what I do for you. Want me to help clear up?"

"No, no that's ok mum. Khush said he'll help once the game is over. Henna is still around, too isn't she?"

At the mention of her name, Anita's sister walked in carrying a small pile of plates, "Damn, we should have gone with paper plates," she said, "this is going to be some washing up. Want me to stick about and help?"

"No thanks. You've done enough. Both of you have. Not much left to clear and Khush is going to help me. And we have a dishwasher."

"When he finishes watching the game," her mum added rolling her eyes at Henna, who looked at Anita with a frown.

"Yes, mum, he will help," said Anita slightly agitated at being caught in her lie. "Come on, you ladies need to go home too. Thanks again for an amazing day. I loved it so much more than I thought I would."

Anita hugged both her mum and sister in one big bear-like hug, which was hard to do with such a sizeable bump in the way. They all giggled and walked out of the kitchen.

As Anita watched her family get into their cars and leave her home, she felt a pang of longing. She wanted so much for her mum to be here all the time with her to help her prepare for the baby and to soothe her whenever she became overwhelmed, which was becoming more and more often now that the due date was looming. She thought that she could have relied on Khush for that, but he seemed to act as if his job was done and it was all up to her now.

As the one who didn't really want a baby in the first place, Anita felt anxious about everything and knew if she brought it up with Khush he would say that she was being silly and paranoid and that he was doing lots to support her and the baby; he bought all the things they needed. Khush would say that everything would feel good and be alright when the baby arrived and her being this nervous was harming his baby and she needed to calm down. But he didn't exactly do anything to help calm her nerves at all.

As she cleared up the plates, picked up the rubbish and filled the dishwasher, Anita replayed these conversations with Khush repeatedly in her mind and eventually she would come to one conclusion; Khush did care, in his own way, he cared a lot. He had prepared the home to be baby friendly and bought her so many gifts and the spared no expense on baby things, so whenever she felt like this, she chided herself for thinking he didn't care. Khush was amazing, he was loving, caring and attentive…in his own Khush way.

Chapter 10.

If someone had told Anita that all the pre-natal classes, books on babies and all the gadgets and gizmos she had persuaded Khush to buy, weren't going to mean anything when the baby actually arrived, she would have never bothered getting them in the first place. It wasn't that they didn't really work (which they didn't), and it wasn't that they seemed to be designed for those naturally loving and adoring mums making Anita feel worthless and like she was an imposter (which they were and she did), but it was that she wasn't confident in her own abilities as a mother and the baby wasn't exactly helping.

Anand had been born a few days after the due date and Anita was already feeling uncomfortable from the pressure the bulge placed on her already swollen ankles. The labour itself had been straight forward for the most part; although when she had suffered some serious contractions that almost floored her, Anita has asked the midwife for an epidural, and as the midwife went to get the ball rolling on this common request, Khush stepped in.

"No," he said sternly as he rubbed Anita's back, "I don't think we should have one of those."

"Why the hell not?" asked Anita through gritted teeth, the pain pulsating through her lower body and across her back, "I'm in fucking agony."

"It's a sound option," agreed the midwife looking pityingly at Anita and then back at Khush, "If she wants the epidural, we can do it. We only have a small window now to get the process going before it's too late to give it to her."

"But I don't want it," said Khush stubbornly, "I've read up on it and there's so many things I'm not comfortable with."

"When did you read up on it?" breathed Anita beginning to get agitated.

"The other night, you were sleeping again and I thought I'd read up on it," he huffed and added icily, "you know I do take care of you and the baby too? It's my child too Anita."

"I know," said Anita sneaking a glance at the midwife who was starting to look uncomfortable at the door waiting for a decision, "but hon, it hurts so bad."

"I know it does, but you can get through this, you're strong. Just think our mothers did all this without drugs, and the side effects are scary."

"Actually," said the midwife walking towards the couple, "an epidural is not-"

"Excuse me," cut in Khush standing up straight and seemingly towering over the midwife, "Can my wife and I have a moment to discuss this in private?"

Anita watched in horror as the woman who had been nothing but helpful and soothing, mumbled an apology and skittered out of the room. As the door clicked shut, she turned to him.

"What was that for?" she asked mortified.

"What? She needed to know her place. She's not married to me and so she doesn't have a say. She's not part of this family."

"What about me? Do I get a say?" Anita asked holding on to her bulge as she began to cramp up again.

"Of course, but I wanted her out. Look Anita, I know you're in pain and I am so proud of you for doing all this for the baby, but I really don't think drugs are a good thing. There's so much that can go wrong, and I think you can do it without them."

"I can do it with the drugs too...and probably better. Khush it hurts, you can't imagine how much this is hurting me, the drugs will help. I promise it'll be fine. Please just let me have the epidural?"

Khush looked at Anita's pleading eyes, her hunched shoulders and her sore ankles, his expression softened a little and he put an arm delicately around her shoulders, "Ok, Anita, if you want to do this, I guess I have no say in the matter. It's just that the drugs they use can get into the baby's bloodstream and harm the baby. It can harm you. I don't want to put you or the baby at risk…but it's your choice, I just ask you think of all the consequences."

Anita closed her eyes, she knew what he was saying was all a tactic to scare her into saying she no longer want the epidural, but she knew he was right about the side effects. She had been at the classes when the midwives and nurses went through the options, and they had decided that she was going to do this without, but right now, right here with the agony, she really wanted the drugs. Anita looked up at her husband and sighed, "Ok, I won't do it. I'll power through."

"Because you're awesome," said Khush his smile growing.

"Because I'm awesome." Anita repeated looking away from her husband and towards the closed door, "Please can you get that midwife back in and I'll tell her my decision."

After that it had all been a blur of screams, pushes, agonizing rips and unhelpful attempts by Khush to soothe her.

Anand Govind was born after 5 hours of labour and as Khush held his baby boy, Anita drifted off into a jaded sleep.

**   **   **

Sleep.

How quickly that has been ripped from their everyday routines. Now that is what Anita craved so intensely in the first few months. She hardly slept and when she did sleep, it was broken by Anand crying for food, or crying for a nappy change, or crying because he had wind. Or just crying because he wanted a cuddle. And when Anand decided to sleep, Anita kept waking up thinking she'd heard him make a noise and something was wrong.

To say Anita's paranoia about everything with lack of sleep was intense, was an understatement. She needed some sleep, just a night of unbroken slumber, or even rest that lasted longer than three straight hours was all she was looking for, but this was impossible. Khush had become less helpful since the baby shower and when Anita had asked for help from Khush, that had not gone down well.

"What do you mean you want more help?" he questioned when Anita had brought the subject up earlier that evening when Anand was having a nap, "I do help. That's what I am doing now, looking after Anand while you get some 'you time'. What else am I supposed to do? You look after him at night so I can sleep and go to work to earn money for you and him, and when I come home, I don't get a rest, I have to look after him in the evening."

"Yeah, that's just whilst I'm cooking dinner though Khush."

"But you can't look after him and cook dinner. What am I supposed to do to help then? Do dinner and look after the kid? I will if you want me to. Just say the word, but I thought we were doing this as a team."

"We are, look Khush…" said Anita wearily.

"No listen. I don't get any time to myself at all. When I am awake, I am either at work, or looking after Anand, and he's not an easy kid you know."

"You don't have to tell me."

"It's not like I'm not making any sacrifices too," continued Khush only acknowledging what Anita said with a fierce look, "my social life has disappeared too. I don't go out."

"I know, sorry, I'm just so tired hon," said Anita realising she was losing a battle she had no energy to continue.

"You're tired? You can sleep when he does during the day? I can't. He keeps waking up at night, and when you sort him out it's not like you're quiet about it. Between his screaming and you stomping and banging about with his milk and nappy changes, it's like being at a concert in here. I have to go to work, you can stay home and have a lay in with the kid, and he doesn't do much anyway, lots of sleeping during the day. So you get to rest. I don't."

Khush's rant had become increasingly louder and louder, and he had ignored Anita's pleading looks to keep his voice down. Only Anand's loud and foghorn sounding cries stopped him from continuing.

"Oh," said Anita looking up at the ceiling feeling her life drain away from her, "Look what you've done."

"Me?" cried Khush clearly angry at the accusation, "Fuck's sake. I need get out of this damn house with that damn kid screaming. You sort him out this time."

"Where are you going?" said Anita starting to panic at the thought of being left alone with her child.

"Out. For a walk or something. Just out."

"When will you be back? What about the dinner I've just cooked?"

"Dunno when I will be back, and don't worry about dinner for me. I'll eat it when I get home or I'll grab something from the shops." With that Khush swept up his wallet, phone and keys from the counter, slipped his trainers on, and walked out the door.

Anita closed her eyes and sobbed.

This was not what she was told parenthood or marriage would be like. She stood crying quietly at the bottom of the steps a moment longer before Anand's relentless crying became too much to listen to.

"Coming baby," she said more to herself than Anand, "mummy's coming."

That evening Anita went to bed exhausted and with a pounding headache. Anand had eventually settled when she allowed him to sleep on her for most of the night. Her eyes were sore and dry from crying throughout most of the evening, and when Anand was placed in his cot for the night, Anita crawled into bed without changing into her nightshirt and slept.

When she woke a few hours later to Anand's shrill cries again, she noticed she was alone in the bed. She squinted her eyes at the clock on her phone and saw that it was 1am. She realised two things; one, Anand had slept for a straight four hours without waking, and two, Khush hadn't come to bed. As she went into her baby's room, she passed the spare room, the door was closed which was unusual. She stood by the door and listened for a moment, almost instantly she heard the low rumble of Khush's familiar snoring and was conflicted. Should she be relieved that he had come home and not stayed out at God knows where with God knows who, or should she be annoyed that he had decided to sleep in the spare room instead of beside her? Before she could react, Anand's impatient wails filled the hallway and she quickly and quietly went to see her son.

A mere four hours later, she went through the same routine with Anand and settled him. As she watched him sleep soundly, his tummy full of milk and a fresh nappy on, Anita knew she wouldn't be able to get back to sleep. It was 5am and instead of trying to catch a few hours of sleep before it all started again, she chose to freshen up and go downstairs for a much-needed cup of tea. Anita wasn't a major tea drinker, but since giving birth to Anand, she had realised that the one thing she needed more than a shower in the morning, was a giant mug of very sweet tea. That, and a bacon sandwich.

As Anita sat nursing her tea at the kitchen table with the baby monitor right next to her freshly made, still untouched bacon sandwich, she could hear Khush moving around upstairs getting ready for work. He wasn't big on breakfast and usually a strong coffee did the trick so when he came downstairs and saw she had made only herself a bacon sandwich, Anita knew last night's argument wasn't over.

"Where's my one?" he asked straightening his tie and putting down his bag.

"What? Bacon sandwich? I didn't know you wanted one."

"You didn't ask."

"You didn't come to bed," Anita said, but instantly realised that was the wrong move.

"I came home didn't I? Be glad of that. Fine, fuck it, I don't want breakfast anyway, I'll get something at the train station."

He moved away from her, grabbing his bag, picking up his coffee and pouring it into his travel mug.

"Here, you can have mine," said Anita feeling frustrated at the way her grown up husband was behaving, "I can make myself another one. No problem."

"No," said Khush not turning to look at her, "I don't want it now. I'm off to work, see you when I get home."

"But it's only six," she called to him. The door slammed and she whispered to no one in particular, "you don't usually leave until seven."

Anita placed her mug down on the table and looked at her bacon sandwich, no longer hungry. Feeling like she was going to be sick instead, she picked it up and threw it away. Before she could sit back down, the baby monitor came to life, emitting such a high-pitched sound that it made Anita wince. It was the signal telling her Anand was ready to be seen to, his day had started. By the time Anita had changed Anand's nappy, fed him and carried him downstairs, her much needed tea was cold.

"Shit," she said shaking her head and pouring the cold tea down the sink. This was going to be another bad day she could feel it in her bones.

Chapter 11.

Over the next few months, Anita had fallen into a routine with Anand; he had stopped waking up several times in the night and now only woke up twice for feeds, he slept better during the day so allowing Anita to get on with the house chores, his screams had become less nails down a blackboard and more sounds of hunger and tiredness (something she could cope with), and his feeding routine had finally improved.

In the first few weeks Anita had struggled to feed her son. In the hospital she had been encouraged to try and breastfeed which she was very eager to do. In all the research she had done on breastfeeding, she knew that this was the best start for her baby, so she knew this is what she had wanted. But, like all things in her life recently, Anita had not managed to get her way. On the first night, she had sat on her bed and had picked up the yet to be named Anand, ready to feed him. But for some reason Anand wasn't happy, he was terribly hungry, and Anita could not get him to latch on to her breast. She tried twisting herself at an angle, holding him in a different way, lifting her breast to fit her nipple onto his mouth, but nothing.

The midwifes and nurses had come to help her and with different hands holding, twisting, angling and pressing at her and her baby to no avail. Eventually, Anita had broken down and cried. Her baby was hungry and she was unable to feed him her own milk. One day in, and she was already failing as a mum. In the end the midwife had given Anand formula milk to settle him and said she would come back to help Anita later on; Anita was tired, and probably thirsty, and that was not the best way to be in order to produce milk. She told Anita to get some rest.

Since coming home with Anand, Anita had tried several times to breastfeed Anand, often only producing a few mouthfuls before going dry and needing to use formula milk. She had panicked the first time Khush had watched this happen as she knew he also wanted her to breastfeed her son like his mother had done for him as a baby.

"What's wrong?" he had asked looking at her as she changed to bottle, "What are you doing?"

"I can't get him to have a full feed on me," explained Anita feeling small and inadequate, "he just won't feed."

"Maybe he's not hungry."

"He is, he's crying for food Khush."

"Then, what is it? Is it you?"

Anita looked at her husband and felt instantly ashamed of herself. She couldn't even provide for her son, she felt useless and Khush had seen that too. She ducked her head so a strand of hair fell over her eyes and whispered, "Yeah, I can't seem to make enough milk for him."

"Did you try the other one?" Khush asked ignoring her state of despair.

"Other one what?"

"The other breast of course" he said.

"Yeah of course I did, I can't produce milk in either. Not enough for Anand, only like a mouthful or two."

"Why?"

"Why?" repeated Anita, she wasn't sure she had heard right, "Why can't I produce milk? God Khush, I don't know. Maybe I, maybe..." Anita couldn't think of any reason other than maybe I'm just not a good enough mum but she couldn't bring herself to say it out loud for someone other than herself to hear.

"Maybe...?" Khush was waiting for a reasonable explanation, he looked frustrated at Anita's inability to string a sentence together and give him something he could accept. "What is it Anita? Are you not trying to pump other times?"

Anita was gobsmacked, not trying was what he said. Didn't he see that she was upset and in turmoil about being unable to feed her son? Didn't he realise that scolding her about it wasn't going to help her produce more milk? Didn't he even care how she felt about breastfeeding?

"Of course I am," Anita mumbled her eyes stinging with tears, "I am trying. I wanted to breast feed but for some reason, I can't. I will ask the midwife why when she next comes to check on us."

"She's coming again?" Khush said sounding irritated about the notion of someone coming into his home when he was at work and judging them as parents, "Why again?"

"I don't know, just to see how we are and to help. That's what they do."

Khush wasn't convinced, "well when she does come around, ask her what's wrong with you not making any milk ok? And don't go gossiping about our private life like last time."

"Ok," said Anita.

She looked down in her arms at her now asleep baby with his empty formula bottle still in his mouth and felt a rush of anger towards him. She gave him a hard squeeze which made him cry out a little and then eased him back comfortably in her arms. *You can't even feed your own son* she thought to herself as Khush left the room and left her to deal with this failure of hers.

When visitors started arriving, Anita found that she was on edge all the time. She felt like everything that was said by either Khush or the others was a judgement on her inability to raise her son. The only time she felt that she could relax a little was when her mother came to visit. When Anita looked at her mum at the front door, she had swept the little woman up in her arms and hugged her hard. After a few moments of tears and laughing, her mother had asked to see her grandson. Anita watched in awe as her mother cooed and cuddled Anand, making him giggle more than she had ever done, and showered him with kisses until he squirmed.

"He's adorable," said her mum stroking his face the same way she had done for Anita and Henna when they were younger, "my little Anand. Do you know what Anand means Anita?"

"Yes mum," said Anita bringing in some tea and biscuits for her parents, "It means happiness."

"That's right," her mum said nodding enough to make her bun on the top of her head bounce about as if it were to fall off, "It means happiness and joy. And here he is, your bundle of happiness and joy."

Anita smiled, watching her parents flutter around after her son, she knew she could never tell her mum that the name felt so ironic to her at this moment in time. She didn't want them to know that this 'bundle of happiness' had brought her to tears more times since being born than she remembered ever doing before. She couldn't tell them that the only time she felt happy was when he was asleep and out of her hair, even if that was only for a few fleeting moments throughout the day. She dare not confess to them that since having the baby her relationship with Khush was tense and even though he had wanted a child more than she had, that he had spent more time away from them than with them at home as a family, making her feel so alone and helpless. And she definitely couldn't admit that when Khush left for work, which had become earlier and earlier since Anand was born, that she would close the curtains, roll herself up in a ball on the sofa and sometimes cry along with Anand for a little while before finally seeing to his needs. She no longer felt like her own person in control of her body, she felt like a broken machine, erratically going through the motions just to keep her son alive. She felt like each time Anand cried that she was falling deeper into this vast sense of nothingness and she couldn't see a way out.

"Anita," called her mum, snapping her fingers in front of Anita's dazed face, "I said how are you doing?"

"Yeah, we're good thanks," Anita replied automatically, "just getting into routines, feeding, sleeping and that. Anand is a good boy, love him such a cutie."

Even as she was saying all this and smiling, she could tell her mum wasn't buying any of it.

"No. Are you ok? I didn't ask about Anand, I can see he is happy and healthy, I asked about you."

"Me?" asked Anita, "why are you asking about me? I'm ok, I just said that."

"Beta," said her mum. Beta was a term used to mean child, and her mother only used it with Anita when she was worried about her, "I think you don't look well."

"I'm ok mum," said Anita her hands instinctively going to tidy her hair back, "trust me, I am ok. Just tired."

"Well why don't you rest a little then?" said her mum giving her a cuddle and looking over at her husband who was tickling Anand with his growing beard, "me and your papa will look after Anand for a few hours whilst you get some rest. Ok?"

"But..." started Anita but she couldn't find a reason why resting wasn't an appealing idea.

"No beta, you need some rest. Now go upstairs and get some sleep. I will call you down in a few hours."

Anita didn't have the energy to argue with her mum as she was led up the stairs. She remembered mumbling some instructions about milk and nappies, but her mum gently shushed her and lay her down on her bed. Anita closed her eyes and heard her mum softly humming an old Indian lullaby that she used to hum to Anita and Henna to help them sleep. Anita smiled, and then drifted off into a deep sleep.

When Anita woke a few hours later, she found that her house was quiet, too quiet. What's going on? she thought as she wandered down the stairs. She could hear the faint sound of the radio on in the kitchen and some soft talking in the living room.

"Mum? Dad?" she called out, "Is everything ok?"

"Yes," called back her mum from the living room, "We're in here."

As Anita walked into the living room her heart skipped a beat and she went numb; there, sitting in the living room was her mum, dad and Khush. Khush and her dad were in polite conversation about something that was on the news channel they were watching, and her mum was sitting in the single armchair cradling a cooing Anand in her arms.

"Khush?" she asked, eyebrows raised, "You're home from work early today?"

She glanced at the clock on the wall and realised she had been asleep for longer than she wanted, "Mum, it's so late, you should have woken me up ages ago. I said only an hour or two."

Anita moved quickly to her mum looked down at Anand. She was avoiding looking at Khush as she could feel his angry eyes burning into her back. Anand was happily babbling away at her mum and when he looked at Anita his arms reached up for her comfort too. Anita took him in her arms and gave him a little cuddle and kiss on the forehead. He smiled at her and then turned to his grandad.

"Your mum and dad have been looking after Anand while you slept," said Khush only just masking the annoyance in his voice.

"That's ok," Anita's dad said standing up and taking Anand into his arms, "it's not work when it's our grandchild, is it Anand beta?"

"Plus, she really did need some rest Khush," said Anita's mum also standing, "and now that she has had some, we will give our grandson a kiss and make our way home too. Anita come to the kitchen with me I want to show you something, let's leave these three men here."

Anita's mum led her to the kitchen. "What's this mum?" said Anita as she looked around.

The dishes that had been piled for the past day and half had been washed, dried and piled neatly on the counter, the floor had been mopped and all of Anand's bottles had been sterilized, dried and placed back in the holder next to the microwave.

"Just thought I would help out a little Anita," said her mum shrugging her shoulders, "I came in here and thought I would help tidy some bits for you, and make it easier on you...and Khush."

At that last word Anita let out a snort she was unable to hide.

"Thanks for this mum, but you really shouldn't have. You know how he gets with guests doing stuff in his house."

"Lucky I am not a guest," said her mum walking to the cooker, "I am your mum. And it is perfectly ok for me to help my daughter out a little bit. I also made dinner for you two tonight."

Looking passed her mum Anita saw that her mum hadn't just made dinner for her and Khush but had made a banquet of different dishes. She had done that Indian mum thing where they say that they will cook one dish and end up producing a plethora of mouth-watering cuisines. Anita counted three different curries; one meat based since Khush only liked meat curries nowadays and two vegetarian curries as she knew that Anita had gone off some meat since having Anand, she saw rice and one of Anita's favourite dahls too.

"Wow, mum, all this? You shouldn't have."

"Well, I wanted to. I didn't make all these here, I brought a few bits over too. Anything that I couldn't find in your kitchen, I got your dad to pop home and collect or grab from the shop around the corner. Did you know they have an Indian section in that little shop at the end of the road?"

Anita shook her head. She walked up to the potato and spinach curry her mum had made for her. "Mmm, my favourite," she said picking out a potato and popping it into her mouth.

Her mum tutted, slapping at her hand, a ritual both had become accustomed to over the years, "I've also made some rotli and they are sitting warm in the oven. You and Khush need to eat. Both of you are looking too thin, especially you. You need energy beta, you must eat so you can be strong for Anand."

"I am eating," said Anita lying to her mum and avoiding eye contact.

"Not enough and not enough of the stuff that will keep you healing and healthy."

"Mum," complained Anita rolling her eyes, "don't worry about me, I have Khush here to look after me."

Silence was her mother's response. She looked at Anita with her greying eyes, "make sure he is looking after you and Anand, he needs to do his fair share too."

"He does," said Anita feeling a lump form in her throat thinking about the late nights, the lonely days and the empty bed.

"Good," she said walking back to the living room, "right, let me give my grandson a kiss before we go."

Anita watched her parents kiss Anand goodbye and shower him with blessings and saw that Khush was rolling his eyes. She felt a spark of anger towards him, her parents had done nothing but helped and there he was rolling his eyes at them blessing their child. *Fuck you Khush* she thought to herself.

It didn't take long for her parents visit to turn into another argument. Khush was upset that they had just 'showed up' out of the blue without a phone call or text, and Anita was annoyed that he didn't see how helpful they had been.

"And to think she was cooking in my kitchen! Like I can't make my own wife and kid dinner?" Khush was building himself up into a frenzy.

"She was just helping me out," explained Anita trying to ease the tension but getting nowhere, no matter what she said it just fired him up even more.

"I can do it."

"But you didn't and she did. It's ok, gives us both a night off."

"Both? Looks like you had more than just cooking done for you."

"Hey, that's not fair," said Anita frowning.

"How long were you sleeping for while you mum baby sat our child?" he said raising his voice along with his arms.

"I was shattered, and mum could see that, so she just helped out. You weren't here to help as you were at work, so she just helped. What's so wrong in that?"

"She basically threw it in my face when I got home Anita. Saying she had done all this while you were resting."

"Exactly, resting. I needed a rest. I didn't ask mum to clear things up, I didn't ask her to cook for us. I just needed two hours to catch up on sleep and get some energy back."

"Well she did clean, and she did cook. Like it was her job to do that. It's not her job to do that Anita!" Khush was shouting now and getting red in the face.

"I know it's not her job to Khush. I know. She's just helping me."

"It's not her job to get in the way Anita."

"No, you're right," snapped Anita, "It's your job and you've not been here to do it. She just helped me. Helped. That's all. Why are you getting so angry about it?"

"This again?" Khush boomed spraying spittle in her direction.

Just at that moment, Anand began to cry in the living room. He had a knack of stopping the arguments in an instant. Breathing hard, Khush looked at the living room door, then at Anita. She took the hint and went straight into the living room feeling his eyes burning into the back of her head. She walked over to Anand, he was crying but not because he was hungry or had filled his nappy, Anita had checked, but clearly because of the raised voices. He stopped as soon as he saw her, smiled, giggled, and reached out his arms.

In that instant, Anita felt something in her heart that she hadn't felt since giving birth to him months earlier, something she was told she would automatically feel when she became a mother but hadn't. Looking at her baby reaching out to her with a smile that melted her heart, Anita felt a kind of maternal warmth and devotion that overwhelmed her. She picked up Anand up and gently soothed him, giving him kisses and stroking his face just her mum had stroked her face, and immediately she knew things with Anand were going to be alright.

She understood, that now, he needed her just as much as she needed him.

Chapter 12.

The months flew by, and before Anita knew it her baby boy was reaching his first birthday. It hadn't been the easiest year as Anita's relationship with Khush became more strained as Anand needed more of her attention and Khush got less of it; but she'd made it through. Just.

It wasn't all bad, Khush had moments where he had become his caring, attentive and sensitive self again, and in those moments, Anita believed things would change for the good and that he really was the man she had fallen in love with. They naturally slipped back into their passionate love making, small gift giving and spending the night's talking about everything and nothing. But those days were short lived, it only took something small and inconsequential to revert Khush back to the distant, uncaring and often mean person Anita was now coming to know.

Her new normal with her family had become something she didn't recognise; Khush ate at separate times to Anita and Anand, often making his own food and leaving what Anita had made; and he spent less and less time with his wife and only showed true affection to his son.

At least Anand is getting some of his love Anita thought as she watched Khush play with his son on the living room floor one day, *it doesn't matter if he's not the same with me all the time, as long as he's good with Anand. They look so happy.* Looking up at Anita from the floor, Khush shrugged and continued playing races with the toy cars and his son.

Routines had become some form of salvation for Anita throughout the months, if she knew what was happening and what was coming she was able to control the situation and feel less like she was spiralling, especially on the darker days when everything became overwhelming. The days would feel structured and safe and when Khush had his bad days, Anita would be able to escape into her own mind and sort through the tasks of the next day or two enabling herself to have some sense of normality in life.

Khush barely spent any time alone with Anita and only shared the same space when Anand was with them. Once Anand was in bed for the night Khush would retreat to the study and spend the night in there. He spent most of his time sleeping in that study too, and if he wasn't sleeping on the pull-out sofa bed he would come upstairs and use the spare room. For the first few months of Khush doing this, Anita's heart sank a little more every morning when she would wake and not find her husband there next to her, but just like his mood swings, Anita got used to the disappointment of being alone in her bed and made it more of a safe haven for herself. She kept the room as it was because she knew this was still his room too, and change could start him off on another rant instantly.

Anand was becoming such a little character; he had a very cheeky smile and the personality to go with it. With his first birthday within a month, Anand was babbling more, attempting to communicate and make conversation with people around him. He loved his cuddles, toy cars and his teddies, of which he had many. Every time Anita's sister Henna would visit, she would bring him a small soft toy. Anand insisted on Anita naming every single one of them…well that's what Anita told herself he wanted her to do. His favourite toy of all was one given to him by Anita's mum, his aajima, a super soft grey and yellow elephant, with a bright yellow star on its tummy. Anand took this teddy everywhere they went and would hold him at night until he fell asleep, with the teddy eventually ending up squished against the cot bars right next to Anand's head. When he wasn't holding tightly on to the elephant, he would be cradling a bright orange dinosaur Henna had given him.

"You know you don't have to bring him something every time you come here," Anita said to her sister as she watched Henna hand Anand another teddy, this time a tiger with thick stripes and a toothy grin.

"I know," said Henna smothering Anand in kisses as he giggled and kissed her back, "But he is my nephew and I will spoil him. No one will ever stop that."

"He's so spoilt already," said Anita laughing.

"No, he's so loved," corrected Henna looking at her sister. She put her nephew down and watched her sister carefully. "How are you doing?"

"I'm good," said Anita avoiding her sister's stare, "we are good, just same old same old. He's so funny. You should watch him trying to waddle about – looks a bit like a drunken cowboy."

Henna laughed at the image of her cute nephew waddling about, "Maybe next time I should bring him a cowboy costume?"

"Oh god no." laughed Anita placing down two tall glasses of orange juice, "Khush would hate that."

"He hates everything Anita," said Henna scornfully, "is he still 'busy' with work?" Busy was accentuated with finger quotes and eye rolls.

"Hey," said Anita defensively, "he is busy with work. He's doing really well actually. Might be up for promotion soon."

"Hmm," said Henna not convinced taking a sip of her drink, "What's he like with you guys then?"

"He's good," said Anita a little too abruptly, "he is so good with Anand, spends the evening playing with him and then when I have bathed him, most nights Khush reads to Anand too. It's so sweet. Gives me time to give the kitchen a little clean too."

"So he plays and reads to Anand," said her sister raising her eyebrows, waving her had around the room she added, "And you do everything else."

"Yeah, because I'm home to do it aren't I?" said Anita repeating a line Khush had fed to her time and time again. Looking at her sister, she sighed, "look he works hard, he comes home and is amazing with Anand. He's doing well. Anand loves spending time with him too. It works. Our system works."

Anita realised as she was saying this, she wasn't just trying to persuade her sister of this set up but trying to persuade herself. Henna wasn't the only one who noticed that all Khush did when he came home was spend time on his own or spend time with Anand. She didn't get more than a word or two from him, he didn't eat the meals she continued to make for him, and once Anand was in bed, Khush would hide out in the study and leave Anita to the housework and tidying up. She felt more like a nanny and housemaid rather than a wife to Khush. It was only when he wanted something from her, usually sex or a favour, that Khush ever approached Anita. Anita wanted to say something, but she couldn't find the courage to deal with the argument that would inevitably follow a conversation like that.

"What's he like with you then? Does he even talk to you?" Henna said interrupting Anita's thoughts.

"Yeah of course he does," said Anita shaking her head. "We chat, although by the time Anand is in bed and I've…we've tided up I'm too tired to say much. Just a couple of hours in front of the TV and I'm in bed. He works at home too, says he's busy with trying to get the promotion that his boss is dangling in front of him. So, we are busy parents. You know how it is."

Shit. Anita had got so into her defence speech that she totally forgot that her sister couldn't have kids.

"No, I don't" said Henna smiling sadly.

"Oh, I'm so sorry, I didn't mean it that way. I didn't want-"

"It's ok," said Henna, "Don't be silly, a mistake. You know, I do hope he looks after you too. You're looking tired. Those bags under your eyes are looking pretty rough."

She added a wink and grin to the last comment showing her sister that there was no offence meant.

"Oi," said Anita throwing one of Anand's teddies at her sister who was laughing, "my bags are not that big. I get sleep. Anand is a pretty good sleeper, so all is good. Promise."

"Promise?" asked Henna concerned. She had a knack of using tone so well to turn a conversation from light-hearted to serious instantly.

"I promise," said Anita feeling her eyes welling up, "I'm all good. Anand is a gem and Khush...well he's a grumpy man. We are all good though. I'm good," she lied.

It was obvious Henna didn't believe her, but she wasn't going to say any more and Henna wasn't going to pry.

"So," said Henna changing the subject as Anand waddled up to her with an armful of teddies, he was bringing to show her, "He's almost one eh? Will he go to nursery?"

"Yeah," said Anita feeling relieved the conversation was moving away from her mental health and back to her little cowboy with an armful of soft toys, "I'm thinking he'll go to nursery full time and I can get back into my psychology work. I almost got there before little man arrived. Plus, I have reached out to a few people I was in training with and they say there are a few spots opening up and a couple may be perfect for me. I have to apply for the job, of course, but they say that it's worth it and I could easily get in with my qualification and training grades too.

I'm so excited about this I feel like I need more adult conversation and I so desperately want to be a psychologist. Actually, I'm thinking, since having Anand, I kind of want to go into child psychology. I'm learning so much from watching him grow and learn how to do things, I think this is where I want to go with my career."

Anita didn't realise but she had become more animated whilst talking to her sister about the potential of getting out of the house and starting her career, her dream. Her arms were flailing around, her breathing had become more erratic and her smile was one Henna had not seen in a long time. Henna smiled at her sister and felt a pang of worry.

"That's awesome. Not to put a dampener on things," she said slowly with Anand on her lap now playing with her bangles, "and not that I care because this is what you need to do by the sounds of it, but what did Khush say to your plans?"

"Khush?" said Anita forgetting herself for a second, "Well, I haven't actually told him yet. He's been busy recently. But I am sure he'll be fine with it all. It makes sense for Anand to go to nursery now, he needs to play and integrate with other kids his age more, plus they'll be starting to do some early learning stuff I think, so he needs to go."

"I agree," said Henna, "I just wanted to know what Khush thought since you've been with Anand all this time."

"He should be fine."

"You need to talk to him about it. Soon too, so you can get the ball rolling on the opportunities your mates are telling you about."

"I know Henna," sighed Anita feeling like she was getting told off for something, "I will."

"When?"

"Soon."

"Anita," said Henna frowning, "tell me you'll do it within the next week. You have to get Anand registered at a nursery, so you gotta be organised."

"I am organised." stated Anita defending herself automatically.

"I know you are. That's why I'm saying take the first step and do it."

"I will."

"Good."

The conversation had become strained and Anita was starting to feel a little irritated with her sister for not believing she would talk to her husband. Although if she was being honest with herself, Anita had been putting off the conversation with Khush for a couple of weeks now, she was not quite afraid, but anxious about bringing this up with him. It's not like they talked much anymore any way, so bringing all this up would mean intruding on Khush's evening, which Khush had made clear he hated her doing. Anita was desperate to get out and start becoming her own person again, but the thought of a confrontation with Khush just made her feel uneasy; all she wanted was a simple life without the hassle of arguments and tension in her house. Anita knew however, this discussion needed to happen, she needed to carry on with her life and pick it up where she left it when she had given birth to Anand.

That evening, after she had bathed Anand and as Khush was reading to him in his jungle themed room, Anita prepared herself for the conversation she had been putting off for weeks.

"Khush, can we talk please?" she asked as he gently closed the door of Anand's room.

"Talk? Right now? You know I'm busy Anita," sighed Khush.

"I know, and I'm sorry to disturb you but we need to have this conversation. It's about Anand." Anita added knowing this would get his attention better.

"Ok, what's up?" said Khush following Anita downstairs and sitting in the guest chair in the living room.

"Well, Anand's almost one now and I think he needs to go to nursery so he can socialise with other kids and start learning with them at nursery," Anita said, then quickly continued so she could get it all out before her nerves took over and stopped her, "and if he's going to nursery full time, then I think I could go back to work. I really want to be working again. Is that ok?"

Why am I asking you? Nikita thought, *I should be able to just tell you I'm going back to work.*

Khush looked at her and then at the box of Anand's toys taking up a corner of the living room. He took a few minutes before he spoke, and Anita didn't realise until he did that she had been holding her breath.

"Ok, so I agree that Anand should go to nursery."

"Oh great," sighed Anita, "So we-"

"Wait, let me finish," said Khush shaking his head and rolling his eyes.

"Sorry."

"So, yes he should go to nursery, full time if needs be…but I don't think you should go straight into looking for a job until he is settled in, just in case."

"But Khush, a mate from training said there is a place open that I would be great for, but not for long, so I think I need to-"

"I think you need to think of your son first, not yourself," cut in Khush.

A blow which took Anita by surprise and felt like a brutal gut punch.

"I don't think going for a psychology job will be good. You'd be too busy with work to help out around the house. You'll have too much stress and that won't be good for us all. You'll have to catch up on your studies and we don't have time for that and Anand."

Anita was stunned, she knew this may not go as well as she wanted but to be called selfish and told she wasn't thinking about her family was unconceivable. That's all she had done, and with less than a week to apply for her dream job, Anita had thought of all the scenarios in her getting this job. It would work. She would make it work.

"Khush," she started, breathing carefully and making sure not to get too emotional, something else Khush said she kept doing to manipulate him, "Look, Anand is doing amazing, and I need to get out and work, so I can provide for us all too. I have this job opportunity here and I know I can sort it so my hours fit in perfectly for Anand."

"And me," added Khush scornfully.

"And you. I won't have to study more, I won't have to catch up because it's only been a year since I finished training, not much has changed. Plus, this role is flexible, and I know I can do it. I need to do something for me now too. If Anand is at nursery all day, what would I do at home all day?"

"You won't be at home all day. You can work."

"So, I can apply for this…?"

"No. I mean you can work. Just not that one. You can find some part time or even full-time work but someplace that doesn't mean you'll be bringing work home with you and your mind can be here, at home with Anand and me, instead of at work all the time. I know how you get Anita you'll get all worked up in the cases and the people you see and forget all about us."

"I wouldn't," protested Anita, but she realised her words had fallen on deaf ears.

Khush had that look on his face that meant he wasn't going to change his mind or be persuaded any other way. He didn't want her to apply for the job that would be perfect for her and would be her dream career. All because he wanted her home, to what? Look after Anand? Anita had doubts as to what Khush was playing at, but she knew that she would have to search for other jobs.

"So, what jobs do you think I should apply for then Khush?" she asked close to tears.

"Dunno, if you still want to stay in that area of work then care worker jobs, that kind of stuff. I don't know Anita, I'm not going to go and find all the jobs available for you, you have to do some things yourself."

At that, Khush decided the discussion was over and walked out of the living room, leaving Anita quietly crying at the crumpled remains of a career she hadn't even had the chance to begin building.

Chapter 13.

It was a warm and sticky morning, and the overly cheerful man on the radio seemed to think it was only going to get worse. Today was Anita's first day at work, she had prepared her clothes, her lunch and Anand's nursery bag the night before; she wanted to be ready and not rush around. She needed to go into work calm and ready for a challenge. A new challenge. Something she had never done before but was surprisingly looking forward to. Her heart still longed for the career she had dreamt of since she met a psychologist at the school's careers day, but she hoped this wasn't going to be soul destroying.

The people and the care home where Anita now worked, were lovely. They had welcomed Anita's application and during her interview they were visibly impressed with her. They knew that her working for them was something of a blessing for the care home and the residents that lived there. Walking around on her induction, Anita had felt a warmth from the people that she hadn't felt for a long while and she knew she could do some good here too.

It wasn't her ideal job, but she had interviewed well and the manager of the care home had openly spoken about using her expertise and knowledge in psychology within the care home and with those who would benefit from her skillset the most. This excited Anita a lot as she could now see a way into her dream job, and although she wasn't going to charge right into pushing for a psychology role, she knew that the chances were there, and they were good.

Stepping out of the shower Anita could hear Anand babbling to himself in his room. He had started nursery a week earlier and had settled in very well. He had enjoyed the settling in sessions she had taken him to, and even cried a little when she had come to pick him up. This was a good sign for Anita, it meant that she could go to work without the guilt she had felt about leaving her son. Anand was happy, which meant she could be happy.

Khush was also happy. Not because she now had a job but because she had succumbed to the pressure and chosen a 'plain old any job' like he had told her to. Her hours also pleased Khush because it meant she was around to drop off Anand at nursery and pick him up on her way home from work too. And as much as Anita's mum and sister had moaned that she was doing everything and Khush was again, doing very little, Anita's preferred it this way. She got to spend time with her baby boy and wouldn't miss out on his growing up. She could be there to feed him in the evenings and help to provide for him. Her money was nowhere on par as what Khush was bringing in, but by being in work, Anita felt like she was slowly becoming her old self again.

Dropping him off to nursery, became the same routine every morning; she dropped him in his ladybird room, he would instantly waddle off and start tipping out all the toys he would play with and ignore her calls for a cuddle and kiss goodbye. Anita smiled and watched him for a moment before turning to the lead carer for the Ladybird room, Daniel.

"Thanks, have a good day, let me know if anything goes wrong and you need me to come by," she said handing Anand's bag to him.

"Don't worry, I'm sure he'll be fine. He's settled in so well compared to some kids we have come here." Daniel looked at Anita and smiled, "Looks like you're off to work? New job?"

"Ah yes," said Anita straightening her pale purple tunic, her uniform for the care home, "Yeah, new job, starting today."

"Excited?"

"Yeah, I am thanks," she replied smiling back at Daniel, "I think it's time, been home with the little man for just over a year and now need some work."

"Somewhere to be an adult again without having a child hanging on eh?" Daniel said nodding his head, "Makes sense and is probably good for you as well as Anand."

"Yup" said Anita breathing a sigh of relief. Daniel always had a way of making her feel at ease and like she was a great mum.

"That's cool. Well, have a fab day, I'm sure Anand will want to hear all about it when you pick him up."

Anita smiled, waved at Anand who was making his way to Daniel for his morning cuddle, and turned to leave.

The care home was just as pleasant as Anita remembered from her induction a week ago. She walked into reception and told the lady her name, and was told her manager, Emma, was coming to pick her up. After a few minutes, a plump, confidently walking woman came through the locked doors smiling at her.

"Ah Anita," she said as if they were long lost friends who hadn't seen each other in a millennia, "Good morning. I'm so glad you're here."

"Why wouldn't I be?" asked Anita smiling and following her through the door that led through to the interior of the building.

"Well, let's just say, sometimes we have people who say they are coming in for work, and then never turn up," Emma had a strong Scouse accent; she spoke fast, and Anita had to listen carefully and look at Emma's lips in order to fully understand what she was saying.

"Really?" Anita laughed shaking her head.

She was led into a small room which was clearly the staffroom. The walls were dotted with display boards and these in turn were full of posters; some clearly many years old and never taken down, just hanging there out of sheer stubbornness. Alongside the back of the staffroom, lockers stood rigidly along one wall looking a little old and scratched; most clearly being used to keep personal belongings in. The room was split into two distinct halves; one with a range of soft chairs and small sofas circling low coffee tables which were surprisingly clean and clear compared to the walls; the other half of the room was converted into a small kitchenette with a fridge, kettle, toaster, small sink and taps, microwave and the all-important coffee machine.

At this time in the morning, the room was quiet, most of the carers were already on the morning rounds and taking care of their allocated residents. Anita smiled and looked around as Emma walked over to a lone man sitting at a table in the kitchenette sipping a coffee and munching on a slice of toast, clearly lost in his own world.

"Eddie," Emma said making the young man jump, "this is Anita. Anita this is Eddie. He'll be your buddy for this week until you settle in. He's been here for a while, he knows everything there is to know about the job and the care home, and he'll take you through the procedures for everything today."

"Hi," said Anita feeling like she was a new kid in a school.

"Hello," said Eddie shaking Anita's outstretched hand, "Nice to meet you. As Emma, the boss, said, I am your mentor for the week. Ask me anything and I shall do my best to answer your questions. This place is lovely, and the people-both patients and the staff, are too."

"You mean residents," corrected Emma smiling, "been here years and still calls them patients. Ed, they are residents."

"Yes ma'am," said Eddie saluting Emma as she walked back towards the door.

Anita giggled as Emma waved a hand as she left, "Have a good day Anita! Be good Eddie."

Finishing off his coffee in one big gulp and shoving his toast into his mouth, Eddie turned to Anita and shrugged his shoulders, "Shall we get going then?"

"Let's do this." said Anita feeling good.

It didn't take long for Anita to get into the routine of how things worked in the care home. Her first impressions of the place and people were accurate, she felt happy working there and began to make some very good friends. Her mentor for the first week, Eddie, had become a very good friend and someone she could trust very quickly. Eddie was a tall, broad shouldered man. He was young, Anita guessed about thirty, but behaved like someone who had been around for much longer. He was wise, well intentioned and very caring when he interacted with the residents, and silly, immature and playful with his peers. Eddie was a fantastic carer and all the residents and staff at the care home adored him. He was the life of the party and good natured; he had a way of making even the most shy and anxious person around him feel at ease and confident. Anita included.

Her belief in herself was returning and she was starting to see the person she was, even before she had met Khush. Anand was happy and doing well in the nursery and even things with Khush had become less tense. Although Khush still spent a lot of time in the study, Anita found that he had started to join Anand and her at dinner time and would even ask Anita about her work. He would occasionally join her in the living room and watch mindless TV with her, joking about characters and poorly put together plot lines making Anita laugh at the stupidity of the shows. Anita was feeling things were starting to look up. Khush had become more intimate with her again, making her feel like the woman he had fallen in love with. Showing her attention and affection like she had longed for, the old romantic Khush was back and Anita was happy. Things were starting to fit back into place and she couldn't have been happier and more content. She just hoped it would stay like this.

"Let's go away for a weekend," said Khush one evening as Anita rested her head on his shoulder whilst watching a movie that they had watched many times before, "just us. What do you think?"

"Really?" said Anita lifting her head so that she was inches away from his face, "just us? You want that?"

"Yes," said Khush kissing the tip of her nose and ticking her with his newly grown beard, "Just us. Somewhere like a city break. We can go for walks and a meal that doesn't involve a highchair and ducking and diving to avoid spaghetti in our hair!"

Anita giggled, "That sounds amazing Khush. When were you thinking of doing this?"

"In a few weeks, we can ask one of our family to look after Anand, and it'll be nice as it's our anniversary soon isn't it?"

Anita's eyes widened with surprise, "Yeah, in like a month, I didn't think you wanted to do anything for it."

"Well, I do now. Is that alright?"

"Of course," said Anita enjoying the slow stroke of Khush's hand along her arm and placing her head back on his broad strong shoulders, "Where do you want to go?"

"You choose. Any place, as long as I can do this," said Khush lifting Anita's chin back up to face him and kissing her deeply, pulling her close to him.

Chapter 14.

It was surprising how it only took a few simple things for Anita to feel like her life was looking good and going in the right direction again. Khush decided to organise a lovely weekend away, not telling her where just to surprise her, he was being attentive, romantic and everything she had fallen in love with. It was just perfect. Anand was at Anita's mum's place with Henna joining them to look after Anand, Khush's parents were unable to look after Anand as his mum hadn't been feeling well, and Khush said he wouldn't even bother asking his brother since they had two kids to worry about already. Everything was sorted for Anita and all she had to do was sit back and enjoy her special time with Khush.

Khush took her to York, one of her favourite places to go and to visit; she loved the historical castles, dungeons and the landscape in York. It was a place that cried romance to her. The hotel was grand and Khush had spared no expense in getting them a deluxe room with a private hot tub and seating area too. The room was vast, almost as big as their downstairs at home, the view from the window overlooked a large park and there were steps leading up to the bed.

"Wow," said Anita spinning around the spacious room and taking in all its glory, "this place is lush Khush, I feel so spoilt. Thanks honey. It's so big, and romantic. I love it. And I love you."

"You're welcome," said Khush dropping their bags at the foot of the bed and smiling at his wife, "happy anniversary."

"Happy anniversary to you too." said Anita walking into Khush's open arms and kissing him on the lips, "thank you. I can't wait to get exploring around, have you ever been to the dungeons?"

"No," said Khush laughing at his wife's enthusiasm, "Maybe we can leave that for tomorrow."

"Ok, no worries," said Anita walking to the window and looking out at the afternoon sun shining on the park below, "so what shall we do now then? What shall we do for dinner?"

Khush sidled up to Anita and slid him arms around her waist as he kissed her neck softly, his tongue flicking out caressing her making Anita moan with pleasure.

He nibbled at her ear and whispered, "Well dinner reservations aren't until 7, that gives us three hours."

"Mmm," murmured Anita closing her eyes and pushing her hips against Khush, "what do you propose we do then?"

"Well," said Khush pulling Anita closer to his body and kissing her neck with more vigour, his breathing becoming deeper, "I think we should start with the bed, and then move to test out the hot tub."

Anita could feel herself melt in his arms and as she turned around to face her husband, she could feel that he was already as turned on as she was. She kissed him hard and ran her hands through his hair and down his chest. Pulling away slightly she looked at him and smiled.

"I take that as a yes," said Khush smiling back and leading her to the fancy four poster bed.

"I like that idea," said Anita reaching to unbutton his jeans as he kissed her again.

The restaurant that Khush had chosen was just as fancy as the hotel they were staying in. Both Anita and Khush were wearing smart evening clothes; Anita choosing to wear a dress that hugged her figure and showed off her toned legs, and Khush wearing a shirt with smart jeans and shoes, his muscles accentuated by the short sleeves on his shirt. They were given a table close to the back of the restaurant which was more private, and looking around the room Anita thought more for couples, there was also a single red rose placed in the centre of the table alongside a lit candle. The lighting was low and romantic, both joked it meant they couldn't see the menu and what they were ordering. The hostess appeared with a complimentary bottle of Prosecco on hearing they were celebrating an anniversary.

Khush was going all out and was making such an effort to be the man Anita had fallen in love with. Everything seemed to be back to normal. Conversation was seamless and not at all awkward unlike the last year. Khush wanted to know about her work and he was even pleased to hear that there may be a chance to work towards psychiatry with her residents there where she worked. They talked about Anand, Anita filling Khush in on what he was like at nursery and how they were planning on a summer show of some sort. They laughed at the concept of the nursery staff trying to organise twenty children aged between one and four to say their lines at the right time. It was something that Anita was definitely going to film and planned to show Anand when he got older and thought himself too cool for.

"So," said Khush after a few minutes of comfortable silence between the couple, "I need to say something."

"Ok," said Anita smiling at Khush as she sipped on her second glass of wine.

"I know we've not had the best year this year, and I know you blame me."

"No, I, look we both-"

"No Anita, let me finish please," Khush cut in softly, "It has been hard for me. Even when you got a job, I couldn't help out much. And I know I may have been…I should have been here for you and Anand. I feel like I have missed out on some of his first year because of it and I know I haven't been a good husband to you."

He paused here to take a sip of his wine and Anita could see he was starting to get emotional. For a moment she wondered if it was the wine making him well up or if he was genuinely sorry. Then she scolded herself for thinking so cynically especially after the passion in the hotel room earlier.

"So, what I wanted to say was that I am sorry. I know I have been such a dick to you. I know that I didn't give you the love and attention you wanted after Anand was born and that I saw you to struggle through some shit on your own instead of doing it with you."

"Khush…"

"I want to promise you something. I want to promise you that I will change, that I will try to change my ways and be more supportive and we can be a proper team. I'm worried I pushed you away and I want to be the man I should be, we can both do it."

There was a long pause, a silence that for the first time this weekend felt strange, and in that pause Khush looked at his glass, took a big gulp and then at Anita who was still holding her glass to her lips, unmoving.

"Anita, will you help me?"

Wiping away a stray tear rolling down her cheek, Anita smiled at her husband. "Of course. And I promise to be better for you as well. I didn't realise you were going through things too and I just let my shit take over when I should also have been looking out for you. I am sorry, I am in the wrong too. It's my fault that we didn't communicate properly. Can you forgive me?"

"That's a deal then. I forgive you," said Khush smiling broadly, he raised his glass and added, "a toast, to us, to new beginnings, making changes and to not being dicks."

"Cheers," said Anita giggling and clinking glasses.

"Now that's over with, where do you want to go after dinner? We still have some time if you wanted to go to a pub or bar?" said Khush polishing off his wine and waving down the hostess for the cheque.

"Well…" Anita said also finishing the wine in her glass and sensing that Khush really wasn't in the mood to go anywhere else. She had to choose their next move carefully, Khush's mood could easily swing hostile so quickly, especially after a drink or two, "how about we grab a bottle of wine and take it back to our room? I think there is some more testing out to do in there."

She winked and giggled as Khush smiled.

"That's a plan," he said grinning, "Now let's get the bill paid, a bottle bought and get back to the room to celebrate our anniversary."

The weekend away in York had been amazing and flew by so quickly. Anita and Khush had rekindled their love for one another and apart from one trip to the dungeons and walking about in the park, they had spent most of their time back up in the hotel room making the best use of the facilities in there. As they drove back home late Sunday night Anita gave her mum a quick call to see how Anand was doing; she wasn't going to pick him up until after work on Monday but thought she would check in with her mum. Anand giggled down the phone and her sister told Anita that their aajima had been trying to teach Anand some Gujarati too. Anita rolled her eyes and she and her sister joked at memories of aajima doing the same to them.

"Give my mum a call too please," asked Khush as she said her goodbyes to Anand, "She's not been too well so I just want to check to see if all is ok. She asked me to."

"Sure thing," said Anita as she found her mother-in-law's number on her phone, "Shall I put it on speaker?"

"Yes," said Khush.

As the car echoed with the phone ringing Anita looked over at Khush and squeezed his knee. The call went to answer machine to their surprise; his parents were always home and always answered the call.

"That's weird," said Anita cutting the call, "Shall we try your dad's mobile?"

Khush nodded.

Anita scrolled down the list of contacts eventually finding her father-in-law's mobile number, a number she rarely called or received calls from. She felt on edge as she rang.

"Hello?" came a gruff voice on the other end after what seemed like a lifetime, "Who's this?"

"Hi, dad?" said Khush looking confused, "It's me dad, why do you sound so weird? Is everything ok? You didn't answer the house phone."

"Oh, Khush," said his dad, his voice sounding a little softer, "we are not at home."

"Why? Where are you?"

"At the hospital."

Anita looked over at Khush who was now gripping the steering wheel tightly.

"Dad, why are you at the hospital?" Khush urged speaking louder.

"Beta, I think you should come to the hospital. It's your mum. She's here. She is here at the hospital."

"Mum? What's happened to mum? Is she ok?"

"I think you should come to the hospital first beta, easier to explain it all to you when you get here."

"We're on our way, we should be there soon. Is that ok? We're nearly home."

"Ok, see you then."

Before Khush could add anything more his dad had cut the call. "What the fuck?" he said looking at Anita.

"No idea."

"How far is the hospital from here?"

"About 20 minutes."

"We're going there."

As Anita looked from her phone to her husband, she began to feel panic rising, *please god let there be nothing bad* she thought to herself, closing her eyes and saying a prayer mentally that her aajima had taught her years ago. She opened her eyes and stole a glance in Khush's direction, his hands still gripped the steering wheel tight, his breathing had quickened, and his eyes were glassy and full of tears. Cars streamed by the window in a blur of colours and the once light sky seemed to darken and turn heavy.

"It'll be alright," she said soothingly although she wasn't sure if it was Khush she was reassuring or herself, "it'll be ok."

Chapter 15.

Anita looked out of the window at the sky, it was streaked with hues of red, pink and orange making the sky look stunning. *What a beautiful sky*, she thought to herself as she turned back to the mirror and adjusted her plain white sari, *too beautiful to look at on such a horrid day.*

"Shit," she yelped as a pin slipped its hook and dug deep into her thumb, "Damn saris. Damn pins. Damn everything!"

"You ok sis?" Henna said as she came into the room holding on to her nephew against her hip.

"No. These pins won't do what they're told to," hissed Anita sucking on her bleeding thumb.

"Here, let me help." said Henna putting Anand down on the bed and walking to her sister, "Let me do the pin. Calm down sis, it's ok, it's going to be ok."

"No, it's not," said Anita her eyes red and brimming with tears, "she's gone. I know I didn't always speak to her lots, but she was his mum, and she's gone now Henna. It's not fair."

Anita began to cry softly on her sister's shoulder. After a few minutes she stopped and dried her eyes. "Sorry."

"Don't be, you have every right to be upset today Anita, it's your mother-in-law's funeral. You can cry. No one can tell you to be brave or anything. You loved her. She loved you. You can be sad." Henna adjusted the sari and giving her sister a little hug.

"Poor Khush." said Anita allowing a fresh set of tears to roll down her puffy cheeks.

"I know sis, I know. You don't have to be strong for me, or Anand, but you will need to be strong for Khush when you're there today ok? Have a cry here and now but be there for him at the funeral."

"I will," sniffed Anita. Taking her son in her arms for a cuddle that made her not want to ever let go she added, "thanks for looking after Anand for the day."

"It's fine, no one wants to have a baby at a funeral. I'm more than happy to watch him for you and Khush."

Anita could hear Khush stomping around downstairs and muttering to himself. She gave Anand one more kiss on the cheek and walked down the stairs ready for the funeral. This was going to be dreadful and Anita was not looking forward to it.

The funeral itself was straightforward for an Indian funeral. Everyone wore white-which was customary- and ladies from the community that had known Khush's mum sang sombre hymns and songs throughout the morning making Anita cry even though she didn't know the meaning of the words; the melody was enough. Khush, his brother and his father had decided to use their home for the final prayers, so when the undertakers brought the coffin into the house on the morning of the funeral and opened up the lid in the cleared out living room, Anita saw her mother-in-law looking like she was sound asleep. She was dressed in a beautiful sari and her make-up had been applied to make her mother-in-law look elegant.

It was an overwhelmingly emotional vigil, but at the same time it felt cleansing. Being able to adorn her mother-in-law with a garland made from subtly scented flowers, touch her feet to ask for a final blessing and place an item in the coffin with her to take with her to the next life was very moving and spiritual. Her casket was simple, and flowers, dried fruit, nuts, and prasad (blessed Indian food) were placed inside the coffin with her to serve as gifts and offerings to God and her ancestors. Anita wasn't a big believer in God, in her Hindu religion or in reincarnation for that matter, but she thought that this small ritual was something that allowed her to mourn, celebrate and remember her sweet mother-in-law. There was something so divine about it that brought a sense of closure for Anita.

Khush and his brother, Pritesh, had taken it upon themselves to keep the diwa lit for the duration of the mourning period; they stayed in the living room in the evenings with an enshrined picture of their mother and took it in turns to sleep whilst the other watched the diwa and added more fuel to the cotton candle when it was going to die out.

Khush's dad, normally a strong and lively man had retreated into himself, losing his wife had made his usually large exterior seem smaller and less formidable. His voice was now a whisper compared to his foghorn-like bellows of before and his bearded face and hair showed signs of neglect. He spent most of his time in silence when people came to pay their respects, leaving the hosting to the others, and he only spoke once the house was empty of visitors.

Khush's sister-in-law Payal was the only one who really spoke to Anita during those days. She was a quiet, small and a serious woman; she looked petite next to her much larger husband, but she could hold her own. On several occasions Anita had heard Payal defend her against Pritesh when he was making snide comments towards her. Payal, and her mother-in-law were the only people who were truly nice to Anita in the family; they had shown her compassion and even when she didn't do things the 'usual Indian way', they accepted her and encouraged her to be her own woman. They did this more than even Khush.

The evening of the funeral when all rituals had been concluded, Payal and Anita were washing up the dishes from dinner, the men had retreated to the living room to watch the TV which had been left mounted on the wall during all this time.

"Thanks for helping me," said Anita as she soaped up the dishes handing them to Payal to rinse them and stack them on the draining board.

"That's ok Anita," Payal said quietly, "It's been crazy these few days."

"Yeah," agreed Anita, "It's going to be strange her not being here."

"I know," said Payal. Then almost as a whisper she added, "we're on our own now. Us girls, the outsiders. She always used to stick up for us and if the boys didn't like something we did, she always told them to leave us alone."

"Really?" said Anita, although she had assumed some of this already it was strange hearing it from Payal's mouth, "she stuck up for me?"

"Yes, you and me."

"You? But you're the perfect daughter-in-law!" said Anita grinning and giving Payal a little nudge with her hips.

"Ha," she laughed back, her eyes glittering, "I'm not as perfect as they all think I am. I have my demons."

"Demons? Oh do tell."

"Sorry, no can do. Those secrets will stay a secret between mum and me."

Anita and Payal laughed quietly so not to disturb the men in the room next door, and then fell into a sombre silence remembering why they were there and feeling the hole that was left with their mother-in-law passing.

"So," said Payal placing the final plate on the draining board and drying her hands on a towel, "Any plans to have a second kid?"

"What?" said Anita spluttering.

"Second kid. Are you guys thinking of having another one?"

"God no," said Anita starting to wipe down the table and surfaces in the kitchen, not because they were really dirty, but because she was avoiding looking at her sister-in-law who was standing there staring right at her, "No way. Anand is amazing, he really is, but no I don't want another kid at all. One is hard enough. I don't know how you do it with two."

"They pretty much look after themselves and each other now," said Payal watching Anita fuss nervously around, "are you alright Anita? I haven't said something I shouldn't have I?"

"No, no you haven't said anything bad," said Anita turning to face Payal, "just, I was surprised. Wasn't expecting that at all. No we don't really want to have any more kids, work for me is great and I'm doing really well and already taking on some more responsibilities and Khush's work is keeping him busy too, so I think another kid now would just be too much."

"That's nice that work is good for you," said Payal fiddling with her sari pleats, "I get what you're saying about kids. I wish I had pursued my work a little more."

Anita looked at Payal and in that moment she saw regret and unhappiness in her eyes. Anita admired Payal a lot, especially with putting up with Khush's brother Pritesh, but she didn't realise that giving up a career and spending all of her time looking after the boys was something she had not been completely behind. When she first met Payal, Anita had found out that she was training as a dental hygienist but gave that up as soon as she had become pregnant, which was less than a year after marrying Pritesh.

"I always thought I would go back and finish my training and get a full time, or even part time, job, you know?" said Payal wistfully, "I didn't realise that Pritesh wanted me to be a stay at home mum and deal with the housework and family stuff while he went out to work."

"Oh Payal," said Anita putting an arm around the small woman, "I didn't know that. I thought that was a choice you made."

"Unfortunately not," Payal said glancing towards the living room, "You're lucky Khush was alright with you having a job."

"Yeah well…" said Anita, "he wasn't really. Took me a year to persuade him to allow me to work, and he wouldn't let me carry on with the psychology angle. Said I would be working too hard to look after him and Anand."

"That sucks," said Payal shaking her head, "but you're doing well now though?"

"Yeah," smiled Anita, "it's working out. Maybe now the boys are both in school full-time you can persuade Pritesh to let you go back to work?"

"Yeah maybe," said Payal hopefully, then giggling she added, "but then how do I carry on being the kept woman? I have a perfect respectable persona to uphold don't you know?"

At this they began laughing and within an instant they heard an angry voice bellow from the living room, "Why can I hear laughing?"

"Sorry papa," called Payal adding a twinge of an Indian accent. This made Anita laugh some more and she stifled it with her hand over mouth.

As Khush and Anita drove home that night after picking up Anand from her sister's place, Anita thought about her conversation with Payal.

"Did you know that Pritesh didn't allow Payal to work once she got pregnant?" she asked, talking quietly so not to wake her son in the back seat.

"So what?" said Khush, his voice was gravelly and dry, he was frowning and staring too intently at the road.

"I was just saying," said Anita feeling the base of her neck starting to heat up, "just because she mentioned it and was happy for me and the fact that we both work and look after Anand."

Khush huffed, "Pritesh may have been right."

"What do you mean?"

"Well, he asked her to stay at home with the kids and look after the family, just like mum did with us boys, and we turned out alright."

"Anand will turn out fine," defended Anita feeling annoyed at what she had just heard, "even with us at work, he will be perfectly fine. He gets everything he needs."

And you and your brother did not turn out fine at all she thought.

"He would benefit more if you were at home," snapped Khush finally looking away from the road and casting an obnoxious look at his wife. After what seemed like an eternity he added scornfully, "if you were like my mum."

Chapter 16.

After his mother's funeral Khush became distant and quiet again. He retreated to his study space and although he still ate dinners with Anita and Anand, he didn't involve himself in family time properly; once he had eaten, he would walk back into his study and spend the rest of the night in there, alone. Anita was worried.

She had enjoyed the few months of bliss and happiness that they all had shared and now with that version of Khush being locked away again, she felt even more depressed and lonely. She believed, and hoped, that this would not last long and slowly Khush would come out of his misery and be himself again, but it was going to take a lot of patience from Anita. Patience she wasn't sure she had.

Khush still played with Anand but was less animated and often his mind was elsewhere. Anand would poke and prod Khush to try and get his full attention, but this didn't work and when it all got too much for Khush he would yell at Anand and leave the room. Anita began the old routine of walking on eggshells around Khush and slowly Anand was learning to do the same which broke Anita's heart.

After one such evening, and after Anita had calmed Anand down and put him down to sleep for the night, she went to find Khush. She knocked on the door to the study.

I can't believe I'm knocking on a door in my own damn house, she thought chastising herself.

"Yeah?" came the hassled voice of her husband.

"Hi Khush, can we talk please?"

Anita stayed by the door, like a stranger in her own home.

"What about?" said Khush, his eyes still not leaving the television he clearly wasn't watching.

"I think we need to chat about things with us and especially Anand."

"What about him?"

"He's really upset you know," said Anita taking a step into the room and manoeuvring her way into his peripheral vision.

"He's upset because he got in trouble and doesn't like being shouted at."

"But it was over nothing."

Khush turned to Anita and glared at her, "you would say that. You spoil him. you're too soft on him."

"No, I'm not," said Anita feeling that all too common emotional mix of annoyance and fear, "I tell him off when he's done something wrong. It's just that he didn't this time. It was hardly anything."

"So?"

"So, you blew up at him over a simple thing."

"He didn't say please or thank you. Manners matter Anita."

Anita pressed her lips together; she knew his comment about Anand was a dig at her- most of his comments were aimed to wound.

"I know manners matter," she said her voice as void of emotion as she could get it, "but it was once and you went mental at him, as if he's sworn at you or something."

"He won't learn any other way."

"You haven't tried any other way."

Anita's breath caught in her throat as Khush turned to finally face her. His face was sullen, and he shook his head.

"Why are you telling me all this bullshit, Anita?"

"It's not...I'm saying that maybe we need to talk it through or seek some help on how to deal with Anand and his tantrums."

And maybe some of your tantrums and mood swings too.

"I don't think we need to at all."

"But I do, you can't keep shouting at him for nothing."

"And you can't keep pussy-footing around him as if he'll break if you tell him no."

Anita stared at her husband in disbelief. He truly believed what he was saying, and he delighted in seeing her reaction to such an insult to her parenting skills.

"It's not nice hearing that is it?"

"I wasn't trying to upset you," said Anita taking a step back towards the door, "I just wanted a civil conversation."

"You just wanted to bitch at me and tell me I'm a shit father."

You are.

"I'm not saying you're a shit father," said Anita, her throat had gone dry, "I'm saying you don't have to shout at him every time he does something wrong."

"How else will he learn?"

"You can talk to him and explain what mistake he's made and how to fix it for next time. Reason with him."

"He's a kid. I'm his dad. I don't have to reason with anyone. You should all just respect and listen to me."

Anita's hands became clammy, and she felt her face flush with anger. But she didn't want an argument, again.

"You and Anand both need to learn to listen to me and respect me," said Khush spitting his words out like venom trying to get a reaction from Anita.

Anita swallowed hard. She licked her lips and took a deep breath.

Don't react Anita.

"Khush, we do respect you and we do listen. That's not the point, I'm trying to say we need to figure out a better way to deal with Anand. Together."

"My dad never got this hassle from my mum."

That was it, the last straw, the one person Khush knew he could get Anita ranting about. He smiled as he watched her hands curl into fists and her lip curl.

"Your dad?" she said shaking her head, "I can't believe you think that the way your dad treated your mum was acceptable. She didn't respect him. She feared him. She did what he said because she was afraid of disobeying him. Their relationship was from another era, an era where women weren't equal and weren't seen as anything important. We don't live in that world anymore. If you want respect from me, you have to earn it."

Anita's control and confidence rapidly disappeared. She was breathing heavy, and her hands ached from her nails pressing into the palms. Looking at Khush's sneer, Anita knew she had said the wrong thing. She watched through wet eyes, paralyzed as Khush stood up slowly and deliberately took steady steps towards her.

"You don't get to talk about my family," he hissed, his sneer replaced quickly with bared teeth and rage, "you don't know the first thing about being a good wife or a good mother. How dare you speak of my mother and say she was scared of my dad. She was everything to him. And you are nothing to me."

Anita flinched and took a step back as Khush raised his hand.

Shit, she thought, *he's going to hit me.*

But he reached his hand to the door, and laughed at her reaction to his raised hand, relishing in the knowledge he scared her.

"You mean nothing to me, you're nowhere near the mother my mum was. Don't ever speak her name."

He shoved the door closed, forcing Anita to step back to avoid being hurt. She looked at the door, her eyes streaming with tears, her chest aching with sadness and hands shaking from fright. She could hear the glee in Khush's laughter echoing through the house as she walked away.

Chapter 17.

Work became Anita's safe place, a place she could be herself, say what she wanted to. She had impressed Emma enough to be given Wednesdays to work with residents with her psychology hat on. She was able to have conversations with the residents and discuss how they were doing and talk through any issues they had. She made notes, and she would make sure they were meticulous and if she needed medical or other professional opinions she would ask. This was an opportunity she was not going to ruin. Anita sometimes worked late on Wednesdays in order to get her files in order, she didn't want Khush to have another reason to have a go at her or get angry with her or to say she wasn't doing enough for him and Anand. Work was almost like a refuge for Anita, a place she could do things right.

Her colleagues were amazing, and she had made many friends, but her closest friend was Eddie. After buddying with her for a week and showing her the ropes, they had ended up on the same shift patterns and became very close. Eddie was hilarious, he would always have a funny comment or amusing story that went with everything that happened during the day. They were a great team, they played to each other's strengths and the residents loved having Eddie and Anita look after them. Some even joked that they were like a perfect couple. Eddie had also become the only person Anita had confided in about Khush's mood swings; her sister and mother had an idea about how infuriating Khush could be, but they didn't know everything, Eddie did.

Within months of working with Anita he was able to detect that something was up, and after a few heart-to-heart conversations over making beds and cleaning rooms, Anita had spilled everything. She sat talking to him about how life used to be with Khush, his mood swings over the smallest of things, the fact that he didn't even eat dinner with his family or speak to his wife properly, only communicating through a few grunts, notes left on the counter and the odd email. Eddie was shocked and annoyed for Anita, he had explained that this was clearly Khush's way of gas lighting her, of making her feel that she was the one doing something wrong.

To Eddie it was clear that after a while of breaking Anita down emotionally and in her self-confidence, Khush would then sweep back into her life as knight in shining armour, shower her with gifts, spend copious amounts of time with Anand and be an affectionate husband again, making promises to change. Khush did this to keep Anita on edge, to keep her doing as he wanted, and most importantly, he did this to keep Anita believing that there was hope for the marriage. Anita had tried to defend Khush whenever Eddie said all this but found more and more that this was becoming difficult. She wanted something to change but was too scared to do anything, she didn't want to break up her family, didn't want the shame of a divorce to be something that she and her family had to deal with. Divorce wasn't the Indian way.

"Divorce isn't something you should be ashamed about." Eddie said as they were on a lunch break. The weather was good, and they had decided to go for a walk instead of sitting in the staffroom.

"But I just couldn't tell my parents. They'd be so upset with me."

"No they wouldn't," said Eddie looking at Anita and frowning, "I don't know them personally, but from what you have said about your family, there is no way they would be angry at you for getting a divorce and being happy. Not even slightly."

"I guess but I don't know, it's so hard Eddie."

"I know mate, I know it must be horrible for you. But you have to look at your own happiness. And Anand's. There are thousands of people out there who live happy lives now that they've managed to escape their terrible relationships."

"But who'd want an old, frumpy, single mum like me? No one will want me with all the baggage I have."

"God Anita" said Eddie exasperated with the way the conversations kept going round and around the same way, "You're not old, or frumpy, and I know, *we* know, plenty of people who have found love again and have kids too. It's not about finding love again though is it? It has to be about getting yourself freed from this cycle of abuse and being yourself again."

"It's not abuse Eddie, he doesn't hit me ever," replied Anita sipping her drink and sitting down at a bench they had just walked upon.

"It may not be physical abuse but it's still abuse. Emotional. Mental. Psychological abuse Anita. You must be able to see it? You're clever, you're more educated than me, and you're a damn psychologist. You must be able to see the signs and see what he is doing?"

"I guess, but-"

"No buts mate," said Eddie sitting next to her and placing a hand on her shoulder, "you have to start thinking about yourself. Anand probably sees the way Khush treats you and he'll end up thinking this is normal behaviour and treat his future girlfriends or boyfriends like this. I bet Khush learnt it from his dad."

Anita smiled sadly at this. The way that Khush treated Anita on the bad days was exactly like the way she had watched his dad treat his mum and this was also the way she saw Pritesh treat Payal. She saw so clearly that this is what the boys had seen and heard when growing up, and must have thought that this was the way to treat your wife. Both Anita and Payal were treated in this arrogant and dismissive way. The way they were made to feel like inferior people just because they were wives and mothers. She told Eddie just what her father-in-law and brother-in-law were like many times before.

"Exactly" said Eddie with an edge of righteousness, "they learnt it from their dad, and if you don't stop it, Anand will learn it from Khush."

"I know." said Anita feeling defeated and helpless.

"Does his brother have kids too?"

"Yeah two boys," said Anita looking at Eddie through tears, "the eldest is a bit of a nightmare towards his mum. The younger not so much."

"There you go," said Eddie raising his hands as if everything made sense, "he's clearly learnt to be a little shit by watching his grandpa and dad be like that."

"Probably," nodded Anita, "but Anand won't be like that. I'll make sure of it."

"But how will you know he's not soaking up the atmosphere, the vibes between you and Khush? How do you know he's not seeing what Khush is like to you, his mood swings and all, and thinking this is how a relationship is meant to be like? Because you and I know it isn't Anita."

"I know."

"It's not a relationship, it's toxic and he's manipulating you. He is gas lighting you into believing you're not able to make it without him, that you need to rely on him, and that you can't take his kid away from the family. None of that is true. You can step away, with Anand, you can get safe and still be happy. It's won't happen quickly, you know this, but you have to start making that choice."

Eddie became more enraged for his friend as he spoke, breathing faster and gesturing his arms further than he normally did. Anita watched him and felt lost. She had only known Eddie for just over half a year, and here he was caring about her happiness and safety more than Khush had in a while. She felt overwhelmed, and her hands were starting to shake, her emotions threatened to spill out and Anita didn't think she had the willpower to reign them in.

"Anita," said Eddie quieter now, he placed a hand on her quivering arm, "Sorry, I shouldn't have said all that, I didn't mean to upset you."

"You didn't," said Anita and then looking at the concern etched across his face she began to sob. Eddie enveloped her in his arms, stroking her head and allowing her to cry hard. After a few moments, when she felt like she couldn't cry any more, Anita lifted her head and plucked a tissue out of her bag.

"Sorry," said Anita wiping her face knowing her make-up had been ruined, "I didn't mean to...I was just overwhelmed."

"It's ok," said Eddie looking at Anita and holding onto her shoulders, "you clearly needed that. Feel any better?"

"Not really," said Anita smiling slightly, "and now I have to back in to work with a messed-up face!"

"So, the usual," joked Eddie pretending to be in pain when Anita punched him lightly on the arm, "I'm kidding. You look great, as always. Sorry I went off on one about him. I'm just so worried about you. I'm your mate and care how you are. He is such a knob. You deserve better. Trust me. And when you do get free of him, and I know you will, there will be someone there who will make you feel as special as you are. I promise."

"Thanks Eddie," said Anita throwing her tissues in the bin and getting up, "I hope you're right. Right now though, I don't know anything about men."

"Women then?" said Eddie walking in step with Anita, "That's a big change. I'm not sure you're ready for that commitment. Women are a handful you know, trust me. I had my fair share before realising men were better. They're simple creatures."

"Simple? Huh, men are idiots."

"And that's why we love them," said Eddie draping an arm around Anita as they entered the building.

Giggling, Anita pushed Eddie's arm off her and went into the ladies washroom to tidy herself up, "I'll be a minute Eddie, just need to sort my face."

"Ok Anita," said Eddie walking into the staffroom, "but you'll need more than a minute to sort that face out."

Anita laughed as she stood in front of the mirror, Eddie had a knack of making her smile and feel better even when things weren't good. Just like Khush used to. Eddie was able to get inside her mind and find out what she was really thinking and get Anita to open-up and be honest. Just like Khush used to. And he had a way of making her feel special, valued and like she mattered. Just like Khush used to. Anita sighed as she tried to make herself look more presentable instead of like she'd just dunked her head in a bucket of hot water; her eyes were puffy and there was no hiding that, but she applied a little blusher and eyeshadow thinking that was as good as it was going to get before beginning her afternoon shift.

"All good?" asked Eddie as she walked out of the ladies and handing her a small post lunch coffee which had become a ritual between the pair of them, "Looking much better Anita."

"Why thank you Eddie," giggled Anita fluttering her eyes at Eddie, "good enough to attract another male?"

"Yeah, I'd say so." said Eddie smiling, "If only I wasn't gay."

"Typical," said Anita, "I find a decent guy and he's gay."

"All the best ones are mate; all the best ones are."

Chapter 18.

When Anita arrived home later that evening, to her surprise Khush was already home and sitting in the living room. He didn't look happy and Anita could tell by the look on his face something was wrong.

"All ok?" asked Anita tentatively whilst putting Anand down who was wriggling to get to his dad for cuddles. *Please please don't be a big issue, I'm too tired.*

"We can talk later," said Khush gruffly. He picked up Anand and gave him a kiss and cuddle, "Hey mate, how are you doing? Good day at nursery?"

"Good daddy," said Anand giggling as Khush tickled him.

Anita stood at the living room door sensing that she shouldn't enter the room and ruin the moment. In her mind she could hear Eddie and she replayed the conversation they had at lunch earlier in her head.

"I'm just going to get changed and then get dinner on," Anita said as she turned to hang up her coat and begin walking up the stairs, "are you eating with us today?" *Please say no and go hide in your little den.*

"I will today," said Khush walking to the doorway with Anand hanging on to his arms like a monkey.

"Pasta ok for tonight?" she asked looking back at him and smiling although the air was charged with something that made her feel on edge.

"Yeah, pasta. Not too greasy this time though."

"Ok."

Anita walked up the stairs feeling her body tense up at this snide remark. Once. It was just once that she had somehow done something with the dinner that had made it all very greasy and inedible. They had thrown it away and bought take-out in the end. Anita walked into the bedroom and began to undress. She looked at her hands and realised that her hands were trembling, and she wasn't sure if it was out of anger at the comment or the unease she felt at Khush being home and saying he wanted to talk.

What did he want to talk about? Anita searched her brain for something that she may have done wrong in the past week or two that he may have an issue with but couldn't think of anything. Khush had barely been around for her to do anything to annoy him. She was unsure and anxious.

"This is going to be a fun evening," she muttered to herself in the mirror. She scraped back her hair into a bun and walked down to her son and husband.

At the dinner table Anita felt tense, her whole body felt like it was twisting into a knot at the nerves of this impending conversation with Khush. Anand was his usual bubbly mischievous self at the dinner table, trying to feed all the vegetables to Anita but keeping all the cheesy pieces of pasta and chicken to himself. He was chattering away throughout the whole meal which was a blessing since Khush had not said a word. He moved his food around the plate and deliberately scraped the fork across the plate knowing it would make Anita wince every time. Anita had tried to spark up some form of conversation, but she only got grunts from Khush, and when she pushed too hard Khush has snapped and said "later, like I said. Just listen to what I say. Later."

The rest of the meal had been spent in silence. Anand was feeing the mood change and he became agitated, looking at Anita with his innocent eyes wondering what was happening.

"Are you done Anand?" she asked him sweetly pointing at his plate, "ready for some fruit?"

"Foot," squealed Anand, he couldn't quite say fruit yet.

Anita got up from the table and went to cut up the apple she had laid out ready for Anand's pudding. Even though she had her back to the dining table she could feel Khush's eyes burning into her.

Stop looking at me, please.

"Do you want any fruit Khush?" she asked. Her answer was given as he left his half-eaten bowl of pasta on the table and walked out of the kitchen.

Anita was afraid of what was to come, she still couldn't figure what she had done to upset Khush and wondered what he was in such a foul mood about. She bathed and chattered along with Anand and sang him a bedtime lullaby that her aajima has taught her when she was pregnant. Anand had played lots with Khush this evening and was very tired by the time Anita tucked him into bed and read him his bedtime story.

She could hear Khush move around the living room, changing channels and being generally restless and she couldn't help but feel like she wanted to curl up with Anand and go to sleep to avoid the inevitable confrontation. But she knew he would just be there until he got whatever it was, off his chest.

She walked quietly down the stairs, went into the kitchen and grabbed herself a drink.

"Want a drink?" she called to Khush. She hoped her voice sounded airy and light and not strained like she was feeling.

"No. When you're done with yours, we can talk."

Anita's shoulders sagged; this was it. Whatever this was about, they were going to talk about it now. On his terms and when he wanted to. Anita walked into the living room and Khush was back at the guest chair, one he hadn't sat on during those months of blissful happiness. Anita sat cautiously down on the sofa and curled her legs underneath her, hoping that making herself seem small would help with whatever was coming.

Keep it light, don't irritate him any more Anita. Don't be stupid.

"So, what's up Khush?" she said her smile faltering a little as she looked at his serious face.

"How's work?"

"Work?" asked Anita taken aback a little, "work is really good. I'm really enjoying it. I like helping the residents and the people I work with are great. How's work for you?"

"Who are the people you work with?" Khush said ignoring the question.

"I don't know what you mean?"

"Who do you work directly with?"

"Directly? Well, there is Emma my boss, who I see every day but only briefly. There's Eddie who is in my team and we work together. There's Sam, Helen, Matt and-"

"Eddie."

There it was. That one word from Khush told her exactly where this conversation was heading. *Ah, Eddie. This is where you've got an issue then?* She thought trying to keep her face neutral even though she was terrified.

"Eddie? Yeah, he was my mentor in the first week remember, helped me settle in, and we've been on the same shift and rounds since. Remember I told you about him. Why?"

"Are you close to him?"

Careful here Anita, watch what you say.

"Close to him? Well, I guess. We work together all the time, so we chat and have a chance to get to know each other quite a bit. But just work friends. Why do you ask? I chat to all the others too. Sam is funny too and Matt is such a-"

"So, do you spend any time outside of work with him?"

Khush was deliberately avoiding all her questions, batting them away as if they were irritating and unimportant obstacles on his way to what he wanted to say. Anita felt her pasta turn stale in her stomach and bile beginning to rise.

"No, I only spend working hours with him. No other time. Then I'm home to you and Anand. I don't do anything else. Why do you ask Khush?"

"What about your lunch break?"

"Lunch?"

"Yes, lunch breaks. Stop repeating what I am saying to avoid this conversation. Answer the damn question." Khush's voice was now hard and cold, there was an edge of anger too.

"Well, we have the same lunch breaks, so yeah we sit in the staffroom and have lunch. With the others too."

"In the staffroom only?"

"Well, yeah. Although if it's too hot in there, or we want some fresh air we go for a walk to the park during lunch. Why?"

What the fuck is going on here?

"Like today?"

Anita's breath caught in her throat. How did he know she and Eddie had gone for a walk today? What was going on?

"Yes, like today," she said slowly looking carefully at her husband whose face was beginning to redden and whose eyes were staring at her hard. He clenched one hand into a fist and the other held a phone tight. Her throat was dry, "What's going on? How do you know we had lunch outside?"

"Surprised I found out?"

"No, we weren't hiding, it was just lunch and a walk."

"We weren't hiding? Ha. You definitely weren't hiding it. You were seen with him, with Eddie."

"By who? We were just having lunch."

"Not what I have been told or what I have been shown Anita."

"So, what have you been shown?" asked Anita.

She was confused about what he thought was going on but felt rattled at the fact that someone had seen her at the park with Eddie on their lunch break and was feeding misguided information to Khush.

"You're going to play innocent with me even though I have picture evidence?"

"What on earth is going on Khush? I am so fucking confused. What do these pictures show? Me eating lunch, walking with Eddie around the park? What?"

"More than that," said Khush sliding his phone across the table at her, "Look. It's disgusting Anita. You're fucking married. You should be ashamed."

Anita took the phone and swiped through the images. Khush was right, someone had seen her in the park with Eddie at lunch time, and they had taken pictures. These were not only pictures of them walking and sitting on the park bench, but these were of Anita's meltdown this afternoon. *Fuck.* Her head on Eddie's shoulder. *Fuck.* His arm around her comforting her. *What am I going to do?* All these images told a completely different story to what was happening. Anita looked up at Khush who was glaring at her. She couldn't speak.

"Well?" sneered Khush, "What do you have to say for yourself? What the fuck are you doing with that guy? Have you no shame?"

It took a moment for Anita to stop her hands from trembling and for her to feel that her voice wouldn't crack before she spoke. "That's me and Eddie in the park today-"

"I know that. What the hell are you doing all over him like that?"

"I'm not all over him," she said as calmly as she could, she needed to explain everything to Khush without telling him it was because of him she was crying, "I was upset, and Eddie was making sure I was ok."

"With his hands on another man's wife? You're disgusting allowing him to touch you like that."

I'm disgusting?

"No, it isn't like that. It's innocent, I promise. He was making sure I was ok because I was upset and crying."

"Why?"

"Because..." Anita paused trying to get her brain to kick into gear and help her explain all this, "because one of the residents had just died, and he was one of my first residents. He was very poorly and died early this morning before I got there, but I was really upset. Eddie suggested going for a walk to get some fresh air, and so we did. We sat on the park bench and I had a cry. That's all. I promise Khush, it's innocent. Nothing to worry about."

Khush scoffed: he didn't believe her at all, "Why are you smiling in some of the pictures then? Why had he got his arm around you when you're walking? What if someone in our community saw you two going on like this? The shame it would bring to my family, Anita."

Going on like this? Shame? What the hell?

"I was smiling because Eddie made me smile and laugh, he was trying to make me feel better."

Like you used to Anita paused. "That's it. He has his arm around my shoulders just because he's that kind of guy."

"A dirty perv, touching another man's wife," Khush retorted.

"A friend, making me feel better about someone dying," Anita corrected gaining control of herself and feeling more confident, "Khush it's sweet that you're a little jealous there, with these pictures, but you don't need to be. I promise you."

"I'm not jealous, I'm fucking pissed off," said Khush, the anger from his voice was clear and frightening.

Anita recoiled in her chair, "there's nothing to be jealous I promise, not with Eddie anyway," she said quietly.

"Why not?"

"Because Eddie's with someone."

"So? People like him cheat."

People like him?

"But he wouldn't choose me."

"How do you know? He's a man and you're a woman. Why wouldn't he try to take advantage? You gave him enough motive being all over him."

"Look, let's put it this way," said Anita with a forced little smile. She realised she could calm the situation down but would end up exposing Eddie's privacy, "he would rather be with you than he would with me."

Sorry Eddie, I had to tell him Anita scowled at having to reveal her friend's situation without his consent.

"What?" Khush said confused. Then slowly, whilst looking at Anita's small smile and her raised eyebrows, the penny dropped.

"Khush, Eddie's gay. He'd fancy you before fancying me so you don't have to worry. I love you and would never betray you."

"Right."

"So, you didn't say who saw me in the park then?" Anita asked carefully although she had already seen who had sent the images whilst she was flicking through the photos when he was accusing her of cheating.

"My brother."

Fucking Pritesh.

"Why didn't he just coming to say hi to me?" she said in as light as tone as she could muster whilst feelings of anger boiled inside her.

"Because he doesn't trust you."

"Wait what?" said Anita frowning, she knew Khush's brother wasn't her number one fan, but she didn't think he would stoop so low, "why doesn't he trust me? Why would that be something that went through his head?"

"I imagine because you were all over that Eddie guy, so he sent them to me. I'm pissed off with you."

"But, why?"

"For being too touchy feely. Just disgusting. You know what our community is like."

"Our community," said Anita getting angry but trying to diffuse the situation that was building up again, "he is my friend, Khush. Only a friend who was helping me out when I was feeling down. That's all. I promise. Look, I can see where you got the wrong end from those photos, but you have to trust me on what I say. Do you trust me?"

There was a pause so long Anita felt like she was going to burst. She held her breath.

"Khush?"

"What?"

"Do you trust me?"

"You? Yeah I guess I do. But I don't trust Eddie. Gay or not I don't trust him. You don't touch a married woman like that even as a friend."

"But-"

"Just make sure he stops doing that, and make sure you tell him. I don't trust him Anita, and if you don't tell him to keep his distance, I will."

With that said, and with him having the final word, which was something Khush always liked in an argument, he walked off to his study closing the door behind him. Anita slumped into the sofa unfurling her legs from under her, picked up a cushion from the side and screamed into it. A long, deep, and guttural scream freeing all the frustration and fear that had welled up inside her.

Chapter 19.

After this confrontation with Khush, Anita kept a low profile with Eddie at work. They still talked lots and had their usual fun banter during the work day, but she didn't go for walks during lunch breaks with him anymore, choosing to stay in the staffroom even on the days that a walk would have been much better. Luckily, the change in weather and the ever-present rain and chill they had now that they were in the winter months, made this easier. Anita also distanced herself from Eddie outside of work; it wasn't like they met up, but it was the texts, WhatsApp messages and Facebook contact that she began to minimise. Eddie wasn't stupid and he had clearly noticed a difference, but he knew it was better to let Anita do what she needed to do than to pressure her, especially with Khush watching her every move.

"So, did you see my Facebook post the other day?" Eddie asked as they worked on cleaning a resident's room.

"Hmm, no sorry. I haven't been on Facebook recently, busy at home," Anita lied.

In fact, she had snoozed Eddie's posts so that she could take a break; most of his posts were rants about politics, LGBTQ support, or pictures of his boyfriend and him- none of which Khush would have been happy to see splattered on Anita's timeline too. Khush insisted in keeping a close eye on all her social media activities since they had started dating; something he declared that was totally fine if she didn't have anything to hide. His jealousy was there from the start.

"Ah, well then you missed a big announcement," Eddie said smiling and looking at Anita.

Anita looked up puzzled. She couldn't read Eddie's face, he had a knack of disguising his emotions well, something Anita was not good at.

"What was it?" she asked.

"Well, you missed my announcement about the big M," he said grinning from ear to ear.

Anita knew this was huge news for him. He had been struggling with getting his brothers, who were a lot like Pritesh, to accept his lifestyle and to get on with his boyfriend. They were very stoic whenever they spent time with the couple and although they didn't make nasty comments or were disgusted like Pritesh would have been, they found it hard to spend time chatting with him. Eddie's parents were happy for him and Callum, and Anita assumed they were just as excited about the wedding as Eddie was.

She looked at Eddie who was moving from one foot to the other like a child in need of a wee and she smiled. She loved her friendship with Eddie and hated that she had missed this big announcement because of her fear of Khush. Anita thought she'd have a little fun with Eddie first.

"Big M?" she said arms outstretched for a hug, "Wow, a mortgage! That is big news. Even Facebook worthy Eddie. Congratulations."

"Mortgage?" he said bewildered, "No you silly tart. Not a mortgage, a wedding. Callum proposed to me last night and I said yes."

He looked at her and realised she was grinning and clearly winding him up.

"You cow," he said laughing and giving her a hug, "You had me going there."

"I know," giggled Anita, "that was fun. Marriage. I'm so happy for you. Congrats."

"Thanks sweety," said Eddie giving Anita a squeeze and then sitting on the chair in the corner of the room, "I'm so excited. Already started planning it all."

"You got a date yet? You need that first."

"I know lady-face," said Eddie rolling his eyes dramatically at Anita. She loved the silly nicknames he used with her, made her smile and feel loved. "It'll be in eight months' time."

"Eight? Will you have time to plan a wedding by then? Venue? Food? Music? All that jazz?"

"Yeah sure I will," said Eddie getting up and helping Anita with the bed sheets, "It's not going to be a massive extravaganza. Mostly family and a few people that we deem special only. We have already booked the venue and the date- I had the place on my radar for months now, so as soon as Callum proposed I booked it. He likes the place and it's a perfect size for a gay old wedding."

Anita laughed. Eddie was so happy and she was happy for him. He had shown her the venue a while back, a large cottage-like house on the side of a golf course. Surrounded by fields and secluded enough to be very romantic. He had sent her pictures of the room they would use and the suite that he and Callum would have for the night. Anita had to admit, it was beautiful, and it reminded her of the manor that she and Khush married in nearly six years previous. She just hoped that his marriage wasn't going to end up anything like hers.

"So," Anita said as she picked up the cleaning gear from the room leaving the old bedsheets for Eddie to grab, "What else have you already planned?"

"Just the guest list," Eddie said closing the door behind them and dumping the dirty linen into a cart, "You're invited Anita. You know that don't you?"

"Aw thanks Eddie," said Anita feeling more emotional than she realised, Eddie's happiness was becoming a little overwhelming for her, "That's so sweet. I will make sure that we can get Anand looked after."

Eddie inhaled sharply and a strange look appeared on his face. He avoided eye contact with Anita and shuffled the cart along.

"What?" asked Anita, "What was that weird reaction for?"

"Well," Eddie said still not looking at Anita directly, "Well it is a smaller wedding than, like most people's wedding, so a shorter guest list."

"Ok, so what are you saying?" questioned Anita although she had an inkling of what was to come.

"Well, you're invited. But not Khush."

"Oh, right." Anita said nodding slowly.

"It's a smaller wedding, and so shorter guest list," repeated Eddie clearing his throat, "And we can't invite Khush...because of numbers."

"Ok," said Anita, "because of numbers...or because you don't like him?"

Eddie looked at Anita, she had a look of understanding and acceptance on her face and he felt that the truth would be better for their friendship.

"Well, yes. But hon I don't want you to feel bad. I'm sorry if you do but I can't have him there. He's too toxic."

Anita smiled and patted Eddie gently on the cheek, "It's ok Eddie. I understand. He's not exactly in a happy place at the moment. Things aren't great again. So maybe him not being there is a good thing. Plus," she added with a wink, "means I can relax and have a good time without worrying about his mood swings."

"That's true," Eddie said smiling and looking very relieved, "we can spend the night dancing and drinking and celebrating without seeing his miserable mug in the corner scowling at you."

"Exactly!" Anita said laughing.

Anita admitted to herself that she was secretly pleased about Khush not being invited to her friend's wedding. Not because he was homophobic but because he had already said he didn't like Eddie, without ever meeting him, and his moods and sulky behaviour hadn't improved either. Anita knew it would be better if he wasn't there. She would be able to let her hair down, relax and have some fun celebrating her best friend's marriage to someone who he truly loved and it wasn't going to be a place for someone like Khush to be at, so she would happily go solo.

A few days later Anita received a brightly coloured envelope in the post; it was her invite to Eddie and Callum's wedding. The card showed two grooms holding hands, looking a lot like Eddie and Callum themselves, under an archway of hearts. A very sweet and subtle design which she was surprised to see, especially since she knew that Eddie was put in charge of the invites. It looked like Callum had some design influence after all. The card was perfect. When she had showed it to Khush he looked indifferent. She had told him about the wedding and that Eddie had asked her to save the date. She hadn't mentioned that Khush, himself, was not invited but she didn't have to as Khush had instantly said that he didn't really want to go, he still didn't like Eddie and didn't want to go to his wedding. This saved Anita an awkward conversation.

"So, you'd be alright with me going on my own then Khush?" she had asked tentatively.

"Yeah, if you want to. Doesn't bother me."

Anita wasn't convinced, Khush didn't like Eddie, and although she had not spoken about him at home much since the photo incident, she knew that Khush was bothered about her going. She wondered what was going on and what Khush's angle was.

"You sure? I really want to go. There are a bunch of us at work going, like a work invite group." Group was a little embellished, in fact only Emma, Anita and another co-worker Sam had been invited. Hardly a group, but Anita needed to make sure everything was ok for her to go.

"Yeah, I can spend some more time with our son then whilst you're out without us."

His tone sent prickles down Anita's neck, it was as if she always spent time with her work friends in the evenings when in fact it had only been one other time she had gone out and enjoyed herself with them all. Even then she had driven so that if Khush had wanted her home, she could come back quickly. Khush had texted her all night and even rang her when she didn't answer his text messages for 20 minutes- checking up on her safety he claimed.

"Ok, cool. I'll RSVP yes then," Anita said cautiously placing the invite on the fridge next to a plethora of Anand's 'artwork' that she felt obliged to pin up for him.

She text Eddie later that night and said that she would be attending the wedding and that Khush was ok with her going without him.

...Really? Mr Moody is alright with it? he texted back almost instantly.

...Yes. He's all good.

...Did you tell him he wasn't invited?

Anita paused, hovering her finger over the keypad,

...didn't need to. He said he didn't want to come as he didn't know you that well anyway.

...you mean he doesn't like me

...Ed, come on...

...Ok, well at least you're coming and he's not. Just what I wanted.

...Exactly.

...so the next plan...

...What plan? For what?

...bachelor party bitch!

Anta laughed softly.

...Oh yeah. Are you having one with Callum? Like a joint one?

...yeah, we pretty much have the same buddies and not going for the whole willy straws, willy hairbands, sweets, and dick t-shirts thing...

...ah ok...on a different note gimme a min I need to cancel an order from Anne Summers...

...Ha ha! Silly woman. Love how you make me laugh! xx

Love you too Eddie. Xxx Right better be off now. Xx Have a child to feed...

...and Anand too. ;) bye love, see you at work xxx

Anita laughed, she and Eddie got each other's humour and delighted in teasing one another. She really enjoyed his friendship and cherished being able to be herself and honest around him. Looking up at Khush as he played with Anand pretending not to watch her, she carefully deleted all the message she and Eddie had just exchanged. *Better safe than pissing him off* she thought to herself. As an extra precaution, she changed her passcode too.

Chapter 20.

Only two months away from her best friend's wedding and Anita was still looking for a dress to buy. She had taken Anand out with her shopping, which normally wasn't a good idea, but she needed to get Anand some new clothes after he had gone through yet another growth spurt, and it meant that she could feel relaxed and not guilty about leaving him with Khush who seemed to always be busy whenever she needed a favour like this.

Anand was beginning to show signs of upset whenever he was left with Khush, and Khush noticed this. He had tried to accuse Anita of pitting his son against him, this didn't go down well. Anita was constantly belittled by Khush and his snide comments, but this was over the line. Khush couldn't win this argument either; it was clear his mood swings were also affecting his time with Anand. He wasn't exactly patient around their son and often would 'give up' or 'tap out' in looking after him, often leaving Anita with a crying Anand.

"What do you think to this?" she asked Anand picking up a royal blue off the shoulder dress.

Anand looked at her with a tilted head and continued to play with his teddy of choice for the day. "Pretty mummy."

She smiled, she would have to make the decision herself. She knew Eddie's colour scheme for the wedding and knew what colours she needed to stay clear of. This dress was the fourth she had picked up and placed on the pram to try on. She knew she needed to be quick as Anand was starting to get cranky being dragged around and being told 'no' when all he wanted to do was wonder around and touch things. Anita would have to take some pictures and send them to Eddie and her sister to get opinions on them. If she was lucky, they'd reply quickly. If not, she would have to make the final choice.

Anita chose a spacious changing room and walked in, manoeuvring some bags so that it blocked the door in case Anand wanted to use his new skill of being able to open doors. She knew she only had a minute or two per dress to try on, to take pictures and to decide which she wanted to wear to her best friend's wedding.

To her relief, Henna had messaged back instantly and the insisted on a video call so she could talk through the dress choices with Anita better. Anand had found a pack of raisins in his snack bag and was content on sitting on the floor and eating them at an unusually slow speed. It took no more than 10 minutes and a dress had been chosen. Anita was delighted with her choice, not just because it was a colour that she knew Eddie would approve of, but because it showed off her legs which were still very toned. She knew she would look great; it had been a while since she felt great too and she was looking forward to that feeling.

That evening Khush was actually talking to her and spending time with Anand, Anita felt good and decided to ask for his opinion on the dress.

"What do you think?" she asked holding it up on the hanger against her body.

"Looks a bit small for you," Khush said.

"No it's not," she said looking at the dress again frowning, "shall I try it on?"

"Go for it," he said, "may look different on you than on the hanger."

"It does," said Anita walking to the downstairs loo to get changed, "trust me. Looks great."

When she came out a few minutes later, Anita felt great. This dress not only looked terrific on her but made her feel confident in herself, which had been something she hadn't been feeling lately. The lack of interest from Khush didn't help her confidence.

"So, what do you think?" she asked smiling and twirling slowly in the living room.

Anand clapped at Anita making her smile. When she looked at Khush, that smile faltered. He was looking at her disapprovingly the way her aajima had used to when she was a teenager and wore a skirt.

"What's wrong?" she said looking at Khush with dread.

"It's, well it's a nice dress..."

"But?"

"But do you think it's appropriate for someone like you to wear?"

"What do you mean 'someone like me'?" asked Anita getting flustered and feeling foolish standing in the living room in an evening dress and fluffy socks.

"Well, it's a bit short isn't it?"

"Not really, shows off my legs too."

"Yeah, maybe shows off too much of your legs."

Anita felt her whole-body buckle, her legs were her favourite asset and they had also been Khush's favourite thing about her. Now, here he was, unhappy about the amount of flesh on show. Whatever was left of Anita's confidence was beginning to dissolve.

"Well, I like the length. I don't think it's too short," whispered Anita close to tears.

"But you don't want to show it all off. You know like some floozy looking for a bit of attention," his words were a punch in the gut, "You're older now", a slap in the face, "and well you'll look desperate if you go all-out like that. Plus you know it's too much for a respectable Indian. Why don't you wear a sari?"

Anita could no longer stop the tears from falling down her face. She was torn with the desire to run upstairs and cry until she had nothing left or to shout and scream at Khush for being such a shitty husband. In hindsight, she should have just walked away at that moment.

"What the fuck?" she spluttered through tears, "that's such a horrible thing to say."

"You wanted my opinion," Khush said shrugging his shoulders.

"I wanted to know if the damn dress looked good, not what you really think of me going to the wedding," her anger was starting to build, and Anita felt herself unravel.

"Alright, Anita," Khush said as if she was a nuisance and wasting his time, "it looks good. Calm down. You're getting hysterical over a dress. Why you want to go to that wedding anyway I don't know. I thought you weren't chumming up to him anymore."

"Oh, fuck," Anita said burying her face in her hands, "So this is what it's about? It's his wedding. He's not after me. How many times do we need to go over this? He is with Callum and he's happy. We are friends that all. Please believe me: a friend."

"So, why haven't I met him before?" snapped Khush looking at Anita as if she were hiding something from him.

"Because..." Anita felt herself lose herself, there was no getting back from this, "because he doesn't like you Khush. OK? He doesn't like the way you treat me; he doesn't like you. Is that what you wanted to hear? You've made no attempt to meet him either."

The deafening silence that followed her outburst was only second in comparison to the darkness that appeared on Khush's face. Anita breathed hard. She knew she had said too much, but she needed to show Khush she wasn't taking his hurtful words anymore. She stood her ground, face red, hands clenched and tears streaming down her face.

"He doesn't like me," repeated Khush, "he doesn't know me does he Anita? He's never met me."

"He knows what you're like," Anita said through gritted teeth.

"What I'm like?" he questioned looking hard at Anita, daring her to stand up to him. Anita couldn't back down, the adrenaline forced her to react instead of back down.

"Yeah, what you're like with me. How you treat me. He knows what you're like."

Khush smiled. Anita's stomach turned with fear. Khush let time pass before he spoke with a snarl, "Well, I don't think he knows what I am like. You've told him your pathetic bullshit about me, so I'll show him what I am like. I'll come to wedding anyway, you're not going on your own dressed like that and I'll show him on his special fucking day, what I'm like."

"Khush, what...?" Anita voice had gone, her legs were shaking, and she felt clammy all over. The silkiness of the dress no longer felt smooth against her skin, instead it felt like it was smothering her all over.

What had Khush just said? He was coming to the wedding. For what? To ruin it for Eddie? Anita's mind rushed with questions and terrifying thoughts. But before she could say anything, Khush stood up, patted a scared looking Anand on the head and walked out of the room into his study. The smile on his face distorted his usual rugged features making him look unrecognisable to Anita; and not for the first time, Anita saw the monster he hid so well out in the open.

Anita stood there for what felt like an age before Anand's whinging became louder and more piercing.

"Shit," she said picking her son up and kissing his cheek, "It's ok bubba, it's ok. Shhh." She whispered soothingly in Anand's ear, took him upstairs for his bath and bed, and muttered "I need to talk to Eddie."

Chapter 21.

"What the actual fuck?" shouted Eddie the next day, pacing outside of their work. Anita had messaged him after Khush's threat and said they needed to talk urgently. She had asked to meet him half an hour before work so she could speak to him and warn him.

"Eddie, I'm-"

"No, Anita," said Eddie swivelling to face her, "This is fucked up. You have an argument with your husband about a fucking dress, and now he's threatening to ruin my wedding. I'm not having that."

"I know I know," said Anita, "I'll talk to him. Talk him out of it. I promise."

"Promise? Fuck's sake Anita you can't tell him anything, you wouldn't be able to persuade him. He's a tyrant. He's nasty. He's such a fucking dick! I'm so fucking angry." Eddie was pacing again, his face red, spittle flying from his mouth and his breathing heavy.

"I will talk to him."

"But you ain't gonna change his mind are you Anita?" he said accusingly, "How are you going to stop him from coming to my wedding? A wedding which he isn't even invited to! He doesn't listen to you or care, so why would he now?"

"I don't know, I will though. He's not going to ruin it, I promise that."

Eddie stopped pacing, he leaned on his car and put his head in his hands. His shoulders shook and Anita couldn't tell if he was crying or not. She didn't know what to do. Slowly, and after what felt like hours had passed, Anita put a gentle hand on his shoulder.

"Eddie."

"What?" he shrugged her hand off his back.

"I'm sorry about all this. So sorry. I'll fix it."

"I'm sorry too," he said after a pause.

He lifted his head to look at Anita. He had been crying.

"Why are you sorry?" said Anita close to tears herself, "It's not your fault, it's mine."

"It's *his* fault Anita. His. Not yours. Not mine. HIS. I'm sorry Anita."

"What are you sorry for?" repeated Anita feeling panic rising inside, "don't be sorry."

"I have to think about my wedding. I have to think about my husband, my family, my guests. This is my day and I have to…to think about that…" Eddie was crying again and looking at a confused Anita, "he can't come to my wedding Anita."

"I know he-"

"Let me finish, please." Eddie took a deep breath, his eyes furrowed with pain, "He can't come to my wedding. And the only way I can make sure that happens to protect my loved ones, is…is to un-invite you."

"What?" Anita breath caught in her throat and she could feel bile burning as her stomach plummeted.

"The only way to make sure he doesn't come to the wedding, is if you don't come to my wedding. I can't have anything to do with you at the moment. I just can't. I've been trying to get you to leave him, to find your own happiness for months and months now, and you haven't. It's not your fault. I know that. He's toxic. But I can't have that kind of poison near me, not now, not during the wedding, not after."

"Eddie…"

"I can't deal with this hateful situation. I can't be near you or be your shoulder to cry on whilst he's still around. I just can't. I need to pull away from all this and focus on my happiness. I need to make sure my life isn't ruined because of yours. He's nasty, he is manipulative, and I can't be near anything like that now which means..." he sighed heavily, "which means I can't be near you either. I'm sorry Anita."

"Eddie wait..." whispered Anita tears running down her burning cheeks, "Eddie what do you mean..."

"I'm sorry Anita. You can't come to my wedding. I can't be around you anymore. I'll talk to Emma now and sort something so I can change shifts. I'm sorry."

"But-"

"Please don't come to my wedding."

Anita sobbed as she watched Eddie slowly walk, shoulders slumped, through the doors of the care home.

Walking away from her.

Anita felt empty as she followed Eddie's footsteps into work, she had never felt so alone as she did at that moment. She had never felt so heartbroken.

Chapter 22.

Anita stood in the shower enjoying the hot water fall across her face. Thinking about the way Eddie had reacted, Anita felt torn. On the one hand she was furious with him for abandoning her when she needed him and allowing Khush to come between them, but she also understood why he had to distance himself from her and chosen to protect his loved ones and his special day. In any case, she was the one suffering because of Khush's hateful nature. Again.

Anita screamed into her hands and gave in to shudders and sobs that flowed from her as freely as the water from the shower head. This was her fault. If only she had kept her temper, if only she had kept her mouth shut about the invitations, if only she could get away from such a toxic person. If only, if only, if only. If onlys were pointless and didn't help her now.

What am I going to do now? She thought.

A soft knock at the bathroom door caused Anita to jerk her head sideways.

"Anita?" Khush called.

"Yeah?"

"All ok? I thought I heard something."

"No, all ok Khush," said Anita through gritted teeth.

"OK, teas and coffees are brewing and we've got breakfast ready."

Anita frowned. She swallowed hard and felt a knot form in the pit of her stomach.

"Ok," she said unsure why Khush was being so pleasant and helpful.

"Also, I'm going to take you to work today," Khush said with an odd cheeriness.

Anita's eyes widened. The drops of hot water on her body were now sharp icicles.

"Oh, ok," she said her mind raced, "you know I'm happy to drive myself."

"I know, I just thought it would be nice to drive you," said Khush a hard edge in his voice now, "is that a problem?"

"Uh, no problem at all," said Anita reaching a shaky hand to turn off the shower.

"Good, see you downstairs. I'll leave you to get changed."

Anita stepped out of the shower and reached for a towel. Her heart thudded and her skin felt like it was burning at every movement. She looked at herself in the mirror and took a deep breath. She closed her eyes. *In through the nose,* she coached herself trying to calm her nerves and mind- both of which were racing. *Out through the mouth. In through the nose. Out through the mouth.*

She opened her eyes slowly and listened for any sound of Khush still being out there. No sound. He'd gone downstairs. Holding her breath Anita stepped out of the bathroom and out onto the landing, a quick look around calmed her nerves, Khush wasn't standing there as she expected, and she padded across into her room to get ready for work.

Sitting across the table from Khush, Anita picked at her breakfast. Her mind couldn't focus and she wasn't sure how to deal with the sudden news that Khush would be driving her to work. She didn't even know if he was just saying it for effect or actually meant it.

"Not hungry?" Khush asked smiling.

"Not really," said Anita forcing a smile.

Anita watched Khush take a big bite of his toast and imagined ramming it and the plate it was sat on deep into his throat. She blinked and looked at Anand who was happily playing with some cheerios.

"Will you have time to drop me and Anand off as well as get into work on time?" Anita asked, her voice quivering a little.

"Yeah," said Khush gulping down the last of his coffee and standing, "don't you want me to drop you to work?"

A loaded question.

"No, no it's not that," said Anita fumbling to find a good enough reason to avoid this chaperone, "just thought it wouldn't work with being late and all."

"Nope, it's fine," he said moving so he was behind her, "plus it means we can spend time together."

"Oh, ok."

"You need to rebuild the trust that you lost with this whole Eddie situation."

Khush placed a warm hand on Anita's shoulder and leaned in, his lips almost touching her ear, "unless you have something to hide?"

Anita swallowed and shook her head, her eyes focused on her mug of tea. She forced herself to concentrate on her breathing.

"Good," said Khush tapping her shoulder and moving away, "we leave in 15."

       **   **   **

Sitting in the car, Anita felt on edge. She kept her eyes on the road ahead or looking down at her entwined fingers on her lap. It was a short journey to work, but every light turned red for them and every car out on the road was going slower than normal.

"This is nice," said Khush casting a quick glance over at Anita.

Jaw clenched, Anita nodded.

"You're quiet today, something wrong?"

Anita swallowed, put on a smile and dragged her gaze towards Khush who was happily tapping at the steering wheel and watching the traffic lights up ahead.

"Normally it's just me in the car," she said trying to inject some laughter into her voice, "that's probably it."

"So tell me about work," Khush said ignoring her attempt at humour.

Anita licked her dry lips. What could she tell him about work that didn't include Eddie? Even though things were strained, they still had to work together, and Khush still hated him. Did she even want Khush to know how awkward and lonely work was becoming all because of him?

"Unless you want to keep it all a secret from me?"

"Of course not," said Anita looking straight ahead and hoping the truck opposite them would swerve into them and stop this conversation. "There's nothing to tell. The residents are old but they're great. Everyday is pretty much the same thing with them and only changes when they have visitors. We spend time with them to occupy their minds and keep them company. An exercise regime every day, same paperwork, same foods. That's it."

"Sounds really boring," said Khush, a not so subtle him of superiority on his voice, "I don't know how you do it. I'd be so bored."

Anita pressed her lips together and stared intently at the car in front of them. Her eyes began to water. This was the job he had forced her into. This was the only job he'd allowed her to take. She knew it could be boring and so did he when he told her to apply for it. But, Anita wasn't going to let Khush win this conversation.

"I quite like it," she said shrugging her shoulders, "it's quiet yes, but the people I look after are really great and they're really interesting residents. Also the guys I work with are-"

She stopped. She'd walked right into the trap. She looked over at Khush who was trying to hide a sneer.

"Carry on," he said.

"I was saying I work with a great bunch of people and my boss, Emma, is brilliant. She so supportive."

"And Eddie?"

"What about Eddie?"

"Is he great too?"

"We don't talk much anymore as he's on different shift patterns to me," said Anita. Her throat squeezed as she tried to steady her breathing.

"Good. I don't trust him."

Anita looked down at her hands which were now white from being squeezed so tight. She felt a small jolt of pain and relief as her nails pierced her skin.

"I don't talk to him anymore," she repeated, "don't worry about Eddie."

"Good," said Khush.

Anita nodded. Afraid that of she opened her mouth to speak, something terrible would come out. A thick air of silence fell over them and Anita glanced in the back seat to watch Anand blissfully stare out of the window holding tightly on to his teddy. Her heart ached and she just wanted to hold her son tightly and breathe him in.

"We're here," said Khush breaking the silence making Anita jump.

Anita looked up at the entrance and saw Emma standing there and talking to a resident.

"Who's that?" said Khush looking at Anita.

"My boss, Emma," said Anita.

Khush nodded.

Anita reached to unclip her belt when she felt Khush's hand on her thigh. She turned, eyebrows raised, her face a picture of fear.

"No kiss goodbye?"

Smiling tightly, Anita leaned in and kissed her husband, pulling away quickly she opened the door. Her lips burned and her stomach heaved.

"Have a good day," Khush called.

She smiled and opened the back door to say goodbye to her son.

"Bye mummy," said Anand, his smile broad and his eyes innocent and wide.

"Bye beta," said Anita quietly, "have a good day. I love you."

"Love you."

"Love you too," said Khush's voice as Anita closed the door and began walking along the driveway and through the entrance.

Anita noticed that Emma had finished her conversation and was watching Khush's rendition of happy families play out in front of her. Her eyes watched Anita walk up the path and enter the building with a small nod and hello. Emma looked back at the car and saw Khush wave at her, his smile wide but his eyes dark. A quick wave and smile in return, and Emma followed Anita inside.

Chapter 23.

Anita's life became a series of routines that she encountered each day without any real thought or feeling; the only thing that kept her moving on was Anand. He was growing into a fantastic little boy; he was happy, talkative and very affectionate. Especially with Anita. His mother was his world and it wasn't just because she clothed and fed him, but it was because Khush's withdrawal from the day to day family life was so obvious and he was no longer trying to be subtle about the cracks in their marriage.

Anand picked up on all of this, but as a toddler he was unable to understand everything; he just knew that daddy had mood swings and was hardly around, and when he was around, he didn't always want to talk or play with him. Watching her son's heartbreak every time Khush ignored him, told him to go away or lost patience with him was agonising for Anita; she wasn't able to fix the pain and hurt for her son. But she would try.

"Why is daddy sad?" Anand asked one night as Anita tucked him into his bed.

"What?" said Anita shocked that her son had asked such a question.

"Why is daddy so sad?" he repeated.

"Well, Anand, he's very busy with work and he has a lot to think about."

Anita looked at her son's face; confusion mixed with pain.

"So daddy's work is him sad?"

"Uh...yes, work is making daddy sad, and tired, and sometimes that means he gets angry."

"Oh," said Anand looking towards the ceiling, his bottom lip trembling.

"Why do you ask beta?"

"He shouted today. I make him angry."

"Aw honey," Anita said tears forming in her eyes, "you make daddy very happy. He's just...he just is very tired and doesn't always have the energy to play. It's not you, ok?"

"Ok, mummy."

"Ok," Anita leaned in and kissed his forehead and gave him a longer than normal hug, "goodnight, sleep tight, love you, Anand."

"Night, sleep tight, love you mummy."

As Anita walked out of the room and closed the door, she jumped at Khush's looming figure in front of her. His eyes glared at her and he frowned.

"I've just put Anand down, but you can go in and say goodnight if you want?" said Anita trying to find a touch of happiness in her voice but failing.

"What did you say to him?" he hissed standing there with his arms crossed.

"What do you mean?"

He heard it all she thought.

"I heard you bad mouthing me to Anand."

"Bad mouthing? No, I didn't."

"Don't lie to me," said Khush closing the gap between them in one swift step, "I heard you telling him that I'm tired and that I'm angry and all that other bullshit."

What other bullshit?

"Khush you've got it all wrong. I was actually defending the way you are to him."

"The way I am? What do you mean?"

Here we go again.

"Well, he asked if he made you sad and angry."

Khush laughed, shook his head and pointed a finger at Anita.

"*You* make me sad. *You* make me angry. Not that kid. And when he does make me angry it's because he's done something wrong, you've been soft on him again and I end up being the bad guy. You put me in that position."

Anita stood mouth open in shock. How could his mood swings be her fault?

"It's not my fault or my work's fault. It's your fault," continued Khush, "you push and push and push until I snap, and sometimes it's him that gets it. Don't put rubbish into his head about me."

"I'm not," said Anita softly, she needed to diffuse the situation, "but if I am, I am so sorry. I was trying to-"

"Well don't try anything. You don't fix issues, you make them worse," Khush snarled turning away from her and walking down the stairs, "don't speak to my son about me again."

**   **   **

Work was different since Eddie had walked away from their friendship. At first Anita had been angry at Eddie for allowing Khush to come between them. She had felt a mixture of hurt and resentment towards him every time she saw him at work, and he turned away from her, but after a few months that hurt, and resentment became a mere thumping ache in her stomach as she learned to shut down her emotions and get on with her life.

Eddie had managed to get his shift pattern changed with Emma without too much trouble. He had given the excuse of Callum's shift changing at work and wanting to be on the same pattern as he was, promising Emma that he would switch back as soon as he was able to. Emma knew that something had happened between Eddie and Anita, whenever they were in the same room the air fizzed with tension, but she didn't pry and as long as negativity wasn't seeping into the care given to the residents, she was happy to let it roll on. Anita made a point of extending some of her psych appointments in order to try and steer clear of Eddie on the days they did have crossovers; to Emma's delight she had requested more residents to see and to extend these days from just Wednesdays to include Fridays too, all of which was approved straight away. Emma was concerned about Anita though.

"So," Emma said one day when it was just Anita and her in the staffroom making coffees, "are you ok Anita? Everything ok?"

"Why do you ask?" said Anita keeping her eyes focused on her coffee as it swirled with the milk to make the perfect shade of brown.

"Well, you've been really quiet lately, not your usual outgoing self."

Anita held her breath.

"And there is the sudden change in the way you and Eddie are with one another." Emma looked cautiously at Anita as if she wanted to keep the conversation going but didn't want to say anything to offend her.

"Nothing's wrong," sighed Anita grabbing a few biscuits from the tin and sitting down at the only circular table in the kitchen area, "are you worried about the work? Is everything ok with what I'm doing?"

"Of course it is love," Emma said joining Anita at the table, "I'm just worried about you. Eddie is a bit off too, but I'm putting that down to the fact that his wedding is done and the sweet 'honeymoon' period with Callum is over and it's back to normal life. What about you though? How are you doing?"

Anita could feel her eyes begin to sting and her face begin to heat up, but she didn't want Emma to know what was going on.

Not answering the question directly, she said "I'm just a bit tired recently, Anand's in those terrible twos stage now and Khush-"

She broke off suddenly, not know what she was going to say about her deteriorating marriage.

"What about Khush? Is everything alright there?"

"Um, yeah Emma, it's fine. We're both so busy with work we don't spend a lot of time together. He's stressed at work and that doesn't always mean he's fun to talk to. That's it."

"Sure?" said Emma frowning. Anita was a bad liar.

"Yeah, I'm sure Emma. Thanks for asking but everything is fine. Typical ups and downs of marriages. Once his work settles and Anand stops being a pain every second he gets told 'no', it'll all be good."

Emma nodded as she sipped her tea. It was clear that she wasn't completely satisfied with what Anita had said but she also knew Anita well enough not to pry too far, otherwise she would shut down instantly. This conversation was Anita sharing, in Emma's eyes.

"Ok," she finally said looking directly at Anita, "Just know I'm here if you ever need me and if you want someone to talk to. And before you say it's fine, it doesn't have to be me you talk to if you don't want. We have numbers and contacts of people who can help and sit and talk to you. I need to look after my employees, you know. And my friends too."

Anita couldn't say anything, the lump in her throat was blocking any sound from escaping and she was afraid any attempt to push passed it would reveal how she was truly feeling. So, instead she brought her coffee to her lips and nodded at Emma.

"Alright," said Emma her scouse accent stronger, "just know I'm here. I'll let you finish your coffee in peace now, love."

Anita watched as Emma walked out of the room and she was glad Emma hadn't looked back towards her as she left because she would have seen Anita's tears were falling into her coffee and her shoulders sagged as she silently cried.

Chapter 24.

Anita needed a distraction from her misery, and luckily that came in the form of a family celebration. These family get togethers were always welcomed by Anita; lots of family around, which meant lots of people to talk to, lots of children for Anand to spend time with, and most of all, her sister. Anita knew that if there were any awkward questions thrown her way by family members, Henna would be there to divert the attention away from Anita. She'd always had a knack of knowing when Anita wanted space and always helped her out without question. Her parents' 30th Wedding anniversary party was no different.

Anita couldn't believe it, her parents had been married for 30 years; a milestone that Anita couldn't even think about. She hoped that she could be as successful as her parents in marriage but events of late had shown her that more than anything, she needed to start again. That thought, however, always brought out her anxiety and fear.

The celebration was smaller than Anita had anticipated; her parents had only wanted key people at the celebration and instead of the big party in some hired out school hall, they had opted for a meal out with family and a few close friends. They were a big enough group to need a section of the restaurant to themselves, but it still felt intimate. Henna had organised everything for the meal out; the table was decorated with balloons and some table sprinkles with 30 on them, every seat had a small box with a gift inside and everything matched the pearl theme of 30 years of marriage. It was beautiful and Anita felt guilty that she had let Henna do this all on her own.

"Wow sis," she said looking at the table as people sat down, "this is gorgeous. You did all this?"

"No, Anita," said Henna squeezing Anita's shoulders, "I didn't do all this, we did all this."

"I'm so sorry I didn't help" Anita said her face crumpling up with sadness.

"Don't be silly," Henna said, "I know you're busy and have stuff going on, so I did it. One less thing for you to worry about. Plus I love doing this sort of stuff."

'Stuff going on' is what Henna had said and Anita noticed this phrasing, mentally thanking her sister for being discreet. Henna knew something was happening at home between Anita and Khush, but she wasn't sure exactly what it was. Anita had brushed it off as typical marital problems and although Henna didn't look convinced, she nodded and didn't say anymore.

"Thanks sis," said Anita smiling, "right let's get on with the party."

The evening had gone down very well, people came, they ate, they drank and celebrated; exactly what her parents wanted. Even Anita's aajima had stopped prying into Anita's marriage and spent the evening telling stories about her life as a child, stories that Anita and Henna had heard many times over, stories which they told alongside their aajima – often saying the lines even before she did. This made everyone laugh and Anita's aajima would giggle, shake her head at them and waggle her frail old finger.

"One day," she said her head bobbing and eyes glazed with consuming a little too much brandy, "you will do the same. Your naughty grandchildren will ruin your stories too."

"Ah not likely aajima," said Henna giggling and playing with her hair, "I don't have kids."

"Well," said aajima not fazed by this potentially awkward moment, "then Anand beta will do it to you as well as his mummy and daddy. I will make sure of that."

Everyone laughed, even Anita was relaxed and enjoying herself. There was something about spending time with people who knew her, who understood her ways and who were not going to be judgmental that made her feel safe.

"Speaking of," said aajima looking at Anita, her eyes suddenly serious, "where is Khush?"

"Oh," said Anita, her smile falling and suddenly feeling more sober, "He's uh, he couldn't make it."

"To his in-laws' anniversary dinner. Pshh. That's not right, what was more important?" she pried tutting.

"Mum leave it," Anita's mum said putting a hand on her mother's frail shoulder.

"No, I want to know why?" aajima was insistent, she wasn't going to let it go. Another side effect of too much brandy.

"Aajima, Anita's already said he was busy. Work was busy and called him away last minute." Henna stepped in, taking control and helping out Anita whose voice had caught at the base of her throat.

"Work? That's not right."

"Well, that's what it was, isn't that right Anita?" Henna said giving Anita a quick nudge with her arm and kicking her into gear again.

"Yes, aajima," Anita said, her voice small like the woman she was lying to, "Khush got a call earlier saying there was something with some important documents. Something like that. He's in London. Working."

There was an awkward silence as Anita's aajima looked questioningly at her granddaughters, clearly not believing them. Anita could feel her face going red and heating up, her eyes were beginning to sting as the embarrassment of the exchange became too much to bear.

"A toast!" cried Henna breaking the tension, clapping her hands and calling over the waiter for more wine and glasses, "It's time for a toast everybody."

This tactic, thankfully worked, everybody hustled to make sure they had a drink ready for the celebratory toast and speech from the couple, the focus had swiftly moved away from Khush's absence and Anita was again grateful for her sister's help. After the toast and drinks, people began to leave. Anita took this cue to get Anand to the bathroom and clean him up, and to get herself some breathing space.

As she cleaned Anand and made sure that he had a wee, she looked in the mirror at herself and remembered the argument she and Khush had just before leaving for the restaurant. Khush decided not to come but decided he wasn't going to tell Anita face to face. Instead on the bed was a note from him.

Anita
I won't be coming. It's for family only, and you will celebrate better without me. I will sort my dinner out don't worry. Just tell them I have work stuff going on. I'm not wanted there anyway.
Take Anand with you if you want, I'll let you.
Khush.

Anita grabbed the piece of paper and stormed into his study where he was sitting watching a football game on the TV. She had demanded he explain the letter and they had argued about him not attending and how it would look and what she would say when asked about it, which was inevitable. But throughout this conversation Khush had remained calm and said that he simply didn't want to go. He didn't want to celebrate but wished them well.

Anita on the other hand, had lost her temper, she charged about the room, shouting at Khush and gesturing her arms around. She couldn't believe it, with everything they were going through, and all the sacrifices she made for the marriage, he couldn't even be bothered to put on a shirt and enjoy the evening with her family; a group of people who had done nothing but welcomed him into their family.

Finally, Anita had resigned herself to the fact he wasn't coming. She retreated to their bedroom and got herself ready and changed Anand; preparing his pyjamas, night nappies and extra clothing in his baby bag just in case he got himself in a mess and needed a change of clothes. Anita had been tempted to pack an overnight bag for herself too, she was furious with Khush, but she knew this would come with more questions from her family that she wasn't prepared to answer.

"Anita beta," her mum called into the restaurant bathroom snapping her out of her painful thoughts, "are you ok? You've been in here for a long time."

Anita turned to find that her mother and sister were standing at the door looking concerned. She could no longer hold it in. Anita shook her head as she felt her chest explode into sobs. Her shoulders shook and her cries were deep and primal; she finally allowed herself to cry at her life and what had become of it. She allowed herself to cry at the failing marriage she was trapped in and her feelings of not being able to escape. Her mother and sister wrapped her in their arms and allowed her to grieve for her marriage.

Henna decided that Anita and Anand would stay at her place with her and Ash. She texted Khush using Anita's phone saying that Anita wasn't going to drive all the way home because she'd had a few drinks, so it was safer and closer for her to sleep at her sister's place. They would be back sometime the next day. She then switched Anita's phone off, picked up Anand in her arms, and helped Anita to the car. Now exhausted, Anita allowed Henna to do all this, she allowed herself to be taken care of and feel loved, she had no energy to fight this decision her sister had made.

And, if she was being honest with herself, Anita didn't want to fight this decision either.

Chapter 25.

The next morning Anita woke, groggy and for a moment unsure of where she was. Then it all came rushing back to her like a nightmare; the argument with Khush earlier in the day, the amazing meal but the questions from aajima, and then the breakdown she'd had in the restaurant toilets. When she had arrived at her sister's house, she quickly placed Anand in the spare room where the bed was already ready and set up for her; something she knew her sister always done, just in case.

She placed a deeply sleeping Anand gently in the double bed and placed some pillows on either side of him so that he would not roll over, she would be joining him once she had calmed down a little. When she had gone back downstairs she found that Ash was making hot drinks and Henna had already changed into some pyjamas on, she also had a spare pair for Anita to change into.

"So," said Henna curling herself up on the large sofa in her living room and patting the seat next to her, "what's going on sis?"

Anita felt exhausted and she didn't want to go through all this with Henna, but she knew there was no way that Henna was going to let her go to sleep without some form of explanation. She decided to give it her best to explain.

"Well, Khush and I are having some problems," she said, her voice soft and shaky.

"Well duh, sis, I know that. Something's going on and I need to know what? I've never seen you so upset."

Anita looked at the concern etched across her sister's face, Ash had come into the living room, placed two cups of tea on the coffee table and said he was going to go upstairs to read; he would keep an ear out for Anand so they could talk. Once he had gone, Henna turned to Anita, and spoke more forcefully.

"Talk. Please."

"Ok, so it's been going on for a little while now."

"How long?"

"A few years or so."

"That's not a little while," said Henna shaking her head, "What's going on?"

"Well, he's just distant, he doesn't spend time with me or Anand anymore, most of the time he is working and when he comes home, he sits in the study."

"Doing what?"

"Don't actually know," said Anita shrugging her shoulders, "I think watching TV. I know work is tough on him but I don't think he's doing an awful lot of work if I am being honest."

"I don't give a shit that his work is tough," said Henna clearly getting angry, "he shouldn't treat you like this. What's he like with Anand?"

"He's good when he's with him. Honestly," said Anita seeing the disbelief in her sister's eyes, "really, he is a fantastic dad-"

"When he's around," cut in Henna, hate evident in her voice.

"Come on. Yes, he's not around much for me, but he is a good dad."

"Stop defending him. You're always defending him."

"You would too if it was your husband. If it was Ash we were talking about now."

"No," said Henna shaking her head and picking up her steaming cup of tea, "If Ash was anything like Khush is being right now, in the past two years, I wouldn't be fucking defending him. Kids or no kids. He's being a dick."

"Ok," Anita said reaching for her own mug of tea and thinking how she could diffuse the situation like she did all the time with Khush, "yes he is being a dick, to me, but to Anand he's alright.

He gets cranky sometimes, and he can lose his temper with him and shouts, but that's about it."

"Has he hit Anand?"

"No, not really. Like we both give him a slap on the butt when he's naughty, but nothing bad. Nothing like we got when we were kids."

Anita tried to lighten the mood, but the darkness that flashed on her sister's face was enough to make her realise that this was not the situation to try and make jokes.

"Look, apart from being miserable and not always spending time with Anand and often not even wanting to play with him most nights, he is good with Anand."

"And with you?" Henna asked, her expression softening a little.

"With me, he's...let's just say he's someone else. Someone I don't know. He comes in from work, sometimes doesn't even acknowledge me or Anand. He goes straight into his study and pretty much stays there the whole night."

"Even dinner time?"

"Well, even then. He doesn't really eat with us."

"What do you mean?"

"He eats at a different time and eats different foods."

"So you're making two meals?"

"No, I cook for us all, but only Anand and I eat it. Khush makes something else for himself."

"What the fuck? That makes no sense Anita. He comes home, spends time on his own, eats his own meals, and what else...?"

"He spends the evenings sleeping in the spare room or on the sofa-bed in the study."

"Bloody hell," said Henna rubbing her eyes, "that sounds like you have a roommate not a husband and father living with you."

"Yeah, I guess it does," said Anita playing with the hem of her dress, her eyes glistening with tears.

"What kind of life is that? Does he show you any affection? Does he even speak to you?"

"Affection?" laughed Anita scornfully, "no affection sis. He doesn't even say morning or hello or anything like that to me. Every so often I find a note in the bedroom or kitchen or living room. That's how he communicates with me."

"What the hell? What does he say?"

"He...well mostly it's some complaint about something I've done wrong. Something he's noticed about Anand and wants me to stop doing."

"Notes? Fuck sake. What have you done wrong? Compared to him too? Jeez, what's he got to complain about, you're doing everything for the family and he's acting like a bloody tenant renting out a room. Can't believe he's judging you. Does he help at all with the kitchen or cleaning or anything?"

"Yeah, he does some work, when he's made a mess so he clears it up like-"

"Like a roommate. Cooks for himself I bet?"

"Yeah."

"And cleans up that mess but leaves you with everything else?"

"Yeah, but I don't mind clearing up after Anand, he makes a mess and I'm with him when he does so it's only fair-"

"Fair?" exploded Henna unable to hold back her anger anymore, "so you're telling me, he hardly spends any time with you and Anand, then berates you and your ability to be a mother. He doesn't even have the respect to do it face to face and just chooses to write a note telling you what you should be doing and what you've done wrong? No fucking way. Please tell me you tell him to fuck right off?"

"Well, I don't' really..."

"Sis, come on!" said Henna moving to Anita's side and placing a warm hand on her leg, "please, you have to tell him to back off, tell him he has to talk to you like a person and not some fucking maid that he has around the house. He has to take some time and spend it with Anand and not be an arsehole about it. My god, why didn't you say anything before?"

Anita looked at Henna, she was trembling and was close to tears, her hands felt clammy against Anita's leg. She was angry.

"Anita," said Henna, "please tell me you will say something to him. Make him understand this isn't what a marriage should be. No one's marriage is perfect, not even mine, but there has to be some respect, there has to be some form of affection and love shown. He seems devoid of any of that."

"He can be affectionate," Anita said, "when he wants to be. He gets so much for Anand, and he provides for us all. I wouldn't be able to afford half the things Anand had if I was doing it on my own."

"You're defending him again," accused Henna, and Anita realised she was right, "you can provide so much for that kid, and you do. He isn't even half the parent you are, he's basically an absent parent. He has to be there to provide."

Anita looked at her sister who was also close to tears.

"Money isn't everything," Henna continued, "and Anand isn't going to remember the things he was bought but the memories made playing and doing things with him. All those days out you've spoken about in the last year or so, did Khush even come to any of those?"

"He did a couple," Anita said allowing tears to fall down her face at what her sister had said.

She knew that Henna was right, this was not the way a good marriage, or even a half decent marriage should be. She didn't need romancing all the time, she didn't need cups of tea and breakfast in bed, she didn't need kisses and nights of passionate love making; she needed someone she could rely on, some one that would be there for her as well as Anand, in more than just money. She needed a husband who was emotionally there for her and supported her every day in acts not just in bought gifts.

She needed the man she married back.

Chapter 26.

You can do this, Anita thought as she slowly drove her car up her driveway, *you need to do this. Something has to change. You're doing it for yourself, and for Anand. For both of our happiness. This has got to be done. You can do this Anita. Don't back out.*

Her hands were clammy, and she could feel herself sweating, and it wasn't because she was trying to keep a pounding hangover at bay. Anita tried to prepare herself for the impossible talk she needed to have with Khush, and she knew she had to do as soon as she got into the house; putting it off would just make everything she'd practised at her sister's house and on the drive home harder to say and Anita knew she only had the strength in her to do it once. If she couldn't get it all out in one conversation, she would end up backing out. Anita was afraid; afraid of what would happen, afraid of what Khush would say, and afraid of what the outcomes would be.

"Come on Anita," she whispered to herself parking the car. She looked in the review mirror at her sleeping son and smiled, turning her eyes to her own reflection she added, "do it for him. Do it for you. Just fucking do it Anita. You have to try."

Khush was waiting for her in the kitchen as she walked in with Anand in her arms sleeping. She said hello to him pointed to Anand and mouthed that she was going to take him upstairs. She needed Anand peaceful and out of the way. She looked at Khush to see if she could gauge what his mood was like, but he just nodded and went back to his phone. *So far, so good.* This is exactly how Anita had planned everything, she was in control, telling him to wait and taking care of Anand first. On the outside she looked confident and in charge, but how she felt on the inside was the complete opposite. She wasn't giving him the satisfaction of seeing this fearful and crumbling side of her.

"Khush," she said walking into the kitchen, "we need to talk."

"I know," he replied looking up from his phone, "I got your text last night. You were at your sister's place."

His hostile voice troubled Anita, but she needed to keep moving on.

"I know Khush. Look, I need to talk to you and I need you to listen and not say anything until I have finished. Please. Can you do this for me?"

"So speak," Khush looked surprised at Anita's sudden burst of confidence and put his phone down.

"Ok, thanks Khush," Anita said. She poured herself a glass of water, she would have much preferred to have a cup of tea, or even a glass of wine in front of her, but she had to make do with some water. She sat herself down opposite Khush and took a deep breath. Her hands were trembling.

"Look Khush, we both know things haven't been going well between us. It's not even in the past few weeks or months, but if we are being honest, it's been even before Anand was born. Things have been...messy. We've had great times, don't get me wrong it's not every day that it's been like this, but there's more shitty days than good ones now. I'm not sure why either. I know it's not just because of me and not just because of you. Something between us is broken, and we need to decide if we want to fix it."

Anita paused, she felt flushed and out of breath. She needed to calm down a little and stopping to take in a gulp of water helped. Khush had sensed she hadn't finished, and he sat there staring at her, allowing Anita to continue.

"So, I've been thinking how this has affected us, our relationship is like we are strangers living in the same house. Like roommates and it doesn't make sense. We weren't always like this. I know things change and happen once you have a baby but Anand is almost four, and it seems strange that we haven't got back to our usual self. I know it's not just you. It is me too. I know it's me too. You- we have been distant and I don't know why. I don't know what to do but I know I can't stay stuck like this any longer."

Anita stopped and watched Khush look at his hands. She had no idea where they would go from there, but she'd said what she wanted to, almost word for word as she had practised it earlier on. She gave him time, as she reminded herself to, *he needs time to take in everything* she thought *and have time to say what he wanted to.*

Time passed slowly for Anita as she watched Khush fiddle with his hands, the expression on his face changing every so often, and with every moment of silence her brain thundered with noise threatening to expel from her mouth. She needed him to speak, to say something.

"Khush?" she gently pressed.

"Yeah," he said slowly looking up at her. There was something in his eyes she recognised. She nodded but didn't say anything.

"That was a lot to take in," he finally said, "I think some of what you say is correct, and some is unfair, but I agree with something- we need to move forward and change. We can't go on like this. I'm not happy and you're not happy even though I try to give you and Anand everything you need. I love you both."

"And we love you," Anita choked back tears.

"I know I haven't been the best and you haven't either. I'm distant and I don't engage with you and Anand much anymore because it's like you two don't want me around."

"No, Khush-"

"Let me finish. It's like you two have your own secret club and I'm not invited to be part of it. You leave me out. I know it started when we had Anand. I really do. But I know we need to make some changes. We both need to work hard at getting this marriage back on track."

"Ok," said Anita feeling a prickle of nerves spread through to her face, "so what's next?"

"I think," he said taking a breath and reaching for her hands, "I think we need to work on our marriage. Our communication. Talk through our problems. Make changes. I think we can survive this. That's what we should do."

"I agree," said Anita allowing a tear to roll down her cheek, she was smiling and felt a rush of emotions.

"Make it better," he added.

"Make ourselves better," she agreed, "I know I have some things that I can work on and change and I'm sure this will help."

"We don't need anyone to help us," Khush said, "I want to try and make this work. I don't want to be some man who has failed at marriage. Or you be a woman who has failed at marriage and motherhood."

"Motherhood?" Anita whispered.

"Yes, you've failed, and I haven't helped you. I can help you and we will be better. You can be better too."

Just let it go, otherwise this will never end she thought.

Anita nodded and looked down at her hands. She felt a wave of pressure on her shoulders and underneath it a light feeling of relief. This conversation had started better than she had expected it to, but soon Khush's reactions were just what she had expected to hear. She had to show him they were on the same page and things would to improve.

They spent the evening together as a family; Anand playing on the floor with his cars, Khush joining him and Anita sitting on the sofa, legs curled beneath her. Khush and Anand laughed cheerfully, and Anita was happy to hear her home filled with chatter and happiness instead of the cold quiet it had been saturated in for months. Anand made the best of having his dad playing with him and insisted on asking Khush to bath him and read him a story at bedtime too.

When it was time to take Anand to bed Khush was ready and willing, he swept up Anand onto his shoulders and trudged him up the stairs making dinosaur noises, making Anand squeal with delight.

Anita listened to her husband play with Anand in the bath knowing full well that her bathroom floor would be soaked with bubbles, and she would have to clean it up. She picked up her phone and text her sister:

...Hey. Spoke to Khush. All good.

...Yeah? And? Henna replied almost instantly

...Yeah, so sweet. He said sorry and that he would change, and we can go to see someone for help. We both need to change and work together.

...Did he actually apologise and admit he had done wrong?

...In his own way, yes. He said we both need to change, and I agree.

...Both need to change? Did he say that?

...Yeah, and we do. I can be doing things too. Need to make the marriage too work Henna.

...Like what Anita? You've done nothing wrong. I'm confused.

...Look, I know what you think but Khush is happy and he wants to work on our marriage. That's a good thing.

...When will it start?

...Soon he said we could talk.

...As in go to therapy?

...No, just us, talk it through. Well, once Anand is asleep, I think we will talk more about it and figure it out.

...I think it will only work with outside counselling. Otherwise he'll just manipulate you into thinking it's all your fault.

...That's not fair Henna.

...It's the truth.

...Look, I am happy with what we have discussed. And maybe if we need to, I ask him about counselling. :)

...Happy for you too sis, just want you to realise it's not you that needs to change, it's him. Just remember that, and make sure he doesn't blame you for everything ok? Xx

...Ok, sis. Thanks. Speak soon. Xx

...Love you xx

...Ditto x

Anita put her phone down and frowned, why couldn't her sister be happy for her? She was getting her marriage back on track, and so what if she couldn't think of something that she had done wrong when Khush mentioned both of them needing to change. The point was they were going to fix the marriage.

Anita finished clearing up the kitchen and went into the living room; Anand had cheekily left out his toys which was something she was trying to teach him not to do but Khush never encouraged it: he knew Anita would do the clearing up in the house. But Anita didn't want to say anything, she didn't want to ruin the amazing evening they were having. This is what she wanted, a happy home and a loving family. She quickly swept up all his toys into his box and went up the stairs to kiss her son goodnight.

As they sat down with a glass of wine in their hands and watching TV, Anita glanced at Khush nervously. Once Anand had been put to bed, with Khush reading a story for him this time, Anita had poured the two of them a glass of wine and sat on the sofa. She was nervous about taking the next step but knew of she didn't start that conversation now, she would backout too soon. Khush had come in picked up his wine glass, sat down next to her and turned on the TV. He smiled at Anita but hadn't said much since coming down the stairs. It looked like it was Anita who would have to begin.

"Khush," she said quietly sipping her wine, "can we talk about what we are going to do to work on...us?"

Khush took a swig of his wine, gulping almost half of it down in one go and turned to her. He looked hassled.

"Yeah ok Anita," he said letting out a breath and muting the TV, "what do you want to talk about?"

"Well, we said we need to communicate better. I think we need to see someone to help us. Like a counsellor."

"No."

"But I think it would help."

"I said no. No outsider is going to get into my business with my wife."

"But I thought you wanted to work on the marriage."

"By ourselves. I think we can do it without someone butting in. It's not the done thing in our culture Anita, you know this."

"Well, we can find someone discreet. They aren't allowed to say anything to anyone anyway."

"Fuck sake, Anita. You're like a dog with a bone. I don't want counselling. But if you want to get someone involved then ok. If it will shut you up about it. My god, I can't even go one evening without being hassled by you."

"Sorry, I just want to help us," said Anita playing with her hair, "did you want me to check in with Emma at work or any of my mates, see if any of them know someone or recommends someone?"

"Fuck No. Don't ask Emma or your other mates," said Khush frowning and shaking his head, "I don't want any of them knowing our personal business. I don't want it to get back to our community, or my dad. It's embarrassing enough that my wife won't listen to a fucking word I say. If your work find out, they'll gossip. I know what they're like. I'll find someone. Even if it means paying more as it's not someone we know. I don't want anyone at your work knowing about our business. Leave it with me and stop hassling me."

Anita nodded and sipped her wine. Emma already knew some of what was going on, she knew that they were having communication problems and it was clear that there was a strain in their relationship. But Anita didn't want to tell Khush that. She needed him on board and happy with all of this. She needed this to work.

"Ok," said Khush putting down his now empty glass of wine and scooting over to Anita, his mood had changed again and now he was calm, he had control. "So now that's settled, can we move on to other stuff?"

"What stuff?" said Anita confused.

Khush leaned in close and placed a warm hand on her thigh, slowly stroking up to her hip and pausing there. His breath smelt of wine, his face was close to Anita's and she found herself breathing deeply as she felt his thumb caress the groove on her hip. It had been a while since they had been this close and intimate. Anita felt dizzy. Khush gently took the glass out of Anita's hand, placed it on the table and then guided her hand to his lap. Anita's eyes widened at the feel of her hard husband against her hand and Khush moved in to kiss her deeply.

Despite his harsh words and the warning siren in her head, Anita felt herself melt into his embrace and soon enough she and Khush were exploring and kissing passionately; fuelled by wine. Anita's breathing was fast, and she felt her heart beating as Khush lifted her up and across him; his hands moving under her top and caressing her body making her skin sizzle.

Chapter 27.

Things with Khush began to improve; he had gone back to spending the night in their bedroom, they were having sex more and Anita felt their love had rekindled. During the evenings Khush was more attentive with Anand, playing with him when he came home from work. He helped in the house, making things easier for Anita, clearing up more often, and volunteering to cook for them at weekends when he had more time. They ate as a family, spent time together as a family and slept as a family. Anita was shocked that her outburst after her parents' anniversary celebration had worked.

Khush was beginning to be the same man she had fallen in love with, the man she spent a romantic weekend in York with. Their relationship was better, and Anita was grateful. It wasn't until after she spoke to Emma in the third week of family bliss that she began to have doubts about what was happening.

"So," Emma had said as they sat in the staffroom with coffees in their hands, "How's things at home?"

"Good" said Anita and for once she felt happy that she wasn't lying.

"Yeah it seems it," Emma smiled, "You seem happier and there's definitely a spring in your step. Things with Khush getting better then?"

"Yeah they are," said Anita.

It had taken a while, but Anita had finally opened up to Emma about what had been happening with Khush, including some of what had happened between Eddie and herself. Emma had been very comforting and had listened to Anita.

"That's good," said Emma smiling, picking up a biscuit and dunking it into her tea she added, "did you think more about what I said about couples counselling?"

"Actually," said Anita smiling widely, "we have discussed that. Khush said he would be open to it soon."

"Excellent," Emma said popping the soggy biscuit into her mouth before it fell into her mug, "We can get right on it, I know a few people who deal with couples exclusively."

Anita stopped smiling. How was she going to tell Emma that Khush didn't want her to know anything about this and that they weren't going to use any of the people Emma knew, no matter how good. She swallowed hard.

"Uh, Em, don't worry about getting someone you know, Khush is sorting it all out."

"But I know the perfect people for the job. Didn't you tell him that?"

"Yeah I did but I think he wants to find someone he is comfortable with," Anita lied.

"Oh," said Emma.

Her face told Anita that she knew exactly why Khush didn't want her involved, "Well, as long as he actually does it and finds someone. He has to be comfortable since he's got most of the issues to work on."

"Thanks for understanding," said Anita biting her tongue at the snide comment.

"So, when did he have this revelation?" Emma could pretend she believed Anita's excuse but she couldn't hide the sarcasm in her voice.

"Well, after my parent's anniversary celebration we talked."

"That was ages ago," cried Emma shocked.

"Yeah, I know."

"And he hasn't done anything since then?"

"No, but things are good with us right now. So, there's no rush."

"Anita, it won't stay good if you don't talk it through properly. It takes at least a couple of months before you'll get an appointment. That'll be too long since saying he would do couples counselling. Lots can happen in that time."

"He will do it, trust me," Anita said feeling a lump in her throat.

"He better," said Emma getting up from the table and placing her empty mug in the dishwasher, "if he doesn't do it, come back to me and I'll sort you someone I know. Give him a chance to sort it, no more than another month, then you come back to me ok?"

"Ok, Emma, but he will do it," Anita wasn't so sure of herself now.

"Yeah right, talk to him. Things may be going great now, but it doesn't mean any issues aren't still there waiting to surface and mess everything up again."

"Ok, I will."

"Promise me? Talk to him?"

"Ok, I promise I will talk to him- soon."

Anita watched Emma walk out of the room and sighed. It had been several months since Khush had made all those promises to change and to see someone together, and Anita hadn't forgotten it. Every day she hoped he would say that he'd found someone, but every day he spoke about everything else but counselling. Whenever she brought it up to he would snap and say he would sort it, but 'right now' he was busy with work and needed time to research. She'd again offered help from Emma in finding someone, but he waved off the offer as if she were a nuisance and said he would do it.

Anita was slowly losing any hope of them ever going to seek help, but as things were still good with Khush at home, she was content on the way things they were for now. She knew Emma was right though, even thought things were settling, they still had issues that needed to be aired and fixed before they could truly move on with their marriage, otherwise it would eventually implode. Anita needed to speak to him.

Chapter 28.

One evening, after Anand had been put to bed and her and Khush were sat in the living room listening to music and playing cards, Anita took the chance to speak to Khush.

"Can I ask you something?"

"Sure" he said looking up at her then back at his cards, "what's up?"

"Well, I'm loving how things are with us at the moment, like it's like our first few years together again and I know Anand is loving time with you."

"But?" Khush's voice hardened.

"Well, as good as we are right now, don't you think we still need to do the counselling thing?"

Khush stopped looking at his cards and frowned. He lifted his head up and looked at Anita for a long time before he spoke.

"So, you still want to do all that crap?" he sighed.

"Uh, yeah" said Anita surprised at his hostility, "I thought you wanted to do it too? You were happy to do it before."

"Before we were back to normal," he said shrugging, "but now I think we don't need it. Things are good, aren't they?"

"But don't we need to do it so we can keep it like this?"

"You don't need a counsellor to tell me what's up you know? You can just tell me."

Anita was tense and anxious; depending on what she said next and how Khush reacted this could be the end of the harmony she had been experiencing for a while now. She didn't want it to end but she knew they had to seek help.

"No, it's not that, I just think it'll help us change and be better together."

"Be better? So, you think I still need to change?"

"No, it's not that, I think we both need to. It's not just you or not just me. It's us." Anita looked pleadingly at Khush, "Come on Khush, we said we would try it out."

"I'm not sure."

"Why don't we just try it out, like for ten sessions or something and then we can see."

"Ten? Bloody hell that's loads," Khush shook his head, "Look, Anita, I don't think we need it. I don't want to do it. But if it stops you hassling me and getting on my nerves like some fucking parrot, I will do it. But only for five sessions- if we even need that many, and then we can evaluate it all ok?"

Anita sighed, only slightly relieved, "Yeah five is good, Khush. Thanks. Want me to sort it if you're busy with work?"

"Yeah alright but don't go blabbing to Emma or anyone else alright? You find someone, not them."

"Yeah of course," Anita smiled, "I'll do it, and then you can approve them."

Anita picked up the playing cards and shuffled them. She knew this was a win for her, but it wasn't what he had promised. She knew five sessions for a couple wasn't going to be enough to get to the root of the problem, but it was better than nothing; she would have to get it to work as best as she could for those five hours. This was a step in the right direction to make her marriage work.

The next day Anita spoke to Emma about the people she had recommended. She explained to Emma that they had to promise to say they weren't recommended by Emma at all, otherwise Khush would lose his temper and back track on the counselling. Irritated with Khush's terms and stupidity, but happy that her friend was getting some help, Emma reluctantly agreed.

"I really hope this helps," said Emma sifting through her contacts and writing down numbers for Anita, "these two are good and you deserve some happiness."

"Thanks," said Anita taking the pieces of paper knowing that she would have to write them down herself so it was in her handwriting and no one else's-Khush would notice that- "he's not overly happy about it but will do it for me."

"He should be," Emma said rolling her eyes, "you need his commitment. I know after a few months of this, you two will start to see the difference. And if not, you'll know to walk away from each other."

Anita looked away from Emma.

"What?" Emma said her eyes narrowing.

"Well, Khush and I have met half-way with all this. He said he would give it five sessions before he decides if it's working or not."

"Five? Anita, you know that's not enough."

"I know that Emma, but it's what he was willing to do. It's five sessions or none. There's no other option."

Emma frowned at her friend, "there are plenty of other options."

"I'm not going in to all that with you again."

"Just saying."

"I know, let's try this first. This is what we need, five sessions or not. It's a win for me."

"Ok," agreed Emma shaking her head and shrugging her shoulders, "well I really hope whatever happens, makes you happy. As I already said, you deserve to be happy."

"Thanks," said Anita smiling and squeezing her friend's shoulder, "I really appreciate it. And I know you're looking out for me. I know five isn't enough but it's a start, you never know, he may like it and want to carry on. This may be the break we need, and I need a fucking break."

"You do," said Emma grinning at Anita's expression, "go on now Anita, back to work for the both of us. You've got patients to see and I've got paperwork to do. Enough to cover the walls with."

"Residents, Emma, not patients, they are residents remember?" Anita said laughing and leaving Emma shaking her head at her in the room.

Chapter 29.

"So, this is our final session," Khush reminded Anita as they got into the car on their way to see Dr Stephens, "how do you feel about it?"

Anita looked at her husband as he put on his seatbelt and started the car, she was grateful for the counselling sessions and they had got a few issues out in the open. They talked about how Khush felt like he wasn't good enough for Anita's family and how he thought she was too much into her career now instead of looking after the family. He brought up Anita being too Westernised and not wearing enough traditional Indian clothing, especially around his family.

Anita had rebuffed with discussing how Khush's expectations of her were old fashioned and that he couldn't model his expectations on Anita as a mother and wife on his late mother; times were different and life was different. He couldn't possibly expect her to be like his mother had been in such a modern society. Khush had not liked that one bit and had actually stormed out of the session shouting at Anita's lack of sympathy for him losing the one woman in his life who treated him well and devoted herself to looking after him; when he finally returned he whined that he didn't want Anita to be exactly like his mum, but learn from how good a mother she had been and to use that with Anand.

This had been the third session and with time running out and Khush not opening up and talking as much as she and the counsellor had wanted him to, Anita knew she had to be bolder with her comments in order to get communication going. It had taken a lot of persuading on Anita's part to convince Khush to go back for the final two sessions, even promising that he wouldn't have to go again after this and that they could stop the sessions. Eventually Khush had admitted defeat and had gone to the fourth session but returned to being silent again as he had been the first time they had gone.

"Are you listening?" said Khush prodding Anita's arm and snapping her out of her daydream.

"Huh?"

"I said it's our final session, how do you feel about it?"

"I think it's been good for us," Anita said looking out of the window at the buildings and trees passing by, "but I think we need more."

"No, I said-"

"I know I know. It's ok, I think it would be better for more but I know I promised you no more after this one."

"Plus I think we're doing alright now aren't we?"

"Yeah."

"Got a few things off our chests, made some comments and suggestions on how to improve. That kind of stuff. Now we're alright yeah?"

Anita gritted her teeth and continued staring out of the window.

Yes, the sessions had got as well as can be expected, but there was no way enough had been done. She needed to explore his issues further. Obviously, the way his expectations lay with the way his mother had done things was paramount in his own behaviour, and this had been discussed, albeit briefly and tactfully so he didn't lose his temper again, but Anita knew there was so much more.

His dad for instance. The way his father had dominated his wife, the way the men in that family spoke to the women in the family, the downright misogynistic behaviour and viewpoints that women should be home looking after the family, cooking and cleaning, and the men should be out working hard and bringing in the finances. Anita hated it and was growing to resent that it had seeped into their lives and relationship. Just like his dad had been terrifying in the way he not only spoke to his wife, but also the way he was so aggressive towards her: like she was his slave and only there to serve him. This was what Anita saw in Khush.

Khush shared his father's aggressive and hostile traits. But what she loathed the most about this was that Anand had seen this and on a few occasions had spoken to Anita in ways that shocked and hurt her; his demands for food, his expectations that daddy would play and mummy can cook and clean had seeped into his mind. Anita had picked up on this and had swiftly served punishments to this rudeness, but to her dismay, Khush had not. He had just smiled and not engaged in the conversations with Anand to rectify these assumptions.

So much more needed to be done for their marriage and here was Khush thinking everything was ok and that they had done more than enough. Anita knew this was the best she was going to get out of him, and there was no way he would admit anything negative towards his father, the patriarch of the family. She knew that she would have to work on subtle changes in Khush from home and although Anita was terrified at the thought of doing this alone, she knew she needed to keep the momentum up.

"Yeah, things are alright," she sighed glancing at her husband who seemed far too happy to be driving to his final counselling appointment to notice her hesitation, "we can work on things at home, just the two of us."

"Yeah, like we should have in the first place," Khush looked over at Anita and squeezed her knee, "Look, I know I have things to change, and I'll work on them. I am working on them, now aren't I? Making changes to make it better. I'm improving, yeah?"

"Yeah, you are," said Anita smiling at her husband, and feeling a flash of sympathy for his eagerness to please her, "You are. And I am so happy that it's making us better. And I will change some of the way I do things too."

"Yeah, we can both change and we can be stronger at the end of it all. I'm happy we did this Anita. We'll be fine."

**   **   **

"Wait, Khush!" said Anita calling at her husband less than an hour later. He walked out of the final counselling appointment in a huff. Turning back to Counsellor Stephens she smiled and shrugged apologising to him, "sorry about that. Not sure why he went off like that."

"I think it is because I suggested you have some counselling on your own too, Anita," the counsellor stated, "I really think it's necessary so you can have a chance to be completely honest with yourself."

"I am being honest," Anita said knowing that for most of the sessions she had been holding back and tiptoeing around issues so not to set Khush off.

"Well, I'm just saying what I observe. And I think until you can deal with the way your marriage is going, and be honest with yourself about it, you'll not be able to work with Khush."

"Are you saying it's my fault the marriage isn't working?" said Anita standing in the middle of the sparsely decorated room feeling like the walls were closing in on her.

"Not at all," he stood up and walked up to Anita, placing a hand on her shoulder he said, "this is exactly why I think you need sessions on your own. You are taking too much of the responsibility for this marriage. It's not a team I'm seeing here. He has control and you always seem to be stopping yourself from saying something. I've noticed it, and you and Khush really do need more sessions."

"But we won't be having any more." Anita said looking sad and desperate to talk more.

"I know, that's why I suggested you have some time on your own first."

"But you saw Khush's reaction. He doesn't like the idea."

"Come on, we both know there is more here. For him and for you. But if he is resisting and refusing to go, I can't help him, but I am reaching out to you Anita."

"I can't, Khush doesn't want me to."

"Do you want to?"

"It doesn't matter what I want, Khush-"

"Khush is not in the room right now. Do you want one to one counselling?"

"I...I'm not sure," said Anita her voice cracking with emotion, "I wouldn't know how I would, I don't want to lie to Khush. We've just been talking about how we need to communicate more."

"No Anita, we spoke about how he needs to communicate more. Look, all I can do at this point is suggest it. I think it would be beneficial for your mental health and your self-confidence for you to have counselling on your own. But I'm not in control of what you do with my recommendations."

"But what if he found out?" Anita was terrified at the thought of Khush knowing what was being suggested. The blowback would be catastrophic.

"I am sure there can be some arrangement made to help you." Counsellor Stephens went back to his table and picked up a few papers, "when you see Khush, please explain that I needed you to read through these documents and fill out some forms, that is why you have taken this long to leave. Ask him to sign the forms too and I want you to bring them back to me by Friday. I may have sorted something for you by then."

Taking the forms from his hands Anita's eyes welled up, "thank you, for everything. I'll bring these back by Friday."

"Make sure you do," he said opening the door to allow for her to leave, "Doesn't matter what time, I will be here and waiting. Take care Anita."

"Thanks" Anita repeated breathing deeply as she stepped out of the one room she had felt safe in for months.

"And be safe."

When Anita reached the car park, Khush was sitting in the driver's seat tapping away furiously at his mobile phone. He looked ready to explode. As Anita opened the car door, he looked sharply at her.

"Why were you so long?"

"I...he was going through some forms with me on what to fill in now the sessions are done. You need to fill in and sign them too."

"Any parts where I can evaluate what he was like?" Khush said ignoring the papers that Anita was trying to hand to him and started the car.

"Um, maybe. We can do it at home he said, and I will take it in on my way to work or lunch break."

"Whatever," said Khush speeding out of the parking lot and headed towards home, "I'm done with it. I did the five sessions you forced me to do, and that's all I'm doing. We won't be going back there. What a waste of my time."

Anita bit her lip; she was about to argue that she hadn't forced him to do any of them but thought better of it. No need to wind him up even more when he was already wound so tightly.

"Did he say more about you going on your own?" Khush asked a few moments later.

"Um, yeah he did. What do you-"

"I don't like it. Why does he want you to go in alone? So you can bitch about me while I'm not there?"

"I don't think that's what he meant."

"Then what?"

"I…" Anita had no idea what to say to diffuse the tension in the air.

"Well, I don't want you to do it. I think it's pointless you starting single sessions when we've just done couples sessions. That's why we went to work on our marriage, not so that you can go and work on your issues and whine about stuff."

"Ok, I wasn't sure about it anyway," lied Anita trying hard to keep herself from crying.

"Well, let's say then you don't do it then. I don't want you to and you don't want to. So that's settled yeah. You won't go."

"Ok." Anita said feeling her chest tighten and her body ache from the inside.

The ride home was longer than Anita ever remembered it being. Building after building zipped by in a blur. Anita looked at the sky; the sun peaked through the dark clouds which looked like they were threatening to rip apart with rain, the air was thick and humid. The world felt like it was pressing down on her; making it hard to breathe.

A perfect fucking metaphor for how I'm feeling she thought as she blinked back some tears and held tightly on to the forms the counsellor had given her.

      **   **   **

It was Friday. Anita was holding on to the papers that she and Khush filled in for counsellor Stephens tighter than she realised and when she handed them to the receptionist and turned to leave, she was stopped.

"Anita?" called a voice walking into the lobby.

Anita turned around, she saw him walking briskly towards her smiling, a warm comforting expression on his face.

"Hi counsellor Stephens. I was just dropping the forms off as you asked, we have both signed them."

"Excellent," he said picking them up and placing them in his pile of paperwork in his arms, "I'm glad you came. Do you have a minute? This won't take long."

"Um…I guess so, I am on my way to work though."

"I'll be brief then."

He sat down on a long backless sofa in the corner of the large lobby, there was no one else here and the privacy seemed to suit him. He beckoned Anita to sit next to him and then hunched his shoulders, leaning in close to her. His face serious and concerned now.

"So, I hope you've had a chance to think about the single sessions I mentioned the other day?"

"Yes, look, I don't think Khush would like it and I don't have time really with work and then going home to look after the family."

"But would you want it?"

"Um, yeah, I think it would be good."

"I agree. So, I have taken the liberty to speak to Emma about this."

"Emma?" said Anita shocked. She didn't want all this to get back to her boss, she felt a quiver of panic begin to rise in her body.

"Yes, remember Emma and I are long-time friends. She was concerned about you, and we had a brief discussion."

Counsellor Stephens looked at Anita's face and put a reassuring hand on her shoulder, "don't worry Anita. I haven't divulged anything to her, especially what was said in the sessions. That's private and confidential. I did say that I recommend counselling sessions for you though."

"Oh," said Anita feeling a little better, "what did Emma say?"

"She agrees with me Anita," he said smiling, "and she wants to make it so that you're able to see someone without worrying about Khush finding out."

"How would that work?" said Anita.

"Well, you do your own counselling sessions on Wednesdays and Fridays now don't you?"

"Yes."

"So, Emma says that usually on a Friday you are quieter, so Friday afternoons you can attend your own counselling sessions."

"But I can't sneak around. I wouldn't be able to."

"We aren't asking you to sneak around Anita, Emma said that you can have your sessions at work on a Friday afternoon."

"How would that work?" asked Anita confused. There were no more psychologists at the care home except her, and if she wasn't going to sneak around, how would it work?

"Well, I'm not sure of all the details, Emma said she would sort that and speak to you today, but I think the plan is to have someone come to you at the care home. How does that sound?"

"Confusing," Anita said frowning and unsure.

"Well, I guess I'm not explaining it well and I don't know the details of the way you see people. That's why I spoke to Emma. She'll talk to you today and explain all." He stopped and looked at Anita's worried face, there was a trace of fear in it. "Look, Anita. Let Emma explain it to you when you get into work. And I am sure she can answer any questions you have. We won't go ahead unless we have your approval, though."

"Ok," said Anita feeling that all too familiar feeling of anxiety creeping back into her skin.

"Ok, right I have to go now, I have an appointment in five," he stood up and shook Anita's cold clammy hand, "good luck Anita, you deserve to get heard."

Anita watched him walk away as briskly as he had walked towards her moments ago and felt apprehensive. How was she going to do this without Khush finding out? She was desperate to speak to someone and she knew it would help her, but the logistics of this was too much. She needed to talk to Emma, and quickly.

Chapter 30.

Anita walked into her house that evening to hear Anand laughing and Khush making dinosaur noises. It had become an agreement between Khush and herself that on a Friday she would stay back at work for an extra hour so that she could finish any paperwork, and Khush would finish work an hour earlier so that he could pick up Anand from school and sort out dinner.

Even through the more stressful episodes in their relationship, Khush had insisted on sticking to this, and although he didn't admit it, it was clear to Anita that Khush actually enjoyed his Friday afternoons with Anand and he wasn't going to change that special time for anything. Anita didn't mind either, not only did she manage to get paperwork completed for her residents, she would also always find the boys in a great mood, and this always made for a happier weekend.

"Evening gentlemen," Anita said as she popped into the living room to give Anand a big cuddle and kiss, "What are we up to?"

"Nothing much," said Khush winking at Anand and getting up to give Anita a kiss, "we were just playing dinosaur police."

"Dinosaur police?" laughed Anita looking at Anand who had picked up a policeman hat from his fancy dress box and put it on his head with a stern look on his face, "Anand, are you the officer?"

"Yes mummy," said Anand said standing tall and hands on his hips, "I charge and daddy dinosaur in trouble."

"He's in big trouble is he?" laughed Anita and looking at Khush who was grinning from ear to ear at his son, "Well I will leave you to it. Make sure you catch the naughty dinosaur Mr Policeman. Mummy's going to go for a shower and get out of my work clothes."

Anita laughed as she watched Anand stomp after Khush. She turned and walked upstairs smiling at how she loved seeing the two of them playing and having fun.

"Dinner will be ready in half an hour," called Khush from the living room, "It's a simple one tonight...ouch! Mr Policeman not so rough."

Anita's mind wondered as she stood under the hot shower rinsing the day off her body. She thought about counsellor Stephens again and to be honest, she hadn't stopped thinking about him all day. What he and Emma had come up with worried her at first but after talking to Emma, she had come around to the idea and by the end of the day, Anita was in fact looking forward to speaking to someone. The plan that he explained was sound, it was going to work and the doctor coming to see her in two weeks' time, knew some of the issues surrounding seeing Anita and was aware of the level of secrecy that was needed.

Anita closed her eyes and recalled the conversation she and Emma had had earlier on, and she was surprised to find that tears joined the water flowing over her face. She was overwhelmed by the love and support she had somehow managed to find around her, she didn't feel like she deserved it but Anita wasn't going to throw it away like she had let happen with Eddie. She was going to listen to Emma, and start making some changes for herself.

"Knock, knock," said a voice at the bathroom door, "can I come in?"

Anita turned to see a foggy silhouette of Khush standing at the doorway.

"Of course," she said gathering herself and steeling her emotions, "What's up?"

"Just, wanted to join you," Khush said opening the shower door smiling. Anita raised her eyebrows and giggled as Khush stepped into the shower and sidled up behind her and began kissing her neck.

She closed her eyes with pleasure, "Mmm, that feels good," she whispered.

"Yeah it does," said Khush slowly running his hands over her wet body pressing himself against her and not hiding his pleasure.

"What about Anand?"

"He's alright, watching his dinosaur trucks show on TV. He'll be good for ten minutes."

"Ten minutes?" giggled Anita turned herself so that she and Khush were face to face, water dripping over their hot bodies, "Is that enough time?"

"Of course," Khush said slipping his hands between her thighs and kissing at her nipples, "plenty of time."

**   **   **

Life for Anita had finally begun to get to where she wanted it to be. Things between her and Khush had also improved again; he was attentive, caring, passionate and more than anything, he was present. He spent more and more time with Anand and Anita, and he had even taken a week off during Anand's school holiday to spend time with them. Khush had planned a short getaway to the coast, renting out a small cottage that sat opposite the beach front, self-catering meaning they could go out and do whatever they wanted, and there was plenty for a boy to do, including run around on the beach. The week had been nothing but perfect for Anita; there had been no arguments between her and Khush and she couldn't remember the last time she had spent so many of her days laughing and playing.

On their drive home, Anand asleep in the back with his teddy clutched tightly in his arms and Khush singing along to some dreadful cheesy pop music, Anita thought this was how she needed and wanted it to be. They had worked out most of their differences and things were looking up. Anita knew the secret counselling for her wasn't going to last long but was hopeful that she would be able to work out her own insecurities before he found out. Right now, she wasn't going to dwell on the what ifs, she needed to soak up the happiness that her family had been basking in over the past few months and she was damned if she wasn't going to try and keep it going.

Counselling was also giving Anita something to smile about. It had been a couple of months since she had started seeing her psychologist at work on a Friday afternoon. The set up was just as Emma had said, and the doctor she was seeing was an older lady, just about believable to be a resident at the care home. No one suspected anything and it was between Emma, the doctor and Anita. Anita had told Henna of course, but had sworn her to secrecy, even from her parents. Ash would know, Henna didn't keep secrets from him, their relationship was unlike Anita and Khush's; things were said out in the open, even if it resulted in arguments, and they never hid the important stuff from each other. They were a perfect couple in Anita's eyes, and she wished she and Khush could eventually become like them.

"I just can't have mum and dad knowing," said Anita to her sister as they sat at her dining table one evening. Anita had been given a rare afternoon off from Anand and chose to spend it catching up with her sister. "It would be shameful. You know, not the Indian thing."

"Fuck that," said Henna waving her hand, "Indian thing or not, you need it and you want it. If it's helping you, you have to do it."

"It's helping Khush as well as me too."

"Hmm, well if he helps you that's alright."

Anita had noticed that since the anniversary meal, Henna had not spoken Khush's name, always opting for 'him' or 'Anand's dad' instead. She was open about how much she was beginning to dislike Khush and what he had done to her sister, but had promised to keep civil enough so that Khush wasn't aware.

"He did the counselling with me, the couples one too." Anita defended her husband.

"Yeah, for like five minutes Anita, then he quit when the shit got too hard for him to handle and admit to."

"Henna, it wasn't like that," said Anita toying with the placemats on the table and avoiding her sister's glare, "It just wasn't for him, it didn't work."

"Because he had to admit to shit he'd been putting you through and refused to do that. He refused to take any responsibility for the marriage getting worse. Come on Anita, you can see that can't you? He didn't give it more than a few sessions."

"Calm down," said Anita feeling her chest tightening at the memory of Khush and how he behaved in counselling, "we've worked it out between us, and things are really good."

"I'm not sure I believe that."

"It is better, I promise. Do you think he would've been happy to spend time with Anand and give me the afternoon off if we weren't getting along? I'm knackered and he's giving me some time."

"Like a normal husband and father would do without asking for any thanks?"

"Come on, Henna. That's not what I'm saying. You know things are better. And the counsellor I'm now seeing-"

"In secret."

"The counsellor I'm seeing," continued Anita ignoring her sister's last remark, "she's great and she is really helping me."

Henna looked at her sister and her demeanour softened; Anita did look happier than she had seen her look in a long time. Her confidence seemed to be building up again and she didn't seem as nervous as before when talking about Khush or Anand. Whether Henna liked Khush or not (which she did not), she had to support her sister getting some form of help.

"Go on then," Henna said smiling at her sister and placing a hand on hers, "tell me about your sessions."

Anita spent the better part of the afternoon and into the evening talking to her sister about the sessions she was doing, how the counsellor was helping her see what she was able to take control of. How Khush's actions were making her feel and believe. Anita knew that Khush had changed her in ways she would have hated seeing anyone else being changed, but her situation was different. It was always one thing to say it out loud, but it was something entirely different to admit it and see it in yourself.

She'd come to the conclusion that she needed to think about what she could control and focus on those rather than the things she couldn't control; she knew that she had to work through her time and interactions with Khush in small steps. Although Anita knew she wouldn't make huge changes with Khush quickly, she knew bit by bit she was starting to understand her self-worth again and used this to slowly improve her relationship with her husband. Anita was still walking on eggshells whenever she was around Khush, but she had started to feel less scared of saying something the wrong way to Khush; she was feeling more confident about asking for compromise or challenging Khush at times.

Getting in the car later that evening Anita felt like a different person; she felt lighter and more like her old self. Talking to her sister had worked a treat on her mood, just like it always had when she was younger and in need of some support and guidance. She cranked up the music playlist that she had made for herself; a mixture of pop, rock and some Motown that allowed her to sing along out of tune and very loud.

Tapping away at the steering wheel and waiting for the light to turn green Anita replayed her last session with her new doctor. She smiled at the progress she felt she had made in such a short amount of time, especially as the first few sessions has resulted in her spending the better part of the hour session drowning in her own sorrow and tears.

A car beeped, bringing her out of her daydream. The traffic light was now green, and she was good to go ahead. There was a sudden loud noise and the last thing Anita remembered thinking about before everything went blank was Anand.

Chapter 31.

When Anita woke, she could hear a car horn in the distance; the sound quiet but piercing at the same time. Her head screamed in agony and she was sure something was banging against it giving her a migraine. She tried to open her eyes but instantly screwed them shut again, the pain of the light blinded her and making it feel like it was burning away her retinas. She turned her head towards the sound of something rustling next to her ear but again, the pain shot through her neck and shoulder like a jackhammer.

She cried out in pain.

"Anita?" came a distant voice, "Anita, are you ok? It's going to be ok. I'll call someone."

The familiarity of the voice brought Anita back from slipping back into blackness again, *I know that voice* she thought to herself, *I know that voice*. She tried to open her mouth wide enough to speak but her lips were concrete; cracked and heavy, her throat felt like it had been scratched sore and Anita was desperate for some water to stop her throat from burning dry. A moment passed, and Anita made an attempt to speak, but what escaped her split lips sounded like a hissing noise, like air being forced out of a slashed tyre.

"Don't try to speak," came the voice again, "here, have some water."

Anita felt a soft hand stroke her cheek and then move to the back of head, slowly and gently tilting her head up. Her lips slowly parted as she felt the first drop of water enter her mouth. She sipped. She sipped some more. The water was heavenly and cold, a soothing liquid slowly running down her burning throat.

"Slowly, slowly," the voice said, "don't drink too fast or you will choke."

Anita lay her head back and allowed herself to drift into nothingness again, this time she wasn't afraid; the voice was comforting, and she knew it would be there when she woke again.

Anita could hear hushed voices as she slowly woke later on. The beeping sound had steadied and no longer sounded like a car horn. She couldn't make out what the voices were saying but she knew it was about her. She heard the soothing voice again, and this time when she tried to open her eyes and mouth, her body responded.

"Mum?" she croaked.

"Anita beta," came her mother's voice, a little nervous than before. She felt a hand stroke her cheek and her mother kissed her forehead, "Oh, Anita I am so happy you're awake."

"Mum," said Anita slowly licking her lips and flickering her eyes open, "Ma, I need a drink please."

"Ok, beta," she said reaching for a plastic cup with a straw in it, "slowly, ok? Not too fast."

Anita smiled slowly. Even this made her wince with pain.

Anita watched as her mum took a step towards the doorway and wave someone over. What had happened? Where was she? How did she get here? There were so many questions that needed answering. A man in a short-sleeved shirt followed Anita's mother into the room and to her bedside.

"Anita," he said. His voice was quiet and instantly calming, he had a soft Indian accent like he hadn't quite trained it out of his voice yet. "Anita, my name is Doctor Jitesh Ranj. Do you know where you are?"

"Hospital?"

"Yes, do you know who is standing next to me?"

"My mum. Where's Anand?"

"Anita, please answer my questions first then we can answer yours, ok? I need to know what you remember. Do you know how you got here?"

Anita blinked; she searched her mind for the last thing she did remember but it felt so long ago. She frowned as Doctor Ranj checked her over, enlisting the help of the clipboard at the end of her bed.

"Can you remember beta?" her mum chimed in holding on to Anita's hand and stroking it softly.

"I remember going to Henna's house."

"Yes?" the doctor probed.

"Is she ok?"

"Yes, your sister is fine Anita. What else can you remember?"

"I...I was driving home...singing...listening to music...the light, the light was green and..." Anita moaned, her head throbbed and she couldn't think of anything else, "what happened? Is Anand ok? And Khush?"

"Yes, your son and husband are fine, they will be here soon. Anita, you were in a car accident. What you remember, with the lights, that happened. Your car was hit by another vehicle. You were sent spiralling and your car ended up upturned with you in it. Officers got you out and brought you here. You've suffered some injuries."

Anita's heart caught in her throat, what injuries? She couldn't feel anything and yet her whole body ached. Her eyes widened and filled with tears, her mind raced with horrific possibilities.

"What injuries doctor?" she whispered.

"Nothing major," he said. Anita was glad he started with that, and his gentle voice calmed her beating heart somewhat.

"So...?"

"Well, you've broken your left arm in three places, you have a cracked collarbone and you have some severe bruising on your right knee. Other than a handful of scratches and cuts, that's it."

"That's it?" Anita said managing to raise her eyebrows and smiling.

"Beta," said her mother coming close to her face, her own face looking like it had aged a decade, "this is good. Broken bones can be fixed and bruises and cuts are ok. They are fixable too, aren't they Doctor Ranj?"

"Yes, you're right. Anita, we've already put your arm in a cast and set it, your collar bone will need to be looked at again once the swelling has gone down, and you will need to take it easy on your knee for a while. But nothing that can't be made right again."

"Oh ok," said Anita feeling relieved, "so, where is Anand? Khush?"

"Everyone is ok, and everyone will be coming later today beta," Anita's mum cooed stroking her hair, "they know you are awake now and will be coming to see you."

"How long have I been here? What day is it now?"

"You've been here for two days, in and out of consciousness Anita," chimed in the doctor looking at her chart and writing something on it, "this is the first time you've been fully awake. You'll be out of here in no time if you carry on healing the way you are."

"Two days?" Anita found it hard to take all this in. It was all too much.

"Look, don't worry, Khush and Anand are on their way now," her mother said, "They are fine, we have all been looking after each other. You're going to be fine."

Anita looked at her mother and smiled, she believed her, and she knew things were going to be fine.

"Um, is it ok if I have a word with Anita on her own please?" said Doctor Ranj.

There was something in his voice that made Anita's already aching body tense up. Doctor Ranj ushered Anita's mother out of the room and pulled up a chair next to her bedside.

"This seems serious," said Anita trying to lighten the sudden atmosphere, "am I in trouble?"

"No Anita. Look, I need to tell you something. I have not said anything to anyone else yet due to confidentiality and it didn't mean you were at risk at all."

"Ok," said Anita trying to shuffle herself up to a seating position.

"Here, let me help you with that, you're in too much pain for you to do it on your own. I'll raise the bed."

Anita let Doctor Ranj position the bed so she was seated a little. As she watched him work she noticed that his jawline was sharp and his eyes were lighter than she'd seen on an Indian; he was good looking and Anita blushed at the urge to touch his face. She turned her head and winced: everything ached and throbbed but she wasn't going to let that stop her from being alert. She looked at the doctor and pleaded, "what is it? What's wrong?"

"Anita, when you came in you were bleeding a lot."

"But you said only a few cuts?"

"Anita, I need you to listen very carefully. I need to tell you something. You can choose to have your husband in here with you when I tell you if you want?"

"Khush? No, no it's ok. Tell me."

"Well, you were bleeding from your pelvis when you came in. Quite a lot. We took you in to surgery thinking it was internal bleeding but it wasn't that. Anita, did you know you were pregnant?"

Anita's heart stopped.

She couldn't move and couldn't speak.

She scarcely shook her head no.

"I'm so sorry Anita, you were pregnant, early stages, the specialist estimated about 12 or 14 weeks only. So very early stages. The impact of the crash, the fact you were thrown about and spun upside down in the car...it meant you suffered a miscarriage. I'm so sorry."

He placed a comforting hand on Anita's arm and watched Anita silently for a minute. Anita breathed deeply, her mind raced, her body ached, and she had no idea what to think. She just sat their numb and silently looking at her feet.

"Anita," said the doctor softly lifting his hand from her arm, "will you be ok? Would you like someone to talk to? Do you want to be left alone?"

Hearing a knock at the door, Anita whipped her head towards the sound, it was her mother looking concerned. Anita looked at the doctor pleading with her eyes.

"I think Anita needs some rest now," he said understanding Anita's look straight away, "no one is to bother her for at least an hour. Please, you can wait in the lobby, or out here is fine, but please let Anita sleep. She needs to rest."

Anita could hear her mother trying to argue with Doctor Ranj, but he spoke respectfully but sternly, Anita even thought she'd heard him emphasise the Indian accent more. She was grateful to him. She needed time to think. To take in all this information.

Pregnant? Fuck.

Another baby? I'm not sure.

Not that is mattered now anyway, you're not pregnant anymore.

Shit.

Anita placed her hands on her face and breathed heavily. She closed her eyes.

Do I tell Khush? Fuck.

Should I tell him? No. But he has a right to know?

Damn, I need to sleep. I'm so tired. Too much to think about. Too much…

Anita closed her eyes unsure of what she was feeling; she was sad about losing the baby she never knew she was carrying; she had enjoyed being pregnant for the most part with Anand. But another baby? With Khush the way he is? No, Anita knew their marriage couldn't take more stress. And she couldn't either.

Maybe the baby would change him? She thought as she drifted off to sleep, but underneath it all, below all the physical aches and pains, Anita knew how she really felt about the miscarriage. One word summed it all up.

Relieved.

Chapter 32.

Anita spent another week in the hospital going through recovery and physio exercises to strengthen her body again, and she became quite close to Doctor Ranj, or Jitesh as she now knew him by. They had a lot in common and he was kind; they liked the same books, watched the same trashy game shows on TV and they even had the same dry humour as one another. It was the spark of a good friendship, like she had experienced with Eddie, that she longed for again. It didn't take more than a few conversations and one confrontation with Khush for him to understand Anita's reasons and reluctance for not wanting to tell Khush about the miscarriage. One evening when his shift was over and visiting hours were done, Jitesh came to see Anita.

"Do you speak to anyone outside of your work and family?" he asked frowning.

"Like, do I have any friends is what you're asking?" Anita teased.

"Something like that" he said looking at Anita seriously.

"Well, I have some work friends who I talk to and there is a doctor-"

"Doctor? Are you cheating on me with another doctor?" he joked grinning and feigning surprise.

"Well, she is someone I talk to but not a friend."

"Shrink."

"Uh, yeah, call it like it is Jitesh."

"That's good Anita," he said his face turning serious again, "I was going to say, I think you need to speak to someone, like a counsellor. But if you're already doing that..."

"Why do you say that?"

"Well, it's clear that you don't want to go home yet. You've been able to leave for the past two days but you just don't seem emotionally ready. And I know I haven't known you longer than a couple of weeks, but you're different around your husband, like you're on edge. Plus, there is the way your sister looks at him, like she's about ready to punch his head in."

She nodded, "Yeah, you're right. Things with Khush are strained, although we are working to make it better. My sister hates him, and as for staying here, I think I just wasn't ready yet to go out there again. You know, on the road."

"I get that," said Jitesh, he placed a hand on her shoulder, "but you've gotta leave already. And you're healthy. You can survive out there no matter what the world throws at you."

Anita looked at Jitesh, his smile was warm and knowing, and she knew he didn't just mean she could survive the injuries out in the world, but much more than she was willing to admit and face right now.

"Look, I will give you my number and you can contact me whenever you want, ok?"

"Are you hitting on me?" joked Anita enjoying how red Jitesh's face was becoming.

He coughed, "no, I just...was thinking you may want someone to talk to. Sorry, I didn't mean to make you think...I wasn't..."

"It's ok!" Anita laughed, holding on to her painful ribs, "I was just kidding. Thanks, I'll take your number, but I may not call."

"That's ok, it's up to you."

"No, it's just I don't think Khush would be happy about me having your number."

"But I'm your doctor and I want to make sure you get back into good health."

"I know that. You know that. But Khush...well he has a tendency...to, well..."

"Get jealous?" finished off Jitesh raising his eyebrows, "he doesn't need to. But if you want to only text, that's fine. Or put me under a different name in your phone, that's fine. But this is all above board, and I want to keep an eye on you to make sure you're ok."

"Thanks, Jitesh."

"I really hope he doesn't go mad; I just want to help you as a doctor, and as a friend. Nothing more, ok?"

Anita nodded and handed her phone to Jitesh to put his number in.

Please don't let this backfire she thought nervously.

**   **   **

Being at home on bedrest was not what Anita wanted but she was under strict orders and for once, Khush agreed with the professionals. Khush worked hard looking after her and made sure she was doing the stretches and exercises she was given, although he didn't understand why all of them were needed.

"What's this one for?" he asked one day as he watched Anita lay back and twist.

Anita looked at him from the corner of her eyes, "just to strengthen my core and pelvic muscles."

"Why? They weren't injured in the crash."

"But the core helps keeps everything stronger and helps the rest of me recover."

Khush looked at Anita and frowned.

"I don't know Khush," said Anita sitting up, sweat forming on her hairline and the beginning of stickiness forming under her t-shirt, "I'm just doing what the doctors say. Dr Ranj said to do it so, I'm doing it. Following his instructions."

"His instructions," said Khush his face unable to hide the jealously he felt.

"Khush, he's a doctor. He knows what's best. Better than me, better than you, better than any of us. If he tells me to do the exercises, I'll do them. Anything to get me back to fighting fit."

And he's a friend that actually cares about me she thought sourly.

Khush seemed to take an age to think about what she had just said. In all honesty, the exercises for her core and pelvic muscles were given to her by Jitesh to help with recovery after the miscarriage. Yes, they helped with everything else too, which is the story they had come up with together, but mostly, they helped her body recover after the loss of her baby. She just couldn't tell Khush that.

"Look," she said facing him, "I have to do these to help myself. Can you either help or leave me to it? These hurt and I can't exactly sit and talk about them, I just have to do them."

"Ok, ok," said Khush standing and holding his hands up in defence, "I'll leave you to it. I just think if he wants to give you exercises to do, then maybe some cardio would be good too."

His words stung like a slap in the face. Cardio? What was he trying to say?

"Cardio?" she said quietly, "why would he need to add cardio to my recovery?"

"Well," said Khush shrugging, "I just think, with all this sitting around, your cardio and body have suffered a little and adding some cardio in that would help you to get back into shape."

"You mean lose weight," said Anita her voice wobbling.

"Well, yeah, I guess so. If you lose some weight, then your body has less pressure carry you and you can recover better."

"You think I need to lose weight?" said Anita not hearing what Khush had just said.

"Just since being sat down all day."

"I'm in recovery," said Anita anger rising up in her body, "that's why I'm sat down."

"I know," said Khush, "I just mean if you lose weight, you'll be able to recover better and quicker. You were in hospital for a while sitting and laying down, and now you're home, again sitting all day, you have put on some weight, and I am sure you'll want to lose those extra pounds. Losing weight will help."

Anita sat in stunned silence watching her husband. His words piercing her chest and chipping away at her self-worth. As Khush watched her, waiting for a reaction, Anita realised that her recovery wasn't his priority, it was having a slim woman on his arm that he wouldn't be embarrassed by, and right now, Anita was an embarrassment to him. Pressing her teeth together until a jolt of pain shot up her jaw, Anita turned away from Khush, closed her eyes and continued to stretch.

"Fine," huffed Khush walking out of the room, "you asked, I was honest, and said you need to lose some weight. I wasn't being mean but fine, act like a goddamned wounded bird and have a flap. I'm done talking to you tonight. Your weight, your issue."

Chapter 33.

Anita returned to work a month after coming home from the hospital, Emma had insisted that she have an extra week sick leave so that she could recover more and ease herself back into everyday life. Emma had also adjusted Anita's work load so that she wasn't on her feet all day, there were more residents that were on the list waiting to speak to Anita as a formal counsellor and this was the best opportunity to extend Anita's sessions. Now, it was only Mondays and Thursdays that Anita worked the normal care home schedule, all the other days she was based in her new office seeing residents and working on their emotional and mental needs with them. Anita was really pleased with this set up as it also came with a pay rise and her own office; she was finally using the skills and knowledge she had been desperate to use for a long time.

Once Anita returned to work, her own counselling sessions also picked up again. She began to talk about her accident more, her marriage and how that was doing well- on most occasions- and she was able to return to the main issue with her lack of confidence: Khush. Anita felt she was making headway with her mental health and was finally able to accept that she wasn't to blame in the relationship, that Khush's controlling manner and his hostile comments that would break her confidence and make her question everything, was to blame.

Anita felt more in control of situations at home and had started to realise that her worrying about what Khush's reaction to everything she said or did was not her problem to deal with and rectify, but Khush's. She knew she hadn't done anything wrong in the relationship, and was more than accommodating, but she had been ostracised so much by him that she believed that she was to blame and that she wasn't doing as she had promised to do all those years ago when they had married. Now, Anita was breaking free from these emotional manacles and becoming the person she knew herself to be. Yes, things were definitely looking better.

Her relationship with Khush was also slowly improving, they had been communicating before the accident and during her week at home on bed rest, he had been attentive and caring-most of the time. Taking time out of work to look after her and Anand. He was loving and Anita hoped that this wouldn't end. This was the longest they had gone for a while being this happy and Anita believed that Khush had finally got the message to change or lose her. He had chosen to change.

As well with helping Anita at home, Khush had also volunteered to continue to drive Anita to and from work while her knee healed. Anita had ask him to do this for her, saying that she needed more time to strengthen her knee so that she could drive, but in reality she was afraid of getting behind the wheel again. The accident had severely bruised her confidence on the road; she felt twitchy and nervous whenever she got into the car and could feel panic attacks ready to pounce if she let them. Khush had been sympathetic and was happy to drive her for as long as she wanted, but Anita knew that anything more than a couple of weeks would affect his work too, and she didn't want that to suffer. She also knew he had ulterior motives to keep driving her to work.

"Hey Khush," she said one evening as they were at the dining table and Khush was filling the dishwasher, "I think I'm ready to get back in the driver's seat."

"You mean drive to work on your own?" he asked continuing to work.

"Yeah, I think I'm ready now. I need to do it at some point. It's a short journey, and my knee feels much better now. I'll take it easy of course."

"Of course you will," said Khush turning to face her and smiling, "I'm ok with it but only if you are. I know it's only a short journey, but you have to feel comfortable."

"I think I do feel comfortable, and I think I'll still feel a little nervous in the car, but that won't go away until I actually get behind the wheel and drive somewhere."

"Only if you're ready," said Khush walking up to Anita kissing her head, "Want me to come in the car the first time you drive?"

"No, thanks hon. I'll do it. I've got to take the step on my own first."

"Ok. So, what about Anand's pick up and drop off? Want me to do those?"

"No, I can drop him off, and I can ask my dad to pick him up if I'm going to be late. Would that be ok with you? It means you're not rushing back from work on the train."

"I'm ok with all of this. I do need to get back into full days at work, and it'll be good to get back to it all too. But they know the situation and are flexible. I'll go with what you decide."

Anita smiled at her husband; this was the Khush she fell in love with, and she wanted to keep this version around. He was going out of his way to help her, and she felt she owed him this. "Of course it's alright Khush. Come Monday I'll drive myself to work. This will also give me practice over the weekend to drive around on my own."

"Sounds like a plan," Khush said leading her to the living room and switching on the TV, "Now for the next dilemma, what shouldl we watch tonight?"

Monday arrived and Anita was more than a little nervous. She prepared for work the night before and sorted Anand's school bag for him. Everything was set and ready for her to take her son to school and then drive to work; a route she had done over and over, but today felt like the first time and Anita was nervous. Khush had woken earlier and got himself ready for work. He left just as Anand was having his breakfast wishing Anita good luck and a good day. *If only everything could be this simple and right*, she thought as she sipped her morning tea. She had refused to show how anxious she was feeling in front of Khush as she wanted him to set off to work happy and relaxed without worrying about her.

Now, standing on the porch outside the front door with Anand next to her waiting for his mother to unlock the car, Anita wasn't sure what to do. The keys felt alien in her sweaty palms, and her legs felt like led.

She blinked, she breathed, and she looked down at Anand.

"Mummy you ok?" he asked frowning and clutching his teddy, even though he was almost five, Anand still loved to hug a teddy in the car. A trait Anita found sweet, and Khush found irritating.

"Yes, mummy's fine sweety," Anita said smiling. She gave herself a little shake making Anand giggle and got the two of them in the car.

The drive was slow, and a few times Anita felt like the panic was going to overtake, but each time she looked over at Anand who was happily chatting away to his teddy, she collected her thoughts and carried on. By the time she got to work, Anita was aching, her body had been rigid throughout the journey and now her muscles ached as well as her head. She walked in to work and was greeted by Emma with a mug of coffee and a biscuit.

"What's the occasion?" she asked tilting her head in confusion.

"You text me before you left for work saying you were driving today so might be late. I thought maybe you'd want a decent coffee to calm yourself once you got here."

"You're awesome Em," said Anita taking the coffee and the biscuit.

"I know," Emma replied smiling, "give yourself five then you can join Sam on your rounds.

After this, time sped by; getting back into routine was simple and Anita felt like she hadn't been gone for long. Even her confidence in driving had improved each day over the week. Things with Khush were still good although going back to work had clearly started to put on a strain on his good mood. But Anita was ok with that, a little stress and the odd bad mood wasn't going to deter her from fixing her marriage. She had said as much to her counsellor earlier that afternoon.

Driving home from work she recalled the conversation they'd in the office and the 'homework' the counsellor had given her to do. She glanced at her bag and sighed. *How am I going to do this?*

"You want me to do what?" Anita had asked dumbfounded.

"I want you to write a letter to yourself."

"Why?"

"Because I think this exercise will help you come to terms with how you are feeling about yourself."

"But a letter to myself, about what?"

"Yes, for your eyes only. I want you to talk about your marriage with Khush, things before you were married, how they changed after Anand, and how it is now."

"Wow, that's…intense."

"I know, Anita, but I know you can do it. And I think you should. You need to talk and reflect openly on your sessions with me, and I think a letter will be helpful."

"Ok," said Anita uncertain.

"It's just for your eyes, no one else needs to read it. Not even me."

"Ok, then. I guess it won't hurt."

Her counsellor had also asked her to write about the car accident, and more importantly the miscarriage that she still hadn't told Khush about.

No one except Jitesh and her sister knew about that. She had broken down and told her sister about it whilst she was still in hospital and was surprised that when she had told Henna that she wasn't going to tell Khush, that Henna had nodded and accepted her decision without argument. Now the counsellor was asking her to open up about losing the baby in a letter to herself. Just thinking about it made her stomach turn with fear.

Chapter 34.

Dear ~~you~~ Anita ~~me~~

It is so nice to meet you again, it has been a while...too long actually. It almost feels like I have crossed paths with my long-lost friend. Thank you for never giving up; never giving up on life, family, love and most importantly, thank you for never giving up me.

The counsellor has asked me to write this letter to myself, to you really. I'm not sure where to start. 'Start at the beginning!' I hear you shouting. It's just I don't know where the beginning of all this shit really is. One day it was all good, and then suddenly I'm ~~thinking~~ worrying about what I have said to make Khush go off at me. ~~Probably something stupid I've said I know~~. No. I shouldn't blame myself. It's not my fault that the marriage is failing. I'm not saying ~~you are~~ I am innocent in all this, but I honestly can't think of what I have done to make him so hateful towards me.

This is hard to write because these days things between Khush and I are going well. But I know that he has done this before, been horrible, then really loving, and then eventually goes back to being a monster.

Man, this is going to be a rambling letter but deal with it. I still don't know where to start. Maybe at having Anand, that's when I noticed bigger changes. I think. The baby shower comes to mind. I hated that we didn't say anything to him about it all. He was such a dick, hardly even getting involved and sitting there with his ~~fucking~~ dad like they were Rajah's in India expecting to be waited on by the women. Khush ~~wasn't that bad during the pregnancy~~, was more hormonal than I was during the pregnancy. I have to be honest with myself. Not sure why I feel the need to sugar coat it, it's a letter to myself. No other fucker is going to see it. Plus, why am I trying to not swear! If this is my letter to me, then it's going to sound like me. Fuck.

Ok, be serious. Get writing. How does Khush make you feel when he's being horrid?

Honestly? He makes me feel like I'm not worth anything. That whatever I do isn't going to be good enough for him and his high expectations of me. I think it's all to do with his mum and dad. But when I said that when we went to see a shrink, he lost it. Got all defensive and cried like a baby about his poor dead mother. She was lovely. But she was old school; she stayed at home, she spent the day cooking and cleaning after Khush, his dad and his dickhead brother. Oh!

Don't get me started on those two! His mum was awesome really, and I miss her. I really do. I don't think she would've let Khush get the way he has if she were still alive. This is it though, Khush thinks I should be like his mum, but she was old school Indian-she loved cooking and cleaning and being the housewife, and I'm never going to be like that. We're not in back-end toilets-are-a-hole-in-the-ground India countryside, we are in a westernised world and I am westernised, and he has to deal with it ~~doesn't he~~? Fuck, yes he does!

I can feel myself getting angry and emotional. Do I calm it down a little? No Anita, keep going.

Back to Khush- the way he broke ~~me~~ ~~you~~ us down bit by bit, snide remark after fucking snide remark, just chipping away making me feel like I just wasn't good enough. Damn. He was like a magician and I was on the hook with whatever he said and told me, I believed him in the end. Khush has broken my confidence. I don't think I am good enough. Not a good enough wife and definitely not a good enough mother.

Marriage shouldn't be this hard eh? I know it's not always perfect rainbows and shit, but it's gotta be better than what I have? Eddie knew that, that's why we ended up breaking the friendship. He didn't want to be around Khush and his toxic hate. And as soon as Khush threatened him and Callum, that was it. Anita you should've done something <u>then</u>. That was the point you should have walked away. Khush has isolated you *from friends. Anita you've lost some seriously good friends and thinking about Eddie is making my heart ache. Anita, some of the others just can't help anymore. And do you know why? Because they know I'm/you're too weak to leave him. But I am not going to be. I can't leave him, there is too much at stake, but I will make sure we get better. Not sure how but we will.*

We have been through it all, it has been a journey, a journey that you will never forget and one day embrace because it has made you who you are today. A strong, beautiful, independent woman, mother, sister and friend. You've been hurt, by words, manipulation, aggression. The experiences you have been through; a miscarriage, betrayal, and losing trust, faith and hope in the one person that is supposed to protect you and keep you safe. That man who has hurt you in the worst ways imaginable. BUT you have to overcome this one day...one fine day you will...and you'll look at yourself in the mirror and say THANK YOU. Thank you for sticking with me. Thank you for choosing to breathe and be there for Anand. And thank you for having faith and hope that things will turn around and be better.

I thought, and sometimes still do think, everything was my fault. But now I know it wasn't. It was him and his issues. Because when these things didn't matter, and when things between us were good, I realised that I hadn't changed at all. Everything I did then to repulse him, I still did now when he couldn't keep his hands off me. It wasn't me; it was him, fucking Khush was terrorising me, he had me captured and had my will to fight and survive in a vice or something. I am was trapped.

The doctor has also told me to write about the car accident. And what happened afterwards. But I don't know what to say. Things were good but when Jitesh told me I had been pregnant and miscarried, I didn't feel loss at all. If I'm being truly honest (which is what the shrink wants me to be with myself), I wasn't heartbroken that I had miscarried, I was relieved. Happy even. Does that make me a monster? I have to say, I don't care. Most women would have cried and been devastated, but not me. I just don't think I have it in myself to do it again. I don't think I am a bad mother. And I'm happy that what happened, happened. Jitesh knows, and Henna of course. But no one else. They both understood my reasons even without being told. My sister who knows almost everything and a man (a doctor aajima would certainly approve of. Ha!) are the only two people who know, and they don't judge me for it. But I know Khush would have judged me. That's why he can't know and will never know.

Lies. So many lies that only just hold this marriage together. That can't be right? I can't tell Khush about the miscarriage. I would be to blame. I can't tell him about me seeing a counsellor secretly. I would be to blame. I can't tell him how I feel trapped and that somewhere something went so wrong with us. I would be to blame for that too.

But it's not my fault.

I LOVE YOU ANITA- most of the time. On a good day I do but on my worst days I hear his voice criticizing every part of me; the choices I made, criticizing who I am, my family, my friends, my parenting, my lack of motivation, my being selfish, disrespectful, not being humble, and not putting Anand first. The list is endless.

In fact, you hear these words each and every day, you do your best to block them out and not let them swallow you whole. One day, Anita, it will be a whisper in the wind...literally moving past you like a breeze, and it won't even phase you. Truth be told, it may take a long time for that day to come, but know this, it will. And when that day arrives, you will be free, Anita. Free from all the hurt, the pain and misery, the constant mental torture, and free from his manipulation and control.

I haven't told you this in a while Anita, but you're stronger than you realize and give yourself credit for. You've heard these words from so many friends and family yet didn't believe them. I get it. It needs to come from you. From your heart, from a place of self-belief. I am proud of you, more than you'll know. You can keep knocking yourself down (you've had practice and learnt from the best - him!), but you WILL get back up, fucking stronger than ever.

My friend, there are going to be some struggles in life, but remember they will not be as bad as what you have lived through and experienced. There will be hardships, times when you feel like you are going insane and just want the world to open up and swallow you whole - but remember these words:

You are worthy my friend, you are beautiful, you are strong, you are brave, you are intelligent, you are independent, you are a good mother, and you are LOVED.

I am rambling again. You are probably crying as much reading this as I am writing it. Just remember it's not your fault and you'll find a way out of this situation. I'm not sure how or when, but you'll survive.

You have to.

Use the anger and the hurt you feel to build yourself up stronger. You're worth more than you think you are and when you finally believe it, you'll make that change. You have to.

I love you, for you and nothing more and nothing less. Be kind to yourself and I hope to see you again real soon.

Me.

Chapter 35.

Tears flowing down her face, Anita folded the letter she had written and placed it in an envelope, writing her name on the front and 'from you know who' on the back. This letter was meant for no one but herself and as she looked around her bedroom, she had no idea where she was going to put it to keep it a secret. Nothing in the room, or house was out of bounds to Khush; he could go into any drawer and look inside any box. It was his house and he made that very clear.

"Why is this box locked?" he asked one day picking up a lockbox that was in their shared wardrobe.

"Oh, that, not much. It's just got a few things in it that I like to keep safe."

"Why is it locked?"

Anita looked up from what she was doing at the dresser and looked at Khush. She frowned at the ferocity in his face.

"I dunno, I think it's just because there are some important documents in there."

"What's in there? What are you trying to hide from me?"

Anita looked at her husband and something in her brain signalled warnings.

"I'm not hiding anything from you Khush."

"Then why is it locked?" he persisted.

"I don't know. I don't even have the key anymore."

"You're lying."

"What?" Anita turned to face Khush who was squeezing the box hard, his darkness scared her.

"I said you're lying. You're trying to hide something from me."

"No, Khush, I'm not. I promise."

"So, why don't you tell me what's in there?"

"I…I…honestly can't remember."

"Liar."

"No, I just can't remember."

"Or you won't tell me. Open it."

"What?"

"I said open it. You heard me. Stop stalling."

"Open it?"

Anita was dumbfounded. Never in her life has anyone asked her to show anything personal or private to her. Never had anyone insisted the way Khush was insisting, especially as he was thrusting the box in her face.

"You heard me. Get the key and open it."

"But I…Khush…"

"See, I know you're hiding something from me. That's why you won't open it."

"Don't you trust me?" Anita whispered.

"No. If you don't have anything to hide-"

"I don't."

"Then you can open it and show me what's in there."

"Why is this important to you?"

"It's my house, as I've said before, I should be able to open any door, cupboard, file, whatever, locked or not, and know what's inside it."

Anita looked at her husband and knew she would have to give in, again. There was no way he was going to let anything go. She shook her head and opened her make up drawer at her dresser table.

"I think the key is in here."

"Good, find it and open it."

Thinking back at that moment, Anita shook her head and sighed heavily. His persistence in knowing everything and not having any secrets between them was initially something Anita had found endearing, but it very quickly gave way to his jealous mood swings and horrid torrents of abuse towards her. Anita had never had anything to hide from him, until now. Until this letter. She needed somewhere secure, somewhere he hardly ever went.

A sound of laughing and shouting came from the garden and Anita looked out of the window; Anand and Khush were playing with water guns and balloons, both getting soaked. As she turned her eyes away, Anita caught a glimpse of her new car. That's it. Khush never went in her car, not before the accident, and not now. He had his own car and didn't really like her new one. Only she would drive that, and if they went anywhere, they would take his car: the family car.

Anita picked up the envelope with the letter inside, walked downstairs, grabbed her car keys and stole a look towards the sounds of her son and husband playing. Neither of them were paying her any attention but still Anita felt like her heart was beating so hard they could hear it. She unlocked the car, slid into the passenger seat and popped open the glove compartment. It was full of sweet wrappers, spare tissue packets, a de-icer cloth and the car manual. A bit of a chaotic mess, and the perfect place to hide her letter. She hid it inside the glove compartment knowing neither her nor Khush would ever look in there. Her hands were sweaty, and she felt a prickle shoot through her body as she looked over at Khush.

"Hey boys." she walked over to them in the garden, laughing at how much of a state Anand was in, "What do you fancy for dinner today?"

"Pizza!" came the cry from the men in her life.

"Mummy's pizza or the-"

"Real pizza mummy. Not yours," giggled Anand walking towards her dripping from head to toe.

Khush laughed, "Yeah mum's pizza is rubbish isn't it?"

"Yeah!" joined in Anand not understanding the look that passed between his mum and Khush at his last comment.

"Ok, you can have a 'real' pizza as long as you and daddy go upstairs, dry up and get yourselves changed."

Anita put her hand on Anand's shoulder as Khush walked off avoiding his stare.

"Ok mummy. One thing?"

"What one thing?"

"This," shouted Khush who had snuck up behind her when she was messing about with Anand's hair.

Anita screamed and jumped as Khush poured a bucket of cold water over her back. Jumping about and feeling the water trickle down her jeans, Anita saw Anand high-five his dad and laugh.

"Worked daddy," he squealed with delight, "I distarted her!"

"Yeah you did buddy," said Khush ruffling his hair and grinning at Anita, "you distracted her perfectly."

Anita stood dazed and freezing staring at her husband and son laughing. Anand hopped from one foot to the other and Khush grinned from ear to ear.

"What was that for?" she said shivering.

"Just playing mummy," said Anand realising that Anita wasn't smiling, "sorry."

"Don't say sorry," said Khush snapping his head towards Anita and scowling at her, "we were just playing, and mummy is being silly taking it so seriously. Don't be such a spoilt sport Anita. Don't ruin our good mood by being such a sour-face about it."

"It's freezing, I'm soaking," said Anita anger building at the way Khush was dismissing her feelings.

"Get a towel, dry and warm off. Easy." He turned to Anand, "Anand go indoors and get yourself dry ok?"

"Ok daddy," said Anand looking back and forth between them, his face full of worry and confusion.

"See, he can get wet without moaning," said Khush watching Anand skip inside, "why can't you?"

"That was so uncalled for," seethed Anita.

"It was a bloody joke. Stop being so arsey about it."

Khush began to walk towards the house.

"Was it though?" called Anita making him stop where he was.

"Was what?"

"Was it a joke?"

Khush's sneer and aloof shrug gave her the answer she knew was true.

Later that evening, after they had eaten the pizza they ordered, and after Anand had gone to sleep, Anita and Khush sat next to one another watching TV. Khush touched her arm and turned to her.

"Anita," he said.

"Hmm," Anita mumbled still looking at the TV. She wasn't watching it and was still upset form earlier on.

"Are you happy?"

Anita felt a jolt of fear run down her neck, she turned to face Khush slowly and looked at his face. He didn't look angry or upset or anything that would normally send alarm bells ringing, he looked like he genuinely wanted to know.

"Yes, I am Khush," she said, her nerves still on edge, "why do you ask?"

"Well, I've just been thinking. We've been much better recently haven't we? I know I'm not as moody as before and you're better too. So I just wanted to know if you're happy."

"I am Khush," Anita repeated smiling, her guard dropping, "are you?"

"Yeah, I'm happy. I feel you getting back to work has helped too. You've got things to keep you occupied when I am at work and I feel like, well, you're ok now. Does that sound too weird?"

"No it doesn't." Anita said resting her head on Khush's shoulders and smiling, "It sounds exactly how I feel."

"Good," said Khush lifting her head and kissing her lips, "I think we got this Anita."

Chapter 36.

A few weeks later Anita and Khush were getting ready for a week away as a family. Anand was playing happily in the living room with his dinosaur toys and watching some children's show on TV which Anita couldn't stand, Khush was checking his car over; the tyres, the oil, water and all that other stuff that Anita pretended to know how to do, but really didn't. Anita was doing the final packing of clothes and toys for Anand. Their suitcase was packed and ready at the front door. They were going to go away to the countryside and had booked a cabin in the woodlands for their adventure. This was going to be an amazing holiday and well worth it after the car accident.

"Hey Anand," she called from the stairs, "are you ready to go when dad says to go?"

"Yes mummy," Anand said running to the stairs holding his chosen two teddies for the trip, "I got everything."

Anita laughed and carried her son's backpack down the stairs. She pointed at the teddies, "Anand, which one do you want to go in the bag in the boot?"

Anand look back and forth between the two and finally settled on having his oldest teddy with him in the back seat, opting for the newer teddy given to him by Anita's sister, a bright yellow monkey, to be the one to go in the bag. Just as Anita was zipping up the monkey into the bag, Khush came in.

"Ready to go everyone? Does he really need to take a teddy? Anand you're a big boy now, you shouldn't be carrying a teddy like a baby."

"But I want to take him." Anand said holding on to his teddy tightly and giving Anita a pleading look.

"Let him have it," said Anita. Giving Anand a sneaky wink she added, "he'll only need it for the journey. He'll be better settled on the drive."

"Whatever," said Khush walking towards the door, "are you ready to go?"

"Yup," said Anita handing him Anand's bag, "Anand, go with dad and get in the car. Khush I'm just going to do a once over of the house to make sure that we have everything, and it's all locked up."

Khush led Anand to the car, "don't be too long."

     **   **   **

The drive down to the countryside was hectic to say the least; it seemed that everyone had the same idea about leaving early on a Saturday morning and that Gloucestershire was the place to aim for. Sitting in at least a mile of traffic, Anand asleep in the back, Anita looked over at Khush. He looked annoyed; tapping on the steering wheel, muttering under his breath and inching too close to the cars in front.

"What's up?" she asked him, "why so glum?"

"Traffic," Khush said frowning.

"Yeah, it's bad. No idea that it would be this busy. Expected some traffic, but not this much."

"Well, I knew it was going to be bad, that's why I said we should leave early."

"We did leave early. Just that so did everyone else."

"I wanted to leave earlier," Khush said huffing and revving the car more than he needed to, "but you took so long."

Here it is thought Anita looking out of the window.

"Khush, we couldn't leave as early as you wanted. We had to get Anand fed and ready."

"You could've got his bag done last night while I was bathing him, instead you sat and watched TV."

"Come on, that's not fair." Anita protested, "It literally took me five minutes to pack his stuff, and I did that whilst you were checking the car."

"I needed to check the car Anita."

"I'm not saying that you didn't. I'm saying that I didn't waste time, I packed Anand's bag quickly. He needed a decent breakfast."

"Toast would've done."

"Toast? For him? No way, he would've been up and whinging by now about food. I made him some eggs so that he would be fuller for longer. We all had a decent breakfast. And cleaning up was easy enough."

"I would've been happy with toast. None of us needed the eggs. You spoil him."

"You could've had toast only then," Anita grumbled getting annoyed that she was yet again, being blamed for something that was completely unnecessary.

"Fuck's sake," Khush said sighing hard, "just let me drive."

Anita shook her head and groaned inwardly; she knew if she carried on Khush's bad mood would ruin the whole weekend, so she had to let it go. Even though she knew she wasn't the cause of the traffic, she had to let Khush have this so that he could get them there safely and without being too frustrated. She picked up her phone and resigned herself to the silent treatment until they reached the cabin.

Just let it go she thought to herself as she looked at her screen, *let him be miserable.*

The cabin was beautiful; dark wooden floors and walls with a lighter décor, cupboards and large windows allowing for the sunshine to warm through the stylish and modern cabin. The kitchen was simple and small but Anita hadn't thought too much about spending time in there cooking when they had booked the place. There were two bedrooms; one a twin with a bunk bed, which Anand delighted in choosing which bed he was going to sleep in that night, and the other, the main bedroom, a huge bed with a faux leather headboard, large bay windows, room for a vanity table and a small two-person couch.

But the bedroom wasn't the reason they had chosen this cabin; it was the hot tub on the balcony that has sealed the deal for them. Anita and Khush had giggled at all the things they could do in the hot tub, the fun they could have once Anand was asleep when they booked the place. The balcony was so private, only trees surrounded it, life was on the opposite side of the cabin and Anita liked it that way.

Now looking across at the serene view of never-ending fields, paths and streams, Anita felt disappointed. Khush's foul mood hadn't changed throughout the journey; even when the traffic cleared and they were able to get to the cabin at the time they had estimated, he was still frowning. Even when they saw the amazing private place as they drove up the gravel path, he still grumbled at the journey, and even when Anand dragged him around the cabin and showed him the garden which also had a playhouse in, Khush just huffed and shrugged his shoulders. She knew that the rest of the day, and probably evening was going to be a flop; no fun, no happiness and clearly no romance was taking place tonight.

A great family holiday this has turned into she thought watching her son try and fail to make Khush smile.

They had decided to go to the local pub for a meal on their first night, but with Khush in such a foul mood, Anita didn't want to broach the subject. Anand was getting hungry, and if she was being honest, Anita was ready for food too. Khush has spent the last few hours sitting in the living room watching some old detective show re-runs whilst Anita and Anand had gone exploring in the woods. Anand had tried to persuade his dad to come along, but Khush wasn't having any of it. Anita gently pulled Anand away from arguing with Khush and said they could explore today and then show dad it all the next day. That had been something both Khush and Anand had agreed to.

"Khush," Anita said as she flicked through the guidebook left by the owners of the cabin, "what do you want to do for food tonight?"

"I thought we said pub?"

"Yeah we did, I just wanted to check if that was still ok with you."

"Why wouldn't it be?" snapped Khush looking at Anita, probably for the first time since their argument on the road.

"Well I wasn't sure if you'd be up for it...after that drive."

"I was, but then you and Anand left. I was waiting for you two to get back from exploring. I'm ready to eat."

"Right, well let's go then. There is one about a ten-minute walk from here- shall we start with that one?"

"Yeah, fine by me. Go get Anand ready. I'm ready whenever you two are. Just don't be look long this time."

The meal at the pub was warming; the people were extremely friendly, although a little taken aback with an Indian family roaming their local area, and the food was good pub grub. Anand chattered away to the people around him and said hello to the pub dog who was more than happy to get fussed by a child. Anita tried to spark up conversation with Khush but he was having none of it; choosing to stay sullen with his head stuck in a guide book throughout the meal. Anita was left looking around the pub at the families and couples who were wrapped up in each other's company looking happy and content and she felt alone.

That evening once Anand had been wrestled into bed, his excitement making him a nightmare to settle down and put into bed, Anita slumped onto the sofa and tried a conversation with Khush again.

"That was a lovely pub wasn't it?"

No answer. Khush was deep in the football game showing on the TV, it was an old one and Anita knew there were no matches today. Anita grew irritated, there was no reason for him to be so sullen and rude.

"Khush, are you going to ignore me all night?"

"I'm not ignoring you. I'm watching the TV," Khush said not taking his eyes away from the screen in front of him.

"It's an old match. And we came away to the countryside to get away from all this. To spend time together. I know the journey wasn't great but we made good time in the end. Nothing went wrong."

"Jesus. Just give me one evening without you hounding me for attention. I wanted to watch the game in peace and quiet. It's been a long day, I'm on holiday too, and I just want to chill."

"Just without me?" Anita pressed.

"Jeez, stop getting so needy. I just want to chill out with the TV, a beer, on my own. Nothing wrong in that."

"No, nothing wrong in that. Goodnight," Anita said getting up from the sofa.

She picked up her phone, her glass of water, walked to the bedroom and shut the door leaving Khush and his football game in the living room.

Chapter 37.

Flopping down on the bed, Anita pressed her face into the cushion and screamed. She couldn't believe it, one silly traffic jam which didn't even last long had ruined the whole day. Khush had been an arse all day and even Anand had noticed that things weren't as good as they had been before the trip. He had asked Anita about it when she put him to bed, and she had said that it was just because he was tired from a long drive and that daddy would be better tomorrow. Anita hoped that this would be right. She sat herself up on the bed, leaned against the headboard and picked up her phone.

Scrolling through her messages and notifications, Anita noticed there was a string of short messages from her sister. Her heart leapt to her throat and Anita prepared herself for the worst. She opened up the messages and read:

...Hey Anita...

...Sorry just realised you are on holiday away in Cotswolds...hope you're having a good time?

...Just been on Facebook and saw that Reena from school is on there. Remember her?

...Go on FB and friend her. I think you'll want to.

...Let me know when you have!

...I'll leave you alone now.

Intrigued with the messages, Anita opened up Facebook and looked through Henna's friends list and found Reena. She had a look at whatever she was able to, but Reena had a private account, so not much was available. She sent a friend request and waited. She thought back to when she was at school with Reena. Reena had been her sister's best friend at school, but Anita also got along with her; Reena was very popular at school, and just like her sister she was the typical beautiful Indian girl. In fact, Reena and Henna had looked more like sisters than Henna and Anita had. Anita remembered many evenings with the three of them laughing, talking about boys, listening to music and making up their own dance moves to the songs.

Reena had lived across the road from them and her and Anita's parents had been friends, so staying over or staying late at each others' was easy. The only difference between Anita and Reena had been Reena's love for Bollywood; she was a fanatic, she loved the actors, the stories and the songs in the films. She especially loved the dances and Henna and Reena always seem to be able to pick up the moves with ease and grace leaving Anita flailing and not knowing what to do with her hands and feet. It would be good to get back in touch with Reena.

Anita wondered what her life was like now. Her phone beeped.

A notification: Reena has accepted your friend request and sent you a private message.

It turned out that Henna had an ulterior motive for connecting Anita and Reena; within a few messages it was clear what that was. Reena was divorced with a kid of her own. As the evening rolled on, and it was clear that Khush wasn't going to grace her with his presence in the bedroom (not even to sleep), Anita allowed herself to get into a conversation with Reena. It turned out that Reena and Anita had much more in common than Anita felt comfortable with.

Reena had been married to a man she had been set up with by her parents. Things had been great for a while but then he had become controlling and obsessive. He had begun to question everything: what she did; what she wore; what she said to him and others, how she spent her money; the way she brought up their son; her family traditions and rituals; her lack of career and the way she behaved around other men. Anita felt her heart creep towards her throat as she communicated with Reena, what Reena was describing was exactly how she felt and what she was experiencing with Khush. He was controlling, manipulative and hostile just like Reena's ex had been.

As they continued to message one another, Anita thought about why Henna had wanted her to be in contact with Reena; Reena was Anita before she had taken the terrifying step towards independence and happiness. Henna had clearly spoken to her about Anita's issues. She opened up her messages.

...*Hey Henna. I figured out why you wanted Reena and me to connect.*

...*Ok. So what did she say?*

...*she told me all about her life.*

...*good.*

...*you know you shouldn't have connected us.*

...*look I know you think I may be overstepping but I needed you to see there is more out there for you. That there is hope.*

...*I get that.*

...*sorry if I upset you. At least you can say you've got a friend out of it.*

...*yeah. It's ok, just was weird.*

...*tell her hi from me. I've gotta go.*

Anita shook her head knowing that whatever she texted her sister now, would be ignored until much later on. She looked at her messages with Reena.

Reena was open about everything that had happened to her, and Anita had a feeling that Reena knew more about her life than Anita had already told her. The conversation between the two went on late into the night, and by the time Anita signed off she had told Reena a lot about what was happening between her and Khush. More than she thought she would have ever revealed. Reena was supportive and understanding; she was able to give advice and be reasonable about the situation unlike

Henna, but that was because she had been there herself. Talking to Reena had given Anita some hope for a life without the threat and manipulation, but Anita wasn't ready to take such a great step, and Reena hadn't pushed her about it.

Instead, Reena had asked if they could have a play date as she would love to meet Anand; her son was a couple of years older than Anand but would love someone else to play with. Anita agreed to meet for the kids to play when they returned from their holiday. She suddenly felt like she wasn't as alone and isolated as she had been for a long time. Anita went to bed not only hoping that tomorrow would be a new day with her family, but also eager to see and speak to Reena face to face.

Maybe this is what you need Anita she thought as she closed her eyes, *someone that knows what you are going through to help.*

Chapter 38.

As if someone out there had heard her hopes and dreams, Anita had woken up to the sound of chatter and laughter from the kitchen. She dragged herself out of bed, still needing more sleep than she would admit, to find Khush and Anand playing and making breakfast together. The kitchen was a mess, but the smell was divine.

"Morning mummy," squealed Anand running to Anita and giving her a hug that ended up with flour handprints on her pyjama top.

"Woah," said Anita giggling and sweeping Anand up in her arms, "morning baby. How you this morning? Did you sleep well?"

"Yes mummy," he said wriggling out of her arms and running back to what he was doing in the kitchen with Khush, "I didn't fall off the bed."

"Well done beta," said Anita smiling. She looked over at Khush who was just pouring coffees, "morning, smells lush in here."

"Morning," said Khush smiling and walking over to give her a gentle kiss, "coffee is poured, Anand and I are making pancakes with plenty of fruit, you just sit down and chill."

"And chocolate mummy. Daddy said chocolate on pancakes."

"Oh, did he?" said Anita laughing at the jumping child in front of her, "well you better be prepared to exercise it all off today then Anand."

"He will," Khush said placing a great pile of pancakes at the table, "right, breakfast is ready, let's eat all this and get ready for a great day out."

Anita looked at Khush and smiled, he smiled back and shrugged.

"Let's forget about last night, start fresh today, eh?" he said.

"Ok," said Anita clinking her coffee mug with his unsure if that was even an apology, "Let's just enjoy the rest of the weekend."

"Me too mummy," said Anand waving his cup of milk and clinking her mug, "cheers."

The rest of the holiday was a dream; Khush's mood didn't falter again, and they went on walks, adventures and had an amazing time together as a family. Anita and Khush made the effort to get along and even had some genuine romantic moments. They were once again happy and by the time it was time to go home, Anita felt a little saddened to be leaving a place like this. Anand was also sad to leave, as he had made friends with the dog he met in the pub on the first night; each time they passed the pub or stopped off to have a drink in it, Anand had cuddled and played with the dog the whole time. He had even asked Khush and Anita if they could have a dog too.

On the drive back to Milton Keynes, Anita checked her phone, there were a few messages from Henna and some from Reena. Anita chose to reply to her sister first.

...Hey sis, thanks for connection with Reena. Was good to chat to her after so long!

...hey Anita. xxx Yeah I've kind of kept in touch a little, but then thought you may want to get in touch too xx

...Hmm, thanks. I see why you chose to do that xx

...Is that a bad thing?

...No it isn't. cheers sis. Xx Was good to talk to someone like her.

...someone who knows what you're going through? xx

…Yeah. Something like that. We said we would do a playdate with the boys sometime. Wanna join us?

…yeah maybe. Let me know when and I'll see what I'm doing. xx

…Cool. xx

…How was your holiday?

…Started off shit – him in a mood over traffic…but ended really well. All good. xx

…fair enough. Glad you had a good time in the end. Xx

…Yeah we did. Xx

Anita looked over at Khush who was humming away to a song on the radio and then turned her head to check on Anand. He was fast asleep; the excitement and adventure of the short holiday had worn him out. She smiled. This was the week away she and Khush had needed and hoped for. She looked at her phone again remembering that she hadn't replied to Reena's last message.

…Hey mate, how are you doing? Sorry I haven't replied, been busy with the family since we last spoke.

…no worries… came a reply almost instantly …I take it things worked out with Khush then? xx

…Yeah, and we've had a great time.

…That's good…

…So, did you want to meet up with the boys some time? xx

…Yeah that would be good. Let me know when you're available and I'll see what we are doing…probably not a lot to be honest!

Anita laughed; she felt the same. Most of the time, weekends were pretty empty and they never had a lot going on.

"What's that?" said Khush looking over at Anita laughing and typing away on her phone.

"Just an old mate from school. My sister's best mate Reena."

"So why are you chatting to her if she's your sister's best mate?"

"We all used to play and hang out together. She used to be around ours all the time."

"How come I've never heard of her?" Khush said. His eyes had narrowed and there was an edge to his voice that made Anita's skin begin to itch.

"Well, I forgot all about her really," Anita said slowly calculating how she should play this, "Henna found her on Facebook and then I found her. She's got a son a couple of years older than Anand; we are sorting a play date thing."

"Oh, right," said Khush relaxing a little, "that's ok then."

Anita felt the tension ease from her body, she was always on edge whenever she spoke to Khush and for a second, she thought that this was going to become another pointless thing to argue about. Anita smiled at her husband and put a reassuring hand on his thigh.

"Oi," he said looking at her hand and raising his eyes, "less of that while I'm driving. I need to be able to concentrate. When we get home, I'm all yours."

Anita giggled and gave his thigh an extra squeeze before letting go. She closed her eyes, rested her head back on the seat and allowed the sounds of the radio to soothe her to sleep. When she woke, they were just pulling up to the driveway, Anita stretched in the seat and rubbed at her face.

"Sorry about that," she said, "I didn't mean to fall asleep and leave you to drive without company."

"That's alright," Khush said switching the car engine off and opening the door, "I didn't mind. You can get the bags in though if you want to make up for it?"

Anita looked at her husband grinning through the car door and nodded towards Anand still snoring in the back, "you get him, I'll get the bags."

That evening, once Anand was showered and in bed, Anita and Khush sat in the living room watching a film and browsing through their phones. Anita saw that Reena had messaged her a few dates and times for a playdate with Anand.

"Hey hon," she said looking up at Khush, "what are we doing on Saturday?"

"Nothing, why?" he answered not taking his eyes off the car chase on the TV screen.

"Well, Reena wants to know if Anand and I are free to have a meet up."

"Not me too?" Khush glanced at Anita, his eyes narrowing.

"You can come if you want to," said Anita laughing nervously and nudging his leg with her foot.

"And sit and listen to two old aajimas nattering away? No thanks."

"Cheeky," laughed Anita, "we aren't that bloody old."

"You keep telling yourself that," said Khush smiling.

"So, we aren't doing anything then?"

"No. Meet up with her, go for it."

"Cool, I'll message her back and sort a place and time."

Khush nodded engrossed in his movie.

Chapter 39.

The weekend seemed to take an age to arrive, and Anita became more and more nervous about seeing Reena. Especially since she knew where their conversations would end up leading to. She had told Anand about it and he was very excited to meet someone else he could play with that was older which meant he would be treated like a big boy himself.

Sitting on the bench watching Anand play on the swings and waiting for Reena, Anita took out her phone and texted her sister.

...I'm nervous about seeing Reena. That's weird yes?

...yes you are weird xx

...Idiot :) you know what I mean.

...lol yes I do. Yeah it's ok to be nervous Anita. But just remember it's just Reena. You can say as much or as little as you want. Be involved in the kids playing. You'll be fine. Stop acting so scared of nothing...

...I'm just anxious...not sure why...

...because Khush has made you believe whatever you do is wrong. So you'll question it. You're just meeting an old mate. That's it. :) xx

...True x

...does he know you're meeting?

...Yeah, he knows we are on a play date. That she is an old mate. That's it.

...well why are you stressed then? You're not doing anything underhand eh? Just meeting a mate and having your kids play together. Chill out Anita. You stress too much.

...I know I do, I just can't help it :(

...well maybe Reena can help you out with that insecurity. She'll be better to chat to instead of me...she gets your situation...

...True. Cheers sis. Right, I better get back to waiting for her and watching Anand to make sure he doesn't injure himself! X

..haha yeah xxx see you xxx love you sis- give Anand a big kiss from his masi xx

Ditto and will do xxx

As she placed her phone into her jacket pocket, Anita looked up and saw who could only be, Reena and her son walking towards them.

Spending time with Reena was exactly what Anita needed. Having her sister to talk to was great, but sometimes Anita thought that Henna just didn't understand her predicament. She didn't understand that Anita still loved Khush, and she didn't like that Anita defended him when it came to being a good dad to Anand, because he was. So, having someone who wasn't completely judgemental about Khush was useful. Even with all the constant text messages Khush had sent checking up on her and even giving her a call, Reena understood. She didn't say a word when Anita texted back each time nor raised an eyebrow when Anita answered her phone and spoke to Khush is hushed tones- but she did notice the signs.

"Sorry about that," said Anita blushing and putting her phone in her bag again.

"That's ok, I get it," said Reena smiling.

"He was just seeing if I needed anything from the shop."

"You don't have to explain yourself to me, I know what it's like. Better to answer the phone than deal with the bullshit that follows if you don't."

"Yeah," said Anita sighing and looking at her son playing happily, "I don't need the hassle when I get home."

"Even though you'll still get the third degree and a barrage of questions coming your way about me."

"Yeah, sorry."

"No need to apologise, not at all."

Reena and Anita had talked for hours while their boys played around the park, only stopping when they wanted a drink or a snack. Anita started a little hesitant at first, not telling Reena everything that had happened between her and Khush, but by the time Reena had told Anita her story and what she had gone through, Anita knew she could be open.

By the time Anita and Anand got home later that afternoon, Anita was exhausted. Revealing how difficult her life was to someone else, and being honest about it, had drained her; physically and emotionally. Anand was equally drained and opted to spend the evening curled up on the sofa next to Khush watching the football and holding on to his teddy. Anita took this opportunity to take a long hot shower and reflect on what Reena had shared.

She knew that things with Khush were fine right now, but she understood that it couldn't last. Reena spoke of her experience of her ex making her feel like everything was ok and safe one minute, and that one word could see her life crumble the next. She countered every argument Anita had about Khush's behaviour with her own experiences and stories. She helped Anita realise that the relationship was over a long time ago and if Anita was being honest with herself, she was just there and waiting for the ball to drop on their marriage; she was too scared to do something herself, but still she continued to hand onto a thread of hope for her marriage. She wasn't ready to call it done and failed, not yet.

What Anita valued the most about the heart to heart she and Reena had, was that Reena made it clear that whatever happened, whatever decision Anita made, it had to be done at her pace. Reena had admitted to making attempt after attempt to leave her ex but found that something always held her back from actually doing it. The final straw had come when he had cheated on her and managed to get his new girlfriend pregnant. Reena had packed a bag of clothes, some of her most precious belongings and the same for her son before getting into her car and driving to her parent's house. She had never returned to the house for anything, letting her ex deal with her dad instead as she knew if she had spoken to him, she would have probably gone running back, apologising to him instead. She had started the divorce proceedings and spoken to a solicitor but it had taken a week of deliberating before she found a number.

"So, that's my story," Reena said smiling and looking at her son playing.

"Wow."

"Sound familiar?"

"Yeah, I guess it does, but Khush isn't cheating on me," Anita said starting to feel her face turn red.

"He may not do that, but by the sounds of it, he's got you second guessing yourself all of the time?"

Anita shrugged, "I know it sounds like that but-"

"And defending him. That's what I used to do." Reena turned to look at Anita. "Look Anita, there's nothing wrong or shameful in doing something that will make you happy. I know as Indians divorce is seen as taboo and shameful but really, it's not. Parents get over it and they will understand. The rest of the community will just have to deal with it."

Anita cleared her throat, "I'm just saying that sometimes I don't say things clearly."

"Blaming yourself again."

"No, I…ok but it's so hard."

"You don't have to tell me, I've been there. But you know that what you and he have isn't a marriage. Not a healthy one anyway. The letter you wrote for yourself, you say it yourself in that."

"I'm just not ready," said Anita tears welling up in her eyes.

"And that's ok too," said Reena placing a warm hand on hers, "you have to do it at your own pace. No matter what anyone says, only you can walk away. On your own terms, in your own time. But you know the eventual outcome and what needs to happen."

"I know."

"I've been there and done that. And if I got a t-shirt for every time I said I was leaving but didn't, I'd have a packed wardrobes with 'didn't do it' t-shirts in it."

Reena explained that it wasn't easy and she still loved him and missed him in the first year of being apart from him, but she knew that in order to keep herself sane and happy, she needed to do something drastic for herself. And she had.

Anita wished that when the time came, and she had finally admitted that it would, that she would be as brave as Reena was.

Chapter 40.

Over the next few months Anita became close to Reena; often confiding in her whenever things got bad between her and Khush either via texts or whenever they met for a play date, which they did more and more often. Anand and Reena's son, Prem, had become very close, bonding over dinosaurs they loved and detective games. Henna had also joined them on occasion and Anita felt like her life was becoming more and more her own when she was with them but achingly aware that what she and Khush had at home, was not right.

As Anita's friendship with Reena began to grow, her contact with Jitesh also became more frequent. He had contacted her a few times since the week away to see how things were with her knee and shoulder, but the conversations quickly veered from her medical needs to other things. Jitesh was easy to talk to, he was funny and most of all, he listened to what Anita was saying; unlike Khush who had become more distant and less attentive whenever they spent evenings together. It seemed the happier and more relaxed in herself Anita became, the more agitated and controlling Khush was.

Her friendship with Jitesh had blossomed quickly and although Anita knew Khush had nothing to worry about her having a male friend, she kept her contact with Jitesh a secret. The less ammunition he had to ware her down with, the better. His messages were instantly deleted. She texted him one evening after Khush had decided to spend the evening in his study alone, again.

...Hey Jitesh, how you doing? Work ok?

...hey Anita. I'm all good thanks :) work is work- so busy. But all else is good. You?

...Yeah I'm alright. Bored.

...He in his man cave again? Lol

...Not a mancave cheeky. Just his study. But yeah he's in there. Again.

...sorry to hear that mate. What's his excuse this time?

...Just he had a tough day at work and needed time. Anand pissed him off today too

...how?

...Well, he was messing about with the lego pieces around the room, Khush asked him to try and keep them on one side of the room, Anand didn't listen. Khush got mad and shouted at him and that made Anand cry. Khush retreated to the study leaving me to deal with Anand and his tantrum.

...wow. He's just a kid.

...I know, Anand should have listened but he was having fun.

...No I meant Khush! ;) ha ha ha

...Oh. Lol. Yeah, him too. Haha. So, now I'm sitting here alone with a big glass of wine, bored. What are you up to? Anything exciting?

...not really. Just arguing with my mum's mum about marriage. Typical, they think I'm ready to settle down. They want to introduce me to someone. That kind of shite.

...Ha! Ha! That's hilarious!

...No it's not. Every time we see them, they go off on one.

Well you are of eligible age ;)

...Eligible or not, I'm not interested in their perfectly perfect choices. Some ditzy woman who thinks because I'm a doctor, I'm a catch without even knowing me. Bah.

...You're a doctor.

Anita smiled as her fingers hovered over the keyboard, she looked towards the study where Khush was hiding, then she added:

...And a catch!

...aw you think I'm a catch. That's nice. But doesn't help me on this end. Lol.

Anita laughed at Jitesh's mock outrage. They had spoken about the way his family, and all Indian families that they knew of, badgered the young and eligible to get match made. Anita knew that it wasn't always the best choice.

...So, what the plan for the weekend for you oh great bachelor? Anita giggled away at her phone and finished off her glass of wine.

...well unless I can find a way of getting out of it, I have to go to my grandparents...which means more marriage talk. Help! At this stage cutting a homeless man's toenails would be more appealing than spending it with my nagging granny!

...So, would you call meeting up with some ladies and their kids at a park a good enough excuse?

...Yeah, why?

...Well, it just so happens Anand and I are meeting with my sister, Reena, her kid at a park for a catch up and playdate. Wanna hijack that?

...yes please! I'll even take on the duties of chaperoning the children.

... come along then. Saturday, at 10am at the park around the corner from the main Tesco's.

...thanks! I owe you one. That would be great. See you then.

...You're welcome mate. No worries. Xx right I am going to grab another glass of wine and get to reading my book. Night xx

Anita felt excited about seeing Jitesh; they got on so well but hadn't had the chance to meet in person since she was in hospital. She knew her sister would get along with him and she hoped that Reena would too. Even if things with Khush were a little more than pear-shaped right now, Anita felt happy that her friendships were becoming stronger and she was becoming more confident and happier in her own self. She couldn't wait until Saturday.

She warned both Henna and Reena than Jitesh was coming along to get out of being fixed up by his family, and that he was willing to look after the boys to thank them for it. They were sitting in the park watching Anand and Prem climb up the frame and slide down the slide for what must have been the twentieth time, chattering away when Anita's phone beeped.

"It's Jitesh," she said with a grin on her face, "he's here."

"Cool," said Henna raising her eyebrows at Reena as she watched her sister beam, "you seem really chuffed about it."

"Yeah, that's because he's brilliant." Anita said rolling her eyes at her sister, "It's not like that, Henna. I know what you're thinking."

"I'm not thinking anything," Henna giggled feigning shock.

"Whatever, actually I'm happy he's here so he can meet you."

"I've met him before remember?" Henna said smiling.

"Not you, Henna," said Anita grinning from ear to ear and winking at Reena, "I want him to meet *you*."

"Oh no," said Reena surprised, but before she could say anything else Anita ran off to meet Jitesh who was walking towards them from across the park.

"Oh man," said Henna laughing, "an Indian set up. I love those."

"Shut up," said Reena laughing and shaking her head.

        **   **   **

Later on that evening after she read Anand a story and was sat alone again in the living room with a large glass of wine, Anita's mind kept running over the events of the day. She had introduced Jitesh to Henna and Reena and had done everything she could to be subtle about trying to match Jitesh and Reena up. They had a lot in common and they seemed to get on; Reena was a little nervous at first, but Anita put that down to the fact she had just learned of Anita's trickery. However after a while they all seemed to relax and have a laugh together. By the end of the afternoon, it was clear that her sister and Reena both got on well with Jitesh just like she did, and they would all be good friends. Things couldn't have worked out better.

She recalled watching Reena and Jitesh talk about all sorts and felt a jolt of excitement at the thought of helping Reena find someone as perfect as Jitesh was. She also felt a jolt of jealousy seeing the two laughing happily together. He had been moaning about what his parents called him, but Anita had to agree with them: he was a catch. They looked good together too; both about the same height as one another, both good looking and they both had thick straight jet-black hair.

Anita had been taken aback when she had first seen Jitesh across the park as she couldn't remember what he looked like at all from the hospital, and her imagination had not done him any justice at all. He was tall, and had broad muscular shoulders, and his face had a boyish charm and natural handsomeness to it. He was a good-looking man and Anita was happy to see that Reena and Henna's reactions showed that they had thought so too.

This was the start of something special she thought, a group of friends that saw the real Anita, and wanted her to be happy. They had tried to discuss Anita's marriage, however Anita had become good at avoiding questions she didn't want to answer and was able to use the children as distractions and coffees as bribes to keep them focused on Reena and Jitesh. They had even planned an evening get together as a group, this time without the children, for the following week. Henna had announced that she would bring Ash if that was ok with everyone, which it was. Anita did not do the same.

"Khush will look after Anand." Anita reassured them as they all started to look a little awkward. There was no way Khush was going to come, or even be invited. This was Anita's safe circle of people, and he was not going to intrude on that.

Chapter 41.

The next morning Anita woke to find Khush sitting in the living room watching children's TV with a mug of coffee in his hand. Anand was curled up next to him still in his pyjamas, watching along with his dad, and playing with his toys. Looking at Khush's face as she entered the room made her feel on edge.

"Morning boys," she said as cheerily as she could muster.

"Morning mummy," said Anand waving at her, his eyes still on the children's TV show.

"Morning," said Khush looking at Anita like she was a complete stranger walking into his home.

"How are you all doing?" A lump began to form in her throat.

"Good," came the reply in unison.

"Have you had breakfast?"

"Yeah" they said again in perfect time.

"Ok, well I'm going to get a coffee and some food, anyone need anything?"

Anita watched the pair of them shake their heads no, she walked quickly into the kitchen feeling like something terrible was about to happen. As she boiled the kettle, she felt someone watching her. She turned and saw Khush standing at the kitchen door staring at her.

"You ok?" she asked him, her voice catching in her throat.

"I saw this on our calendar this morning. Are we going out for a meal next week?"

"Oh, that," said Anita her defences working overtime, "no, that's just for me. I'm going for a meet up with Henna, Reena and Jitesh."

"Jitesh? Who's he? Reena's husband?"

You know damn well who he is!

"No. Do you remember the doctor that looked after me when I was in hospital after the accident?"

"Yes, what about him?"

"Well, that's Jit. He will be joining us for dinner."

Anita looked at Khush, she couldn't read what he was thinking, but she knew whatever came out of his mouth next wasn't going to be good; his frown lines had intensified, and his face darkened.

"Why is he joining you? Will he be the only man there?"

"He's joining us because he is a friend of ours, of mine. No, he won't be the only man there, Ash is coming too."

"A friend of yours? When did that happen?"

"We got on well at the hospital when he was looking after my injuries, and then afterwards we kept in contact, mainly to talk about my recovery. Then we just became good friends."

"Good friends? Does he know you're married?"

"Yes, he met you at the hospital remember?"

"So why is he hanging around you then? What's he want from you? What are you getting from him?"

"Nothing Khush," said Anita sighing and shaking her head, "we are just mates, and he's met Henna and Reena now, and we've all become close. So instead of the usual park meet ups we've decided to go for a meal out. Just adults."

"And you didn't think to tell me?"

"I put it in the calendar like you asked me to whenever I made plans. That's how you said you wanted to know."

"It's not how I wanted to find out about this doctor who's sniffing around you."

Anita looked at Khush shocked; not at his language or his sudden burst of anger, but at the obvious jealously he was showing.

"He is just a friend Khush. That's it. He doesn't find me attractive, and I don't find him attractive."

"How the hell do you know that, Anita? You're a married woman and he shouldn't be eyeing you up or anything. You're not available to him. You're married to me."

"I know I'm married to you," said Anita her voice hard and her own anger threatening to surface, "he knows I am married too."

"That doesn't seem to be stopping him from sniffing around you."

"He's not doing that he is just a friend."

"He wants more, I know it. I know guys like him."

"Guys like him? what do you mean by that?"

"What are you doing to think he's got a chance with you?" Khush's voice was getting loud.

"What? Khush, I'm no doing anything. I don't think of him that way."

"You'd better not. You're married to me."

"I know, He's just a friend."

"I hope you're not slagging him off to me."

"God, no," said Anita feeling like she was losing control, "we don't talk about you."

"Oh, so you pretend like you don't have a husband?" Khush's words were knives stabbing at Anita.

"No, that's not what I said..."

"I don't like this. Something is going on, I'm sure of it."

"Nothing is going on between us. In fact, Khush, I am setting him up with Reena."

Khush opened his mouth to speak and paused.

"Well, as long as he doesn't come near you in that way," said Khush trying to regain some semblance of control.

"He's a friend. That's it. Even if you don't trust him, trust me. I'm not that kind of person, you know this."

"I don't know what you're like around them. I don't know them, and I don't trust them. Even your sister. I don't want to tell you not to go out with them, but I will let you know that I am not happy about it. You make the choice."

Khush walked towards the door, he turned and snarled at Anita, "I don't think you should go If you want to make me happy, you won't go. I'm going to my study to work now. I didn't get much done because you were sleeping in and I had to look after Anand otherwise he would have gone hungry. Now that you're up I can get on with my work without being disturbed."

Khush spun around on his heels and walked out leaving Anita seething, red faced and breathing hard. Finally making a decision of what she wanted to do, she went into the living room to find Anand in the same curled up position watching TV like nothing had happened. Sitting next to him in the gap Khush had left, and forming fists to stop herself from shaking, Anita kissed her son's forehead.

"You ok mummy?" he asked without looking away from the TV.

"Yeah beta, mummy's ok," she said trying to push past the lump forming in her throat, "Anand, you fancy going to see aajima and bapa today?"

"Oh yeah," he said finally turning his head and looking at Anita, his grin broad and innocent, "is daddy coming?"

"No beta," Anita said smiling through the tears in her eyes, "he's working. Shall we have a sleepover? Let daddy work?"

"Yeah," bounced Anand on the chair.

"Excellent," she said tickling him until he squirmed next to her, "let's go get ready. I want you to pick five of your best teddies to take with you."

"Five?" Anand couldn't believe his luck, normally he was only ever allowed two.

"Yup, five. Now off you go, they need to be on your bed with a pair of pyjamas and two of your night reading books. Before mummy comes up in a few minutes?"

"Ok mummy," said Anand giving Anita a military salute and running up the stairs.

Anita turned her head and finally allowed the tears to run down her cheeks. Her head hurt and her heart ached. She picked up her phone and texted her sister:

Staying at mum's place for a couple of nights. Khush and I just had an argument. I'm so done. Maybe see you there if you're around? Will let you know when we are there. X

Anita went into the kitchen, poured her coffee down the sink, took her wedding ring off and placed it on the counter and walked up the stairs to pack a bag.

Chapter 42.

By the time Anita had driven to her parent's place she had received two missed calls from Henna along with six messages. She hadn't replied to any of the messages or answered the phone calls at all; she needed all her strength to walk out of the door with Anand and drive without stopping to her childhood home. She knew that she would have to let Khush know where she and Anand were and why they were there, but she couldn't muster the courage to do that yet either.

Sitting in the car on her parents' driveway, Anita's heart was beating so fast she felt it would burst through her chest, and as she looked at Anand in the backseat smiling at his grandparent's house eagerly and bouncing his teddy in his lap, she felt her body relax and her mind slow down. This was the right thing to do. It had to be.

She picked up her phone and looked at the empty box and cursor waiting for her, and typed out her message to Khush:

I've gone to my mum's place. Anand is with me. We won't be back tonight, and I'm not sure how long we will be here for. After our last discussion, I have so much to think about when it comes to our marriage. Things are not good- we are not good. I love you so much and this hurts me so much, but I need space to think about us. If you need to call you can, but please do not come over. I still love you. x

Anita could feel her eyes sting with tears even before she had sent it, but she knew it had to be done. She needed Khush to realise that she was serious about their relationship; she needed to force him to have a proper conversation about their marriage; but most of all, she needed time and space to think about what *she* really wanted. Her parent's home was the most loving place she knew and right now, she needed her family and the comfort they brought to surround her.

"Mummy, are we going in?" asked Anand from the back, tilting his head and furrowing his eyebrows.

"Yep Anand, we are going in."

Anita put her phone in her bag and stepped out of the car. An instant rush of cool air whirled around her, making her hair fly about and Anand laugh at her from the inside of the car. She laughed lightly as she opened the door to let him out and watched as he ran straight up to the front door and knocked loudly on the glass. Anita grabbed the overnight bags she had thrown together and followed him inside the house. Her mother and father looked confused but knew she would explain in time.

"Henna said you were coming over," said her mum giving her a kiss on the cheek and taking her bags, "but you talk when you want to ok? Chai beta?"

Anita smiled, that was one of the things that the British culture and the Indian culture had in common; whenever you were feeling down, the first thing offered was a cup of tea.

"No thanks mum," Anita said, "did Henna say she was coming over? She called but I didn't answer, I haven't read her messages yet."

"I think so, but I am not sure."

Anita followed her mum into the living room where her aajima sat on her usual chair watching some Indian game show which looked alarmingly like Deal or No Deal. Anita looked at her mother who gave a slight shake of her head, meaning that her aajima didn't know what was going on.

"Hi aajima," said Anita giving her a hug and kiss on the cheek.

"Anita beta, how are you?" said aajima smiling, "where is my great grandson?"

Anita looked around and found that she couldn't see Anand, but just as she was going to call for him, she heard a thud upstairs and a giggle. Anand was jumping on 'his' bed upstairs and was talking to her dad.

"Upstairs with dad I think aaji," said Anita following her mum into the kitchen, "he'll come down in a minute."

Once Anita and her mum were alone and out of earshot from her aajima, her mum turned to her.

"Is this about Khush?"

Anita nodded, she felt exhausted and her emotions were firing in all directions. She couldn't bring herself to speak to her mum.

"Does he know you are here?"

Anita nodded.

"What did he say?"

There was a pause. Anita swallowed hard trying to control her emotions but failed miserably when she looked at the concern in her mother's eyes. Her mother stepped towards her and wrapped her in her arms. Anita's cries were fierce, and she had no choice but to let them out.

After what felt like an eternity in her mother's arms, Anita slowly lifted her head and looked at her mother. Her eyes wet with anguish matched her mother's which were wet with sorrow.

"What did he say?" repeated her mother gently passing Anita a tissue.

"I just sent him the message before I got out of the car," said Anita wiping her eyes, her voice croaky and hoarse, "he was so horrible and then I had to leave, and I took Anand and I came here. I messaged Henna and that's it. Mum, can I stay here for a day or two please?"

"Of course, beta," said her mother stroking her cheek and kissing her forehead, "stay as long as you need to. You know this is still your home and you can come here whenever you need to, for as long as you need to. Now, go take your bags upstairs to Anand's room and you two can sleep there. The bed will need to be made, if you do that for me I can take questions from your aajima, ok?"

"Thanks mum."

As Anita trudged up the stairs with her and Anand's bags, she passed her dad on the way down with Anand at his heels. He smiled at her softly and nodded. Anita smiled and looked away, tears threatening to reappear with a vengeance. Once in the room, Anita looked at her phone. She had expected messages and maybe even a miss call from Khush demanding they come home or saying he was on his way there, but instead there was one solitary message:

I will call later so we can talk.

Anita wasn't sure if she was angry, offended or just bewildered at thinking his response would show any emotion at all at the fact that she had left with Anand. She shook her head and looked at the messages her sister had sent instead.

Message 1: Fuck, ok. Are you and Anand ok?

Message 2: Hey? All ok? Have you reached mum's yet? Need me to do anything?

Message 3: Want me to go over there and kick his ass? I will. Ash can come too. ;)

Message 4: Anita, are you ok? Just send a quick text to let me know. I'm worried. Love you x

Message 5: I'm going to assume you're driving and can't answer. I'll call you.

Message 6: you're not answering your calls, I'm fucking worried. Answer something please?! We are on our way to mum and dad's place now. See you there.

"Shit," said Anita deleting the messages and turning her attention to the voice message Henna had left her.

It was as she expected, a message asking if she was ok and if Anand was ok, followed by the usual angry rant about Khush, ending with her saying she was calling their mum to let her know Anita was on her way.

Anita was about to ring her sister back when she heard a car pull up to the driveway. For a moment, she was paralysed with fear. Khush.

Is he here to drag us back to the house?

Anita inched her way to the window to see who the hasty footsteps belonged to and sighed when she saw her sister marching up to the front door and Ash following behind. She looked at her phone to see if Khush had decided to send another message or even call, which he hadn't, then went to face her family downstairs.

Everything seemed to be a blur after that; Henna was talking loudly, gesturing wildly with her hands and pacing around the living room; her dad sat stern faced but silent half playing with Anand; and her brother in law, Ash, tried, but failed to calm her sister down. The living room felt smaller than it had earlier, and Anita couldn't help but feel that it was slowly shrinking in towards her too. As Henna paused to take a breath, Anita's mum took the chance to settle the situation.

"Look, Henna, it is not helping you shouting and ranting in front of Anita and Anand. You must be calm," said her mother quietly, "we don't know anything about what happened, so let Anita tell us in her own time. We are here to support her as a family. That's it."

As Henna went to protest her mother gave her that look that only mothers know how to give. The look that turns a grown ranting woman into a meek little child again.

"Sit down Henna beta," her mother said firmly, "let Anita talk before we ask questions. First, Ash please can you take Anand into the playroom and put a film on for him?"

Henna finally sat down, her face flush and her breathing just as heavy as Anita's. She smiled grimly at her mum and nodded at Anita.

"Well," said Anita taking a breath and fiddling with her bracelet, "It started when I came home from the park..."

By the time Anita had told them what had happened, answered their questions as best as she could, and calmed her sister down another three times, Anita was exhausted. Her family sat there in silence taking in everything she had told them. Her mum and dad were stunned. She had finally told them the truth about her relationship with Khush; the lies, manipulation, controlling remarks, the criticisms, the angst and uncertainty she felt about herself. Anita even revealed her miscarriage and how she felt about it all; that she had been supported by Jitesh and Henna and Reena, and hadn't even told Khush about it out of fear of what he would say to break her down. Ash was silent but looked every bit as angry as her sister did. Only when Anand made a fuss that his film was over and came pottering into the living room, did they all begin to move.

Anita's mum picked up Anand and asked if he wanted a snack, she also commented on how everybody needed food and that she was going to bring in some tea and biscuits. Henna, aajima and Ash followed her into the kitchen in silence, needing to stretch out their legs and sort the thoughts in their heads.

Anita was left in the room with her dad.

Since the moment she had come in with Anand, Anita's dad hadn't said a word. He had sat and listened to everyone's comments and input, stock still and barely moving unless he was nodding in agreement with his wife. His eyes always deep in thought and dark. Now, he moved to the seat next to Anita and took her hand in his.

"Anita," he said softly, his voice sounder shakier than it had ever sounded.

"Yes dad," Anita said looking at her hands in his, unable to look her father in the eyes.

"I'm sorry."

I'm sorry. Those words.

They hit Anita's ears and heart like a bullet. She couldn't breathe. She couldn't look at her dad. She felt like she was silently choking on those words. Anita stared hard at her hands looking small and futile in her dad's own gorilla-like paws. She needed to focus on something visual so her body could keep breathing. She closed her eyes as her dad's hands let go and one tilted her chin to face him.

His eyes were wet. Just like hers.

"I'm sorry Anita," her dad said, "I didn't do my job as a father. I am supposed to protect you. I am supposed to help you have a better life than I had. I am supposed to help you be happy. And I failed at all of that. I didn't do it. I'm sorry beta, I didn't know."

Anita opened her mouth, no sound came out, but tears flowed down her face. She could feel her chest ache and her throat close in on her. She raised a hand to her mouth.

"Dad..." she whispered.

Anita's dad continued, tears tumbling down his face, his chest rising and rocking with every sob and his hands shaking with fury.

"No, Anita, I have to say this. I am your dad; I am the first person who should be protecting you. That is my job, my only important job while I live. It is to protect you, your sister and your mother. And I failed you. I didn't protect you from him. How I didn't see that my daughter was suffering, I don't know. But that is my failure," he sniffed and shook his head, "that, I must live with somehow.

But now I am here beta. I am here and I won't let him, or anyone hurt you anymore. Whatever happens with him, I am here to shield you from any more pain. Give me the chance to protect you now. My beautiful daughter. I am sorry."

Anita couldn't say anything. Not one word would escape her mouth. She wanted to tell her dad that it wasn't his fault at all. That he had been the best dad she could have ever dreamt of. That there was no way he could have seen this coming or been able to protect her from Khush's deluge of hurt, even she hadn't seen it coming. She wanted to say how much she loved him too. That every part of her that was once fierce and independent was because of him. That she would promise to bring that part of her back to him one day.

But she couldn't.

None of these words could reach her lips. They were stuck in her throat.

Anita looked at her dad, a crumpled mess in front of her, on his knees now and sobbing, and she hugged him tight and cried.

Chapter 43.

The phone call conversation that evening, with Khush had not gone quite as Anita had thought it would. But she wasn't overly surprised since she no longer any had idea how he would react or what he would say. She wasn't sure how much he was going to engage in a dialogue to mend their relationship, if at all. After spending time with her family, before deciding to call Khush, Anita was confident on what she wanted, however as she dialled his number and sat in the kitchen alone, Anita felt scared. The phone rang and rang like a shrill bird pecking at her ears, and Anita thought that he wasn't going to answer her at all. But, on what could have only been the last ring before she was sent to his voice message, Khush answered.

"Hello Anita," he said. Instantly Anita's heart raced, and her throat caught at the sound of his cool and calm voice. She felt afraid and unsure all over again.

"Hi."

"I thought I was going to call you?"

"I wanted to call now. Is that ok?" she felt her face begin to warm up instantly and felt beads of sweat forming on her lip.

"I suppose so."

There was a long silence. Anita had expected Khush to rant at her about leaving so abruptly, but he seemed unnervingly calm.

"So, you left. You called. You can start talking," Khush spoke, his manner controlled.

"Ok," said Anita taking a breath, knowing what she needed to say to her husband, "so, we need to talk about us. Properly this time. We have to make a decision on where we see our marriage going."

"I thought you had made your decision."

"What?" said Anita confused, his matter-of-fact tone throwing her.

"Well, you left your wedding ring here. On the counter. I'm assuming you've made a decision on us, our marriage, our family."

"Look, Khush," said Anita feeling herself unravel a little, "I have some things to say and I need to say it all. Will you allow me to do that first?"

"Sure" he sighed loudly as if he was bored with the conversation.

Anita took a deep breath and closed her eyes.

"Ok, well, it seems to me that you don't want to be in this relationship. You've stopped talking to me, spending time with me, stopped being with me. You're always off in your study and I know work may be busy, but when you are home, you need to be here with us. You criticise everything I do; my friends, my choices, my work, the way I look after Anand. Everything. And I'm not sure what I have done to deserve such hate from you. I do love you. And I am willing to be part of this marriage if you want me to be. But you need to be part of the marriage too."

Anita sighed, licked her dry lips and continued.

"The bottom line is, we have got to get help, see someone, and not for a measly five sessions and run off when you hear something you don't like. But proper couples counselling. And you have to deal with the issues that come up. And I'll do the same too. We need to work together, and we need to trust each other. Otherwise, what is the point in all of this? We'll end up hating each other and feeling lonelier together than we would if we were apart. You need to communicate with me. We need to work this all out together or decide to get divorced…that's it. That's what I wanted to say."

Anita let out a deep breath, one that she didn't know she was holding. She needed to give Khush time to digest everything she had said but the silence growing on the end of the phone was killing her. She needed to hear his voice.

"Khush? Are you there?"

"I'm here. I'm thinking. Give me a minute to take in what you've said."

"Ok."

Anita watched the second hand on the kitchen clock tick around and around. What felt like hours passed, but it had only been a few minutes.

"So, I've thought about what you said," said Khush so suddenly that Anita jumped, "and to be honest I have been thinking all day about you leaving me, taking Anand and going to your parent's place. I'm not happy about it. We should have been able to deal with this without getting others involved. But I hear you Anita. I hear what you're saying."

Anita sighed, relief washing over her. Her face was sticky, and hands were so clammy, she had to place the phone on the counter and change it to speaker phone. She knew none of her family would intrude or eavesdrop on this conversation.

"So, what's next then?" she whispered hopeful.

"What's next? We get you and Anand home. You and I go seek help. Get it all out and see if we can save this marriage. How do you feel about that?"

"That sounds like a great plan," said Anita breathing heavy running a hand through her hair.

"Good. I know you won't be coming home today. I'm not stupid. You need time away to think, and I guess I do too. But will you come home tomorrow?"

There was a pleading in his voice that Anita's heart reached out for.

"I will come home. But I promised Anand two sleepovers here."

"That's fine. It gives us time to talk more and sort this mess out without him bothering us. We can pick him up the day after tomorrow then."

"Sounds like a plan," said Anita feeling a weight gradually lift from her shoulders.

"Ok, well, I better leave you to it then."

"Ok. See you tomorrow."

"See you tomorrow."

Anita reached down to disconnect the call when Khush spoke again.

"Anita?"

"Yes?"

"I love you."

"Love you too," smiled Anita.

**   **   **

Although Henna wasn't too thrilled about Anita going back to her house as soon as she was, she had to allow Anita to try, and speaking to Khush face to face was the first step.

"Get his agreement down on paper," she said when Anita had told her about Khush agreeing to go to the counsellor, "you don't want him backing out after a few sessions again."

"I won't need paper Henna, I don't think he will back out this time," said Anita smiling. She and her sister were in the kitchen putting together some bits for the dinner their mother had made them, "he really seemed to realise that this was his last chance."

"As long as he knows this.," Henna said sternly. She raised her eyebrows at Anita and added, "remember you said that the last time. Then you gave him another chance. He's getting used to more and more final chances."

"Not this time," insisted Anita, "this time feels different and is different for me. This time I have nothing to hide from anyone."

"As long as you're sure? I'm only saying this to protect you."

"I know you are. I appreciate it, but I know it'll be fine."

Later that evening, once Anand was in bed asleep, Anita's aajima was also in bed and her sister and Ash had gone home, Anita sat on the sofa watching TV with her parents. It was their usual Indian TV channel with the Hindi version of EastEnders which they maintained was more realistic and less sensational that the actual EastEnders. They weren't fooling anyone, least of all not Anita. Anita watched as some busy body rich woman berated her maid for spilling some tea on her dining table cloth; the maid was young and pretty and had been deflecting the advances of the husband and in her haste to leave the room quickly, had spilled the drink. Anita shook her head and sighed.

"This is just as rubbish as EastEnders mum, why are you still watching this crap?"

"I like it," her mother said grinning at her knowing what was to come of this conversation, "it's really interesting, the acting is good, and I like the songs too."

Anita rolled her eyes and groaned loudly; typical, anything from India that was on TV had to have a young pretty girl, a love story, and of course, songs. She half expected to see the characters running around a massive field, lush green grass and tall trees surrounding her, singing about not being able to find love or some other crap like that.

"Leave your mum alone," said Anita's dad winking at Anita, "this is the only time someone sings love songs at her!"

The three of them laughed as a pillow flew across the room and hit Anita's dad in the head.

"You guys are nuts," said Anita, picking up her phone which had been beeping steadily for the last minute.

"Yes, we are. And that is why you love us." Anita's mum said turning back to her show.

"You're also nuts like us," added Anita's dad.

Smiling and shaking her head, Anita unlocked her phone and looked at the messages on there. The group chat with Jitesh, Henna and Reena had ten messages unread by Anita, and there were a few notifications on Facebook she browsed. But the message that made her heart leap was from Khush.

...Ready to make this work. Get a good night's sleep. See you tomorrow. Love you xxx

Anita smiled and typed her reply:

I love you too. We can do this. Night xx

Chapter 44.

The next morning Anita went back home without Anand, who hadn't even bothered asking why he wasn't coming and was too busy wolfing down his aajima's scrambled eggs and toast. She was anxious and felt a nervous energy shooting through her body throughout her entire journey home. Without seeing Khush and talking to him face to face, she wasn't one hundred percent sure that what he was saying wasn't just a ruse.

As she parked behind his car on the drive, she felt her heart swell and a lump form in her throat, she could see him at the window looking out to her. She waved. He turned away from the window. A moment later, just as Anita was about to open the front door with her keys, Khush opened the door. It was like she was a guest and he was inviting her into his house. Anita's mind raced, her heartbeat was quick, and she felt on edge almost as soon as she saw Khush.

She smiled meekly as he let her in and went straight into the kitchen. She saw her ring on the table where she had left it and felt a pang of guilt. Maybe she had been too rash in taking off the ring? Maybe she had made this situation more volatile than it needed to be by doing that? So many questions and scenarios went through her mind, she didn't notice that Khush had sat down at the dining table.

"Sit, please," said Khush. It didn't sound like his voice, it was strained and to Anita, it actually sounded like he had been crying. His eyes were puffy too.

"Ok," said Anita slowly sitting down, not taking her eyes off the wedding ring.

Khush noticed what she was looking at and picked up the ring. He moved it around his fingers and looked at Anita.

"This is yours. If you still want it?" he said softly.

"I do want it," said Anita, her guard dropping slightly, "but before I take it back, we need to talk seriously about us."

They spent the rest of the day talking about their marriage; how they were going to try and repair the damage caused, where they were going to go and seek professional help in couples therapy, how they were both going to change and adapt to better the relationship, and how communication was going to need to improve. They were honest with one another.

Khush made promises to change- some she had heard before and never believed and some new that made her want to hold him tight. She felt exhausted. This is what she wanted to happen between her and Khush for years now, an open and honest relationship, with trust and love at the forefront. It wasn't an easy conversation and there had been tears, from both of them, at times raised voices and a lot of going around in circles, but in the end they each knew they did want to fight for their marriage.

That evening, they ordered in dinner, sat and drank wine and talked. It was like they were in their courting days again, learning new things about one another, things they didn't know all surrounded with a nervous energy. Anita asked about Khush's work and how that had been going, especially with all the extra work he had to do. She learned that it was the same as before, there had been no extra work, he'd just wanted time away from her and Anand. Khush had finally apologised for lying and for avoiding his family. Anita felt confused, she wondered if she should be angry at the lies or happy that he had finally come clean? How did she not realise what was happening much sooner?

They talked about Anita's group of friends who Khush had yet to meet properly, she explained that Jitesh and her had become close after the accident and found they had a lot in common, but that they were friends only. She explained that was in fact trying to set up Jitesh with Reena. She commented that Reena and her son were great to be around and that eventually he would get a chance to meet the boy Anand had been going on about for a while now. She was conflicted; on one hand she wanted him to meet Reena and Jitesh and see how his jealousy was unfounded, but she also felt like they were her friends and they needed to be separate from Khush.

However, she still left out some truths.

Anita couldn't bring herself to tell Khush why Henna had introduced Reena to Anita after all this time and knew that it would be harmful to the progress they had made that day if she did. She explained that Reena was divorced but claimed to not know anything about the reasons behind the marriage ending. She knew that Khush wasn't completely convinced but refused to divulge anything more. She also had kept quiet about why Jitesh had kept in contact with her. The biggest secret of it all; the miscarriage, stayed hidden.

Anita had debated with herself constantly about telling Khush about this, and she was torn. She had walked into the house prepared to tell Khush, but by the time they had sat down and started talking, and seeing his reaction, however much he had tried to hide it, to her connection with Reena and Jitesh, Anita knew this was the one thing she could not be open and honest about. This had to be her secret. This had to be her shame.

That night Khush said that they should share a bed together. All the wine that Anita and Khush had consumed played a large part in that decision and Anita was too emotionally drained to resist even though she knew it wasn't best for them and she wasn't really in the mood to connect with Khush physically. In their drunken haze they fell into their usual routine for sex. Her body felt empty as Khush rocked on top of her, as if it wasn't her own. Her mind raced in a drunken blur and she was unable to be in the moment.

Once he was finished, he lay on top of her for a moment, panting hard and then with a kiss on her neck he rolled off the bed and went into the bathroom. Anita turned to the side and listened to him in the bathroom, her body felt alien to her.

She felt him get back into bed, his head nuzzled against her shoulder blade. *What is going?* She thought to herself, *why doesn't this feel right?*

"Was that ok for you?" he murmured gently stroking her thigh and kissing her back.

"Mmm," Anita murmured feeling cold inside her own body.

"Good," Khush said rolling over to his side of the bed and pulling the duvet over him, "night."

"Night." Anita whispered, squeezing her eyes shut and curling herself into a ball, as single tear rolled down her cheek and onto her pillow.

Chapter 45.

The next morning seemed to fall into simple routines for Khush and Anita again; Anita woke to find Khush was in the shower, so she went downstairs to put the kettle on. He had taken the day off so that once she collected Anand from her parents, they could spend it together as a family, to try and mend the fractured relationship that was starting to form between Khush and Anand. As Khush got out of the shower, Anita walked up the stairs with two steaming mugs.

"Shall I make breakfast?" she asked handing him a mug.

"Nothing in the fridge, we normally do a food shop, but you weren't here," Khush said drying himself and getting dressed into jeans and t shirt.

"Oh, sorry," said Anita feeling ashamed and guilty at not having the house stocked up with food, "want me to go grab some stuff?"

"No, that's ok," said Khush picking up his mug and descending the stairs, "I'll go do the shopping whilst you get Anand. Then we can get two things done and have a day together. Ok?"

"Sure," said Anita turning on the shower and gulping down some of her scolding hot coffee too quickly, "I'm going to jump into the shower now. See you when you get back."

Anita picked up her coffee and took it into the shower with her, something Khush would have admonished her for and normally she wouldn't have for fear of being yelled at, but today, she didn't care. As she stepped into the shower she heard Khush coming back up the stairs.

"Anita, your car is blocking mine," he said through the bathroom door.

"Ok, take my car instead, and I'll take yours to get Anand," she called back.

"Sure, see you later."

Anita heard his footsteps fade and a moment later the front door slam shut. She smiled and hummed a song that had been playing on the radio downstairs and showered. It felt good to be back home. In her home, with her family. This was finally going to be the start of a new chapter in their lives.

"So, how did it go?" asked her mum as soon as Anita stepped into the house an hour later.

"It went ok, mum." said Anita smiling.

"Ok? That's it?"

"Mum, it went really well. We talked almost all day. Got loads of stuff out in the open."

"And what about counselling?" chimed in her dad who had Anand on his lap playing some detective game with his teddies.

"He is open to it. We didn't actually talk much about that," said Anita, "but we didn't ignore it." Anita added quickly seeing the concern on her father's face.

"That's good," he said going back to Anand.

"Yeah, it was. We are going to have a fun day together all three of us once I get Anand back home."

"Is he not working today?" asked her mum picking up and tidying some of the toys that were left at her place for Anand to play with when he was there.

"He called in saying he wasn't coming in. A family emergency. So, we have the day together. I think it'll be really good for us and to be honest, mum, we do need it."

"That's good," said her mother but her face clearly showed her unease.

"Come on mum," Anita said giving her mum a big hug, "this is good. Khush wants to fix our marriage, he wants us to work on it. And he wants to be a family. This can only be good news."

"Ok beta," said her mum forcing a smile, "I just want you to be careful. Don't go and forget all the things he has put you through. Don't forget all those promises he has made too. Be careful."

"I'll be ok mum," smiled Anita, "right, Anand, shall we get going? Say bye to aajima and bapa and then we can go home to daddy. He's at home today so we can have the day together."

Anand jumped out of his grandad's lap and came running to her bursting with excitement.

"A day with daddy?"

Anita smiled, but with her mum and dad watching her, it felt forced. It was a rarity that Khush would be spending extra time with her and Anand, but she didn't want that to show so obviously with her parents there.

"Come on then Anand, let's get going."

As they walked to the car, Anand jumped and pointed at the car.

"Daddy's here?"

"No," said Anita unlocking the car and getting Anand strapped in, "daddy has got my car and I have his today. He's gone to do some food shopping."

"Can I have a mint please?" he asked as they waved goodbye to her parents who were standing at their front door watching her drive away.

"A mint? I don't know where daddy keeps his."

"In the glove thing." Anand said pointing to the passenger side dashboard.

"Oh, right," said Anita reaching for the glove compartment. As she fumbled for a mint, finally grabbing a packet and handing one to Anand. She shook her head to clear the odd feeling in her stomach and popped a mint into her mouth too.

Walking into the house with Anand, Anita could feel something was wrong. That same strange feeling she had experienced in the car but couldn't put her finger on what it was. Her stomach hurt, she felt like something was pressing down on her and making her feel nauseous.

"You're back from shopping quickly. Is everything ok?" said asked Khush who was sitting stone faced on the couch in the living room.

"You tell me."

Khush turned to face her. Anita's breath caught in her throat. In his hand was a piece of paper, and next to him an envelope. Anita looked at the piece of paper and then at the envelope, scrawled on the front it read 'To you know who'.

"Khush," she whispered panic rising like bile burning her insides.

"We'll discuss this later," Khush replied walking straight past her and picking up Anand.

There was a heat coming from him, pure hatred and anger in his eyes. Betrayal.

Anita couldn't move. Her brain willed her to move to pick up the letter that Khush had dropped onto the floor, but she could only manage a slight movement of her fingertips. She tried to calm her breathing, but all she could do was let out rasping hisses from her searing throat. Her heart was pounding like it was trying to escape her body; her face, her eyes, her whole being felt hot and scared. Panic controlled her now.

That letter had been hers. No one else was to read it.

Khush had found it. He had read it. And now he knew.

Hearing Anand squeal and giggle tore Anita out of her trance. She moved. She stepped to her letter and picked it up.

The letter she had written herself months ago. The one she had almost forgotten about. Almost.

The one with the secret.

Holding the letter to her chest she turned slowly to look at Khush. His eyes were dark, almost empty. But at the same time, they burned her, shamed her, accused her. He turned and looked at Anand.

"Anand," he said ruffling his son's hair, "want to go to the park and play?"

"Play in the park?" repeated Anand laughing hard and jumping about, "Woohoo yes please!"

"Come on then," said Khush putting on his coat and slipping his trainers on.

"What about mummy?" Anand asked looking at Anita and frowning.

"Oh, I think she will give this one a miss. She looks like she is poorly. Maybe needs a nap," Khush looked at Anita when he said the last part his eyes blazing.

"Uh…yeah. I have a headache, mummy will take a nap whilst you and daddy go to the park, then you can bring back some lunch. And then I will be fine to play. Ok?"

"Ok mummy," Anand walked over to Anita and gave her little squeeze and kiss, "I won't hug too tight, mummy."

"Thanks beta," said Anita feeling the need to never let her son go, "I'll be fine in an hour or two. You two have fun and bring me back some lunch."

Anand waved Anita goodbye and followed his dad out of the house. Anita watched them laugh and play as they got into Khush's car and drive off out of the road. Her lungs were struggling to function and her head was hammering against her skull. She stood at the window for what felt like an age before looking down at the crumpled letter in her hand.

Fuck she thought walking to her bag and putting the letter inside of it, *should've kept it in my fucking bag.*

Fuck. Fuck. Fuck.

Stupid girl! You're so stupid Anita!

Why didn't you keep it in your bag?

Anita paced around the house unsure of what to do, she felt dizzy and hot. She was terrified of what punishment Khush would dole out for this betrayal. She walked into the kitchen and poured herself a glass of orange juice, took one shaky gulp, paused, then ran to the sink.

Slowly, she opened her eyes and looked at the remains of what had been her morning coffee and a few bites of toast at her mum's house in the sink. Her throat burned, her eyes watered, and her stomach pulsed. She felt terrified. What was she going to do now? She remembered the look of betrayal on Khush's face and her stomach flipped again.

Feeling woozy she slowly walked to the living room. She collected the letter again from her bag and sat down on the couch with it. She closed her eyes and focused on her breathing. She needed to concentrate on something other than the cluster fuck she was now in.

Breathe in. Breathe out.

In.

Out.

In.

Out.

Chapter 46.

Anita woke to the sound of her phone ringing somewhere in her bag. She was confused. It was just getting dark outside. As she moved from the sofa, her legs screamed in agony. She had fallen asleep with them folded underneath her and her muscles had ceased. Limping to her bag which was still on the floor at the living room door, Anita fumbled for her phone, grabbing it just as it stopped ringing. It was a missed call from Reena, she had already missed another two from her already. She put the phone in her pocket and walked into the kitchen. Switching on the lights she called out her husband's name.

"Khush? Where are you guys?"

They should be back from the park by now, she thought to herself.

No answer. She moved to the bottom of the stairs.

"Khush. Anand. Are you upstairs?"

No answer.

As she walked up the stairs her stomach reminded her of the vomiting in the kitchen. She grabbed her stomach and curled over.

"Ow, fuck," she said pulling herself up using the banister, "Khush? Where are you guys? What is this? A joke? I fell asleep, sorry."

Anita reached the top of the stairs and looked up. Darkness. No sound. No movement.

"Anand? Come on, no more hiding, mummy isn't playing now, where are you?" she tried to appeal to her son's inability to hide for too long without laughing or revealing his hiding place but there was no answer.

Panic began to sweep through her body. She went from room to room opening the doors, switching on the lights, looking in every cupboard or hiding space a boy could fit into. But nothing. No one was home.

No one except her.

She stood in the hallway, her stomach threatening to upsurge again, held her hand out on the wall to steady herself, her mind racing so fast she couldn't keep up.

"Khush! I'm not playing any more. This isn't funny. Get out here now. And you too Anand or you'll be in big trouble."

Anita could hear nothing except her own strained breathing; short and rapid. She pulled out her phone and called Khush. No answer. She called again. Nothing.

"Fuck!" she screamed tears falling down her face, panic giving way to terror.

She dialled again. This time Khush answered.

"Khush!" Anita gasped holding the phone tight, "Where are you two? I'm really worried here. I woke and you're not here. What the fuck?"

His voice was calm, cold, and full of loathing.

"You did this Anita. This is your fault," he said and then the only sound was the click of him ending the call.

Anita cried down the phone, tried to ring Khush's number again, but he'd turned his phone off. He had cut all communication with her. Looking at the blank screen on her phone, Anita's hands shook. Droplets of tears fell against her screen, blurring her vision. She leaned against the wall and slowly slid down to the floor as her legs gave way and collapsed refusing to hold her up anymore.

Her shoulders shook. Her head throbbed. Her heart weakened.

This was it. Her biggest fear glaring right there in her face. Khush had taken her son. He wasn't coming back. She'd lost everything.

She was alone.

Anita sat on the hallway floor in her home and cried. She didn't know what to do. This was her fault, and she couldn't fix it. Her head slumped on to her heaving chest and her arms lay by her side. She wanted to give up, but she knew that she couldn't. Anand's sweet face, the face that had made her believe in love again, called out to her. She knew he loved her and would want to see her again.

"Damn," she said, her voice cracking and dry, "what am I going to do?"

Slowly, Anita picked herself off the floor and walked towards the living room. Her head pounded and all she could hear was Khush's last words to her 'you did this' ringing in her ears. Her eyes glanced towards the pile of toys that Anand hadn't quite finished packing away the last time he was home. His favourite teddy peeked out from under the pile, the teddy's eyes looking at Anita longingly. Anita's breath caught in her throat, she knelt on the floor and picked it up, held it close to her and sobbed.

With everything that happened between Khush and her, with all the arguments, the belittling, the way he made her believe she wasn't good enough at anything, Anand was the only ray of hope Anita had. He was the one thing that kept her going, even in the dark days when she thought everyone would be better off without her there, she would only have to take one look at Anand, or receive a cuddle and kiss from him, and she knew he was the reason she hadn't given up on life. Tears streaming down her face and onto his favourite teddy, Anita knew she couldn't give up now.

She stood up, still holding onto her connection to her son, and looked around the room. She needed to think. What next? Where would Khush go? What would he do? Who should she call? Anita looked around for her phone and eventually found it in the hallway where she had been sitting. She picked it up.

"I need to call mum," Anita said out loud, "she will know what to do."

But her fingers hovered over the screen. Something stopped her from calling her mother. She wasn't ready to tell her mum that she had failed yet again. That she was still too weak to keep her family together. That she couldn't stop Khush from taking their son. It was shameful. Her mother might understand but her aajima wouldn't. She would ask too many questions, none of which Anita could answer, but all which would make Anita feel like a failure in marriage and motherhood. Anita wasn't ready for everyone to know she had failed, and in this community, she wouldn't be able to keep anything a secret. Indians talk. They gossip. And they judge.

"No," said Anita placing her phone on a counter in the kitchen, "I have to do this myself. I can't call anyone. I can't go to them as a failure."

She sat down, her legs heavy like her heart, and buried her hands in her head again. After a moment, she picked up her phone again. She had to keep trying Khush. Her call went straight to voicemail.

"Khush, it's me," she said, "please come back with Anand. Where are you? We can talk. Please call me back. I'm sorry."

She looked at her phone. Stared at it for what felt like an eternity. Nothing. No call back from Khush.

"Maybe if I text him instead?" she muttered to herself.

Her fingers shaking, she slowly typed out a message.

Khush, please call me back. We need to talk. Please bring Anand back. We can fix this.

Minutes ticked by as Anita stared at her phone. No reply. No text messages from Khush.

"Fuck," she said anger and fear rising in her body again, *I can't just sit here doing nothing and staring at my phone. He's not going to call. He won't text. What else can I do?*

Anita paced around the house, unable to sit still and unable to do anything. Her mind was racing a million miles an hour, but there was nothing she could think of to do. Nothing except call her family, and she wasn't ready to do that just yet. Not after she had just spoke about how she and Khush would be working everything out. That just wasn't an option.

She looked at her phone again. No messages from Khush. Just a few from her sister.

…Hey, how's it all going? Your family day working out?…

Anita scoffed, her eyes welling up with tears. She replied.

…Hi, all ok. all good. X

She walked up the stairs, still not knowing what her next move would be. Anand's bedroom door was ajar. Her heart skipped a beat. She went into her son's room. It was a normal little boy's room. The bed was small and against the wall, covered with a green and blue dinosaur bed covers and his chest of drawers were splattered with stickers collected over the years. Anita stumbled and sat on his bed, holding on to his pillow she could smell her son; apples and vanilla, his shampoo and cream.

"Anand," she whispered crying into the pillow. She stayed like this until she heard her phone beep.

Chapter 47.

Quickly grabbing it, Anita swiped her the screen hoping it was a message from Khush. It wasn't. It was a message from Payal. Frowning, Anita read the message.

...Hi. Payal here. Just wondering if you were also coming over. Khush and Anand are here and I wanted to know if you were coming too?

Anita's eyes widened. Khush was at his brother's house. With Anand. She jumped up from his bed and squealed. They were there. They were safe. Her heart was beating fast as she plodded down the stairs with her phone to her ear. It rang.

"Hello?"

"Hi Payal. It's me Anita."

"Oh, hi. Where are you? Khush is already here."

"Is Anand with him?" Anita asked pulling on her trainers.

"Of course. Why?"

"Is he safe?"

"Safe?" asked Payal clearly puzzled, "Of course, he is."

"Good, I'm coming over now."

"What's going on Anita? Khush is here-"

"Who are you talking to?" came a voice from the other end of the phone. Anita listened then frowned. It was Pritesh. She pressed the phone closer to her ear, grabbed her car keys and walked to the front door.

"Payal?" she said, "are you there? Is everything ok? I'm coming over now."

"Who's this?" Pritesh's growl stopped Anita in her tracks. There was anger in the voice.

"It's me, Anita. Pritesh I-"

"Khush doesn't want to see you."

"But we need to talk."

"No. He said he can't talk to you now. You've betrayed him. Typical. He doesn't want to see you right now."

"But Anand is there and-"

"Anand is fine. Khush is fine. They are with us."

"Pritesh, please let me speak to him."

"He doesn't want to see you," repeated Pritesh, Anita could hear him sneering, "don't come here. You're not welcome."

"But I need to."

"No, you don't. You are not welcome Anita. Bye."

"Pritesh? No, Pritesh please I-" but Anita had been cut off.

She stood at the front door, her hand hovering over the handle. Khush and Anand were there, at Pritesh's place. She needed to see her son. But Pritesh had told her she wasn't welcome.

"Khush, what did you tell them?" she whispered as she turned back into the kitchen.

She looked at her phone again. Payal said Anand was ok. That was good. But Pritesh was angry. Anita didn't want her son around him, she needed to see Anand. Needed to hold him. Needed to tell him that mummy loves him. She had to go.

**   **   **

Anita parked her car off the main driveway to her brother-in-law's house. She had driven past once to see if Khush's car was there. It was. They were there. She had seen a figure standing at the window, *Pritesh* she guessed, *looking out for me I bet*. She looked at her phone; the neon light burned her tired aching eyes. She typed a message to Payal.

…Hi. I want to come by. I need to see Anand. It's urgent.

She pressed send and waited. She could see that the message had been read. Two ticks beside the message. Anita looked up at the house. The large figure looked to one side, then moved. Her phone beeped.

…I'm sorry. Pritesh says no.

…Anita shook her head in disbelief.

…He can't stop me from seeing my son!

…He won't let you in. Sorry.

…He has to. Please get Khush.

…Pritesh said no. Sorry.

"Fuck!" screamed Anita slamming her hands against the steering wheel. She looked at the window. The figure was there again. She picked up her phone.

Please she typed.

Her phone rang almost immediately. Khush's name flashed on the screen.

"Khush," Anita said breathlessly.

"No, it's Pritesh."

"Pritesh, please, put Khush on. I need to speak to him."

"Khush and Anand are staying with us. They are fine. Khush needs some time, just like you did the other day over that silly argument, now Khush needs time."

"But Pritesh. I need to talk to him."

"I'm going to say this once and once only now. Leave him alone. He doesn't want to see you or speak to you until he is ready. Leave him alone."

"But Anand…"

"Anand is fine here. Leave them both alone."

"Pritesh, please."

"Go home Anita. I know you're outside. This is your warning, go home or you'll be sorry."

Anita's voice caught in her throat. He knew she was outside his house. She glanced outside, her skin tingling with fear. Nothing. Just darkness.

"You thought I wouldn't see you out there? Don't be so stupid. Now go home. I'm warning you," Pritesh's voice was full of malice.

"I need to speak to Khush, please," Anita whispered.

"No. I've made my decision. If he wants to talk to you, he will call you. Bye."

"No, wait!" but it was too late. Pritesh had hung up on her again.

Anita's shoulders slumped and she cried. She was so close to her son but couldn't see him. Couldn't speak to him. Couldn't touch him. Khush had run to his brother and Anita believed the venom in his threat. She had to go home. She had to do as she was told if she wanted to see her son again.

Chapter 48.

Anita sat on her sofa in her cold living room in the dark. But she didn't care. An empty bottle of wine sat beside her and, in her hand, a second. The third sat on the table next to her phone. Guzzling straight from the bottle, Anita felt numb. Her heart was broken, and her life was shattered. Khush had won. She felt nothing. Nothing except the warm tingle of the wine working its way through her tired and aching body. She'd been sat there for hours since returning from Pritesh's house, running over the conversation in her fuzzy mind again and again. By the time sleep came, all three bottles had been consumed and it was almost morning. Thoughts of loss and loneliness, of shame and failure, of never seeing Anand again had haunted her and by the time she gave in to exhaustion Anita had lost all hope. She finally slept.

A faint ringing in her head began to bring Anita out of her slumber. She couldn't quite make out what the ringing was, but it was shrill against her thumping head. Slowly, Anita opened her eyes and as she looked for her phone, it rang. Her heart leapt. Khush. She scrabbled to accept the call.

"Khush? Hello?" she cried desperately down the phone.

"Hi? Anita? Is that you?" a female voice.

"Who? Who is this?" said Anita confused, her eyes too puffy to see the screen properly.

"It's Reena. I've been trying to call you all morning. Are you ok? What's happened?"

"He's got Anand," Anita wailed, allowing fresh tears to form and fall. She walked aimlessly to the front door.

"What? Shit. What are you saying Anita?"

"He's got him. He took him to the park, and I fell asleep. I shouldn't have fallen asleep. But he found out about the letter.

He took him to the park. I fell asleep and now they aren't here." Anita rambled on incoherently.

"Wait Anita, calm down," said Reena calmly, "where are you?"

"At home. He took Anand."

"Ok, you're at home. That's good. Anita, I am coming over to you now. Don't go anywhere and don't do anything. I'm calling Henna too, ok?"

"I'm home," repeated Anita laying down on the hallway floor, "he's taken him."

"Ok, hon, I hear you. I'm on my way."

**   **   **

Anita didn't know how long she had been lying on the hallway floor when she woke to someone nudging her and calling her name, but she knew it wasn't Khush returning.

"Anita! Bloody hell. Are you ok?" cried a deep voice.

Anita felt a gentle shake of her shoulders, she heard other voices too.

"Anita, hon, are you ok? Wake up please!" one voice.

"What has that fucker done?" another voice.

Slowly, Anita opened her eyes and groaned. She felt like she was experiencing the world's worst hangover. Her mind was groggy and her body ached. Then it hit her. Why she was on the floor. What had happened. She sat up like a bolt.

"Anand," she said her eyes wide and burning, "he took Anand!"

"Ok, ok calm down," the deep voice said again, "let's get her up and some water down her first."

Anita allowed herself to be picked up by Jitesh, Henna and Reena. All three looked concerned and Anita could only imagine the mess she looked in their eyes. She voiced this thought and was met with sympathetic, and forced, laughs. They walked her to the kitchen and sat her down at the kitchen table. Henna rushed to get a glass of water whilst Jitesh stood in front of Anita, both hands on her shoulders.

"Anita, I need you to listen to me carefully. Can you do that?" he asked gently but firmly.

"Yes." Anita said flatly.

"Ok, I need you to tell me what happened. From as far back in the day as you can remember."

"Ok, so I went to collect Anand from mum and dad's just before lunch. I took Khush's car because my car was in the way, and he was going to the shops for food. So, he took my car. I took his. When we came home, he was sitting in the living room." She looked into Jitesh's soft eyes and sobbed, "he found my letter."

"What letter?" asked Jitesh frowning and sitting down opposite Anita, his warm strong hands still comforting on her shoulders.

"The letter the counsellor told me to write to myself about everything."

"What was in the letter?" piped in Henna handing a glass of water to Anita and forcing her to take a sip.

Anita swallowed, her throat was raw but the cold water felt soothing, "Everything was in the letter. How I felt about him, our marriage issues, the way he is with me and the way he makes me feel with his words. His controlling and manipulation of me. And…and the miscarriage."

Anita paused as she let the last part sink in. She looked at Reena, her eyes welled up again.

"He told me that it was my fault and that I did it."

"Did what?"

"Made him walk away with Anand."

"How is that your fault?" cried Henna getting angry.

"Look, we all need to stay calm," said Jitesh looking at Henna and shaking his head, "for Anita. So, he read the letter, which had everything in. Everything that he wouldn't want anyone to know and the miscarriage too, which he didn't know."

"Yes."

"And then he just walked out?" asked Jitesh.

"No, he told Anand I wasn't feeling well and that I needed a nap. Said he was taking him to the park. And then I fell asleep, and when I woke, it was dark outside and I was alone."

"I saw him," said Reena after a moment of silence. The three of them turned to her eyes wide with surprise.

"What? Where?" muttered Anita reaching out to Reena as if touching her would bring Anand closer to her.

"In the park, about midday. He was on his phone and Anand was playing on the swings." Reena looked at each of them, stopping when she got to Anita, "I just assumed that he was going to finally spend some time with him and give you a break. I didn't know."

"How long was he there for?" asked Henna.

"Well, I was there on the other side of the park with Prem and my family. We were having a picnic, and I couldn't see you Anita, so I thought I would leave him to it. We were there about an hour before I noticed they had gone. I assumed they had come back home to you."

"No, they didn't," whispered Anita shaking her head.

"That's why I called you. After I realised they had gone, I thought I would give you a call and see if everything was alright. Especially after the other night. But you didn't answer straight away. When you did, you sounded frightened and said they had gone."

"I don't remember."

"No, of course you wouldn't," said Jitesh, "Reena called me and Henna and we all came here straight away."

He went to Pritesh's place with Anand, but I wasn't allowed to see him."

"Right," said henna grabbing her phone, "I'll call Payal."

Anita watched as Henna spoke to Payal.

"Ok, thanks," Henna said, "call if you hear anything."

"What's happened? Are they there?" asked Anita.

"No, they aren't there any more. He didn't say where they were going, just left. He's kidnapped my nephew? Fucker!" cried Henna hands balled into fists and rage burning in her eyes.

"Not really," said Jitesh shaking his head. He turned to Anita, "look, he may have taken him somewhere and you don't know where. But because he's the dad, nothing official can be done."

"What do you mean?" said Anita, her voice catching in her throat as panic began to build inside her again.

"What Jitesh means," said Reena rubbing Anita's back trying to soothe her, "is that because he's Anand's dad, and he's never been in trouble with hurting him…or you. Jitesh means the police can't and won't do anything really. Not straight away anyway."

"What?" said Henna and Anita at the same time.

"She's right," said Jitesh looking at both Henna and Anita in turn, "he's not known to the police for being abusive-"

"But he is abusive!" shouted Henna.

"But it's never been logged or made official. Anita has never gone to the police about it and the school haven't contacted social services as it's not affected Anand. I'm sorry, Anita, but from the outside, he's just a normal dad and husband."

"What do I do then?" asked Anita rubbing her hands across her face, "do I not report it?"

"That's up to you," Reena said, "you can report it, see what they say. Depending on everything, they may take it further, but it depends on what you tell them about this whole situation. But be prepared for them to not jump straight away. Anand is with his dad, so they might not do anything straight away. It's your choice Anita. What do you want to do?"

Anita sat there, taking in everything Jitesh and Reena had told her. They were right. She had never reported anything to anyone. Only her counsellor, her family now and close friends knew, and it was all circumstantial. Her word against his. Her interpretation of everything he said. He had never touched her aggressively or physically hurt her. He had never hit Anand either.

From the outside he was the model father.

"Anita," said Henna pressing on Anita's arm, "you need to decide. Now. What are you going to do?"

"I...I know he wouldn't do anything to harm Anand-"

"Do you though?" challenged Henna.

"I do, he wouldn't hurt Anand, not even to get back at me."

"So, what do you want to do?" repeated Henna.

"I'm not sure. What if the police think I'm overreacting?"

"What if they don't?" asked Reena, "what if everything you tell them is enough?"

"I don't know!" sobbed Anita.

A moment past as she controlled her emotions and calmed herself down.

"I want to go to the police," Anita said finally.

"Are you sure?" asked Jitesh.

"I think I am. Yes. I want to go to the police. My husband has taken my son without any warning, and he hasn't contacted me about it."

"Then let's go." Henna said quickly, not waiting for a chance for Anita to change her mind, "Anita, you're coming in my car. Let's go."

In the car, Anita looked constantly at her phone, willing it to ring. Willing for Khush to be on the other end saying he was on his way home with Anand. She kept refreshing the screen, hoping she hadn't missed anything.

"He's not going to call, sis," said Henna glancing over at her sister, worried.

"You don't know that." Anita pleaded.

"Yeah, I do. And you do too. You heard what he said on the phone. He said that whatever happened next was your fault."

"But he wouldn't..."

"But he wouldn't what? He's used and manipulated you for years now. You've been under his control and out of fear, love or whatever, you've stood by him. You don't think he would use Anand as leverage? Come on, sis. He's taken your baby away. Don't make excuses for him. Not now. Not anymore."

Anita glanced at her sister. There was fire in her voice, but her face streamed with tears. She looked back at her phone.

"You're right. I just want this to be over, I want to be happy and believe in myself again, and..." Anita trailed off as she saw the sign for the police station in front of her.

Henna parked the car and went to unbuckle. Anita placed a hand on her arm.

"No, Henna. I have to go in myself. You wait here."

"Like that's going to fucking happen Anita. I'm coming into the building with you, and if you want to talk to an officer on your own, fine. But I'm not sitting here waiting for you. I'm here for you and I won't be leaving your side until I'm happy."

Anita looked at her sister again. There was no way she was going to win this argument with Henna. No way she was going to change her sister's mind about coming in. She sighed and nodded.

As they walked into the cold and dreary looking police station, they were joined by Reena and Jitesh too. The three of them stayed by her side until an officer came to talk to Anita.

"I'm sorry," said the officer to the group, "you can't all go in."

"Can I come in with her, officer?" said Henna holding tightly on to Anita's hand, "I'm her sister."

The officer looked at Anita's dishevelled state and nodded, "It might be wise if you do. But please, let Mrs Govind do all the talking."

She led Anita and Henna down a corridor and into a small room. Looking back at Jitesh and Reena she added, "thank you for being here."

Chapter 49.

"FUCK!" screamed Anita into her hands as they drove out of the police station car park. She slammed her fists into the dashboard with every word, "Fuck! Fuck! Fuck! Fuck!"

"I'm sorry," Henna said reaching out to her sister.

"How can they be so fucking chilled about it!? I told them everything Henna. You were there, right? I told them everything and they still won't do anything."

"I know, Anita," said Henna, but she knew her words were falling on deaf ears. Anita needed to shout and scream, and Henna would just have to let her.

"They want me to wait? Wait for what? Wait for a call saying they've gone and are never coming back? What's the fucking point?"

Anita broke down and screamed into her hands, her shoulders slumped, and she whimpered.

"Henna," she said a few minutes later, her voice was quiet and defeated, "it took everything I had, and I mean every ounce of my fight to go in there and tell them what I told them. And for what? I've lost."

"You haven't lost sis," Henna said shaking her head defiantly, "you haven't. I know they can't help you out yet. But they will be able to help soon. And we aren't going to just sit about and wait for them to help, we're going to find them. Ok?"

"How?" said Anita looking out of the car window, rain had started to fall, and she watched the drips slide down the window as if they were racing to get to the end.

"Firstly, we need to get you home and fed. I'm going to call mum and tell her and dad to come over to yours. We will be there with you no matter what. Then, we will call all his family in case he's still there hiding out. They need to know what he's like."

"His dad won't give a fuck, he hates me too."

"I don't care. He needs to know what his son is doing, even if he doesn't believe it. And he needs to help. Khush just can't take away your son like that. No way. We won't let him. He's our family too."

Anita sighed and closed her eyes. She felt empty; there were no more tears, no more arguments to be made, there was no more hope. She heard Henna call her parents. The voices were muffled, and Anita allowed the gentle hum of the car engine and the tapping of the rain against the window to lull her to sleep.

**   **   **

"Anita, we're here."

Anita woke to find she was staring at the front of her house; all dark and empty inside like she was now. Henna was nudging her.

"Let's go inside."

Anita climbed out of the car and shivered, the temperature had dropped, and the air felt harsh against her tear streamed face. Standing at her front door waiting for her were her parents and Ash. She smiled, even though she had given her parents a key to her house years ago, they had never used it, always opting to wait outside the front door or in the car until she or Khush had arrived to let them in.

"Beta," her mum said walking straight to Anita and wrapping her arms around her daughter, "we will fix all this rubbish ok?"

Anita said nothing but nodded into her mother's shoulder.

For the rest of the evening, everything was a blur. Anita sat on the sofa in the living room and watched everyone rally around her and do whatever they could to help. Her mum went straight into the kitchen and began rustling up some food for everyone, Henna and Ash made calls to Khush and Anita's mutual friends to see if they'd had any contact with Khush, Jitesh and Reena sat with Anita, checking her phone for her and making sure she was ok, and her dad took control and called Khush's dad and brother, talking to them and explaining what had happened and asking if they had heard from Khush or seen Anand at all that day. The house was alive, more alive in that evening than it had felt for a long while.

"How long did the police say to wait before calling them again?" Ash asked taking Anita's plate from her after they had all eaten. Anita had hardly touched it.

"They said to wait until tomorrow afternoon. Just to make sure. They said to keep calling him- but that's pointless since he's decided to turn off his phone so I can't even locate him, especially as we now know he's not at his brother's anymore."

"Tomorrow afternoon?" said Ash shaking his head, "Anita, I'm so sorry about all this. Wish I had done more to help."

"You couldn't have," said Anita smiling at how the three men in front of her, her dad, her brother-in-law and her friend, were the three that she trusted the most and loved the most right now.

"Still."

Anita returned to the living room with her mum and dad, as Reena, Jitesh, Henna and Ash tidied up the kitchen.

"Anita," her dad said sitting next to her, "I spoke to his dad. He hasn't seen them. He didn't know things were this bad. He...didn't seem too regretful but he did give the numbers of some old friends that Khush may have gone to. He really didn't want to talk about his son doing something this bad. Ash has those numbers and will call them soon, ok beta?"

"Thanks papa," said Anita leaning her head on his strong shoulders, "When will this nightmare be over?"

"When you and Anand are both back home with us, and when you have divorced Khush."

Anita looked at her dad shocked.

"I wish" she said closing her eyes.

"Your wish will come true beta," said her mother stroking her face reassuringly, "we will support you until it does."

"Um, Anita," said Reena at the living room door, "hon I have to go. I need to pick Prem up from my mum's place. Sorry."

"No, that's ok," said Anita standing up and walking over to Reena. She embraced her friend and squeezed tight, "thank you so much for looking out for me. You've been amazing."

"You are welcome Anita," said Reena, then looking straight at her she added solemnly, "it's not over yet, you know. But it's going in the right direction. You're doing the right thing for you and for Anand. It will work out."

"It has to." Anita said forcing a smile and thinking about a life of loneliness ahead of her.

"Have faith. It will," said Reena opening the door, "keep me in the loop. Let me know what's happening ok? I'll be back tomorrow- maybe with Prem, but I'll be back."

"Thanks mate," said Anita.

She watched her friend get into her car and leave. As she turned, she saw Jitesh standing there watching her.

"Hey," she said walking to him and giving him a hug.

"Hey you," he said squeezing back and stroking her hair.

"Are you off too?"

"Not a chance, I'm here as long as you want me to be. Same as your family. I care about you and want to make sure I'm here if you need anything. Even if it's just a cuppa."

Anita grinned, "sorry but there is no way you can make me chai the way my mum does. That'll be her job."

"Then for advice and to be a sounding board."

"Henna and Ash's job. Sorry. What else have you got?"

"Um...someone to hold you and comfort you?"

"That's my dad."

"Well, I'm not sure what else that leaves me with," said Jitesh smiling shrugging his shoulders, "maybe just here to make you smile and laugh? Will that do?"

"That's good," smiled Anita resting her head on his shoulders and listening to his heartbeat. After a moment of silence, Anita stepped back from Jitesh's arms and walked into the living room where her family were all sat watching TV, "your job is to make me smile and be happy."

Anita turned to look at Jitesh and smiled, she looked at her family too, grateful that each of them were putting their lives on hold for her. Pausing whatever they had going on, so they could support her through the worst moments of her life. She smiled.

"What are you smiling about?" said Henna looking from her phone to her sister.

"Just, I love you all so much. Thank you for standing by my side. I love you all."

"Love you too," said Henna, "now stop being soppy and sit down with us. If all we can do it wait, we may as well do it watching some decent TV."

Chapter 50.

The next morning Anita woke with a fright. Her mind instantly when to Anand and hoped he was safe. She jumped out of bed and went straight to his room. No Anand.

Emptiness greeted her.

She walked quietly across to the spare room, the room where Khush spent most of his time, and quietly opened the door. Her parents were sleeping soundly, clearly tired from the previous evening.

Walking quietly down the stairs, she went through in her mind what had happened to her the day before; the look on Khush's face as he held the letter out to her, the threat from her brother-in-law, the sound of his voice when he had told her it was her fault and then put the phone down on her, the frustrating and unhelpful conversation she'd had with the police officer, and the comfort and support of her family and friends throughout the evening. She looked at the time, 7am, too early to call the police. But not too early to try Khush's phone again. As she balanced the phone between her ear and her shoulder she filled and switched on the kettle.

Straight to voicemail.

"Damn you Khush," she whispered putting her phone down on the counter.

As she grabbed a mug and began making a coffee, she heard someone move behind her. She turned hoping to see her son's sleepy face smiling at her holding onto a teddy. She frowned.

"Morning," said Jitesh stretching, still wearing his clothes from the previous night and looking at the disappointment on Anita's face, "expecting someone else?"

"Hoping for Anand," she said sadly, "want a coffee?"

"Yes please," said Jitesh nodding, "strong and sweet, just like me!"

Anita laughed and poured him a cup. "Did you sleep ok?"

"Yeah, ok, I guess," said Jitesh shrugging his shoulders and scratching at his head, "dare I ask you the same question?"

"Slept ok I guess," said Anita sitting opposite Jitesh cradling her own coffee mug in her hands, "dreams felt loud and chaotic, so although I slept, I don't feel rested."

Jitesh nodded taking a sip of his coffee. "So Anita, what's the plan for today?" he asked.

"Waiting I guess. Waiting until midday then I'm going to call the police if Khush doesn't get in contact or come home by then."

"Good plan."

"Yeah, I need to be specific. No room for what ifs and speculation."

"True."

"Jit?"

"Yeah?"

"Thanks so much for staying. You know you didn't have to. I appreciate you so much. Thanks."

"No need to thank me," said Jitesh looking at Anita, "I wouldn't do this if I didn't care about you and your wellbeing. I need to know you're ok and I need to know you're going to be happy."

Anita looked at the sincerity in Jitesh's eyes and smiled warmly. For a moment, the two just stared at one another in silence. It was comfortable and Anita felt safe there in that shared moment with Jitesh.

"I smell coffee," said a voice breaking the silence.

"Morning Henna," said Jitesh standing up, "yeah coffee is made. Want some?"

"Yes please" said Henna raising her eyes at Anita as they watched him find his way around the kitchen and pouring Henna a coffee.

"How do you like your coffee?" he asked.

"Strong and sweet- just like me," Henna said.

Anita and Jitesh looked at one another and laughed.

"What?" said Henna frowning looking at the pair of them, "what's so funny? Why are the pair of you laughing like schoolgirls?"

"No reason," said Anita grinning and winking at Jitesh, "no reason at all."

"Weirdos," said Henna taking the mug of coffee from Jitesh's hands, "thanks Jit. So, what's the plan for today?"

"Wait until midday, then make the calls," summarised Anita nodding.

"Good shout. Where are mum and dad?"

"Still sleeping."

"Ok, let them sleep then," Henna said, then running her hands through her hair she groaned, "I need a shower though sis. I think, if mum and dad stay with you, Ash and I can go home, go get showered. Then when we're back mum and dad can do the same. What do you think?"

"Yeah sure," said Anita waving her hands about, "doesn't bother me. You can all go and get showered if you want, I can handle it on my own."

"No," said Henna and Jitesh at the same time.

Looking at one another and smiling, Henna added, "No, someone will be here with you all the time. You're not being left on your own. Especially if he comes back."

"I have to agree with Henna," said Jitesh, "I'll stay until Henna and Ash come back, then when your parents go, I'll go too. And I'll come back too. I'll call Reena and see if she needs picking up on the way."

"Sounds like a good plan" Henna said smiling, "now we just have to wait for that prick to bring your son home."

Anita watched the clock for the rest of the morning; she tried to keep herself busy emptying the dishwasher but choosing to handwash the breakfast dishes instead of filling them in the machine. She tidied the rooms in the house, changed bedsheets and vacuumed around the house too. Anything to distract her from watching the clock move slower than she could handle. More phone calls were made to Khush's friends and his family, but no additional news came from that. Anita had even started to look at divorce lawyers and the process she would have to go through, but she wanted to wait until Reena came by to speak to her about it.

By midday everyone had been home, freshened up and returned to support Anita. Jitesh had picked up Reena on his way back without Prem, her mum had agreed to look after him again for the day. Anita was surrounded with love, and she finally felt like she could tackle Khush and his scheming head on; she felt strong and confident and she knew this was what she needed to show him in order to get her son back.

At 12.05 Anita looked at her parents and they nodded.

"I'm calling the police," she stated boldly, "He won't answer his phone, he hasn't contacted anyone, and he still hasn't brought back my son."

They all looked at her in agreement. She stared at the phone in her hand and dialled the number the officer she had spoken to had given her.

"Hello, Officer Miller speaking."

"Hello, Officer Miller, it's Anita Govind. I came in yesterday to speak to you about my husband. He took our son without me knowing and hasn't been in contact since and he hasn't come home with Anand."

"Ah, yes Mrs Govind, I remember. So, tell me about what's happened since we last spoke."

Anita filled in Officer Miller with what she and her family had done to try and track down Khush and Anand without any luck.

"Right," Officer Miller said clearly taking notes, "this is what we are going to do. We are going to try and trace his car, it's been 24 hours since he has gone missing with your son, and so we will do this so to make sure they are not in any danger or hurt. I will get some officers to come to your home and take a few statements from everybody. They may ask some of the same questions again, but they need to do this. Please ask everyone to stay there."

"They aren't going anywhere," Anita said smiling at her entourage staring at her in silence.

"Fantastic. We will be in contact if we hear anything about the car. And if you hear any more please contact me on this number."

"Ok, thank you, bye," said Anita putting the phone down and turning to her family.

"So?" asked Henna as soon as Anita had hung up.

"She is putting an alert out for his car. Just so they can check it's not in some ditch somewhere. They are sending officers here to talk to you lot too. Take statements. We don't have to keep calling family and friends and his mobile anymore, but I want to. Just to make sure."

"Good plan," said Jitesh.

"You seem so calm," added Ash getting up and squeezing her shoulder, "are you ok?"

"Yeah, I actually am," Anita said smiling, "I know what I need to do. This is the end of me and Khush, but I need my son back first. He may have broken me down, but he won't take Anand away. Not without a fight. I don't think there is any moving on for us from this. I can't let him take Anand."

Chapter 51.

A few hours later and the police officers who had been sent by Officer Miller had come, taken statements from everyone, including Anita again, and left. Anita's parents sat watching TV as Henna, Ash, Jitesh, Reena and Anita talked at the dining table in the kitchen.

"So," said Henna looking tired, "what's the plan if he comes back today?"

"Well," said Anita looking at her sister, "I guess it all depends on what he does. I would prefer if he came home, and we talked about what's happened-"

"Talk? Again Anita?" said Henna shaking her head in disbelief, "Don't you think you've done enough talking?"

"No, I don't." Anita replied.

"Talk doesn't seem to be working with him, does it though?" Ash asked.

"Not that kind of talk," said Anita smiling at her brother-in-law, "I mean, we will talk about what he has done, then I will tell him what will happen."

There was a pause, they all looked at Anita expectantly; worry, compassion and surprise etched upon their faces. Looking back at the people that loved her, Anita was filled with hope. She felt a desire to live again and be her own person; a chance to change and fight for what Khush had taken away. Her family's brute force and support of her throughout the worst time in her life helped her begin to believe in herself again. She wasn't going to let them down.

"I am going to tell him that I will be leaving him. And I will be taking Anand with me to mum and dad's place."

Anita looked at Reena and smiled, "I will tell him that I have already looked at divorce lawyers and will start the process as soon as I can."

Reena nodded and smiled, she had been spending the past day looking at divorce lawyers and contacting her own one for Anita.

"That's good," said Jitesh placing a hand on Anita's, "we just want to help you get out from his hold."

"And I appreciate everything you all have done. You've all stood by me throughout all this," then she looked at Henna and Jitesh, "and through worse."

"You've been through so much," said Ash getting up and giving Anita a hug, "we'll be here for you. Always."

"Thanks," said Anita leaning into the hug. It was times like these that Anita truly realised that the people around her, were the people she gained strength from too.

A comfortable silence fell upon the group as each contemplated what was to come and how Anita would be cared for throughout.

"Anita!" called her mum from the living room breaking the rare serene moment, "It's Khush, he's called."

Anita's head snapped towards the living room and her body jolted. This was it. This was what she needed to hear. She ran into the living room, almost knocking her mum over who was standing by the doorway looking at her husband.

"What's happened? Where is he?" she asked blood pumping through her faster than she could handle. She reached out a hand to the wall to steady herself.

"Dad's on the phone," said her mum.

"To Khush?" breathed Anita her head swimming.

"No, to Khush's dad."

"What?" said Anita shaking her head, "I'm confused? I thought you said he called?"

"Just give me a minute, wait until dad's off the phone, then you'll know more." Henna said standing behind Anita.

Anita looked behind her, they had all followed her out of the kitchen. As a group, they all walked into the living room, not taking their eyes off Anita's dad who was at the end of the conversation and beckoning them in.

"Ok, thank you Akash. Yes, I will tell her now. Ok, bye."

"Dad?" asked Anita standing up again almost as soon as she'd sat down, "What was Khush's dad doing on the phone? What did he say? Does he know where they are? Are they there?"

"Sit down Anita," her dad said nodding towards the seat she had just vacated, "and I will explain all."

Anita sat down, her hands clammy, her body going cold. She reached for her wedding ring to spin around on her finger, a habit she had picked up during the bad moments with Khush but remembered that she had taken it off and hadn't put it back on. She clasped her hands together instead.

"Ok," her dad said looking at his daughter and smiling, "I will say it all, then questions later?"

"Ok" whispered Anita trembling a little.

"That was Khush's dad on the phone. I called him while you were in the kitchen to see if Khush had made any contact with them. He had. He had called his dad an hour ago saying he needed somewhere to go. So, he is at his dad's house now, with Anand. Anand is happy and safe. When he got there his dad asked what was going on and he had to tell him. His dad knew most of it already and he knew that everyone was looking for Khush."

"Ok, so we go over and get Anand," Henna said nodding and looking at Ash.

"No, Henna," said her dad holding a hand up to her, "Khush said he was going to come home with Anand but knew we were all here, so refused to come in."

"Still trying to hold on to control," muttered Henna gritting her teeth.

"He said that he will let you have Anand back," continued Anita's dad ignoring her sister's comment, "he won't give him up, just let him be with you. He won't give Anand up and said he will fight for custody."

"I don't want to fight for custody," said Anita looking at her dad, "he is a good dad, and Anand needs him. But he can't stay with him now."

"Yes, that's what his dad said. Anita, Khush's dad was very kind to us, he persuaded Khush to come back and let Anand come home with you. Akash wasn't sure what his son had done, but seeing Khush and speaking to him, what he did find out, he did not approve of."

Anita sat there in stunned silence. Her father-in-law had helped her?

"So, what's next then?" asked Jitesh.

"Akash has said that Khush will allow you and me to come and collect Anand from the house. Khush has said if you choose to stay here, in your home, then he will stay with his dad. He said apart from seeing Anand, he will give you space and will accept that whatever you decide about your marriage, although he is not happy about it. He thinks you shouldn't quit on the marriage yet. Says divorce is the easy way out. He thinks you should be together but knows that may not be possible. What happens about where you stay, is up to you. He said he will give you permission to leave."

"Permission? Allow her to go get her son? Ridiculous," scoffed Henna.

Anita closed her eyes taking everything her dad said in and swirling it around her head. *Divorce is an easy way out?* She thought, *so why doesn't all this feel easy?*

"So, I'm getting what I want?" she asked a moment later to no one in particular.

"You're getting what you need," said Reena kneeling next to Anita and placing a hand on her arm, "this is your chance to make the changes you need to make, Anita."

"Anand will be with you beta," said her mum smiling.

"And you won't have Khush controlling your life," added Henna.

Anita breathed, and she felt her head clear. This was far from the idyllic ending, but her body still felt on edge a little. Things could easily go wrong again. Khush could easily change his mind like her had many times before.

"So, what are you going to do sis?" asked Henna, her voice soft and full of concern.

"I'm going to go collect my son."

Chapter 52.

Anita's hand squeezed her father's hand as they stood at the door of the house she had been to many times and lived in over the years; Khush's childhood home. She had felt confident and calm as she and her dad had driven to her father-in-law's house, but now standing at the front door, about to knock, she felt nauseous. Her face was pale and hot at the same time.

"Are you ok?" whispered her dad next to her, placing his other hand over the one she was holding tightly on to.

"Yeah," she said nodding, "I just didn't expect to see his brother's car here too. I didn't know they would all be here."

"Well, just like we are with you, Khush's family will be there to support him too. But don't worry. I'm here."

"Thanks," Anita said smiling. Her dad was always the one who saw reason and was logical, one trait of his she didn't get from him.

She took a deep breath and knocked.

The door opened almost immediately, as if the person who opened the door was waiting right on the other side.

"Anita," said a small voice.

Anita looked up to see her sister-in-law Payal at the door. She looked like she had been crying. She looked smaller than Anita remembered.

"Payal," breathed Anita wanting to reach out and hug her.

"Will you come in?" she asked stepping aside.

Anita stepped forward, looked past the doorway and froze; there, standing at the end of the hallway, was Khush. Fear and panic swallowed Anita's control of her body and she couldn't move. She couldn't breathe. He was staring straight at her.

"I think we will stay here, Payal," said her dad sensing Anita's grip tighten on him, "no disrespect to your Papa, but we will stay here."

"Ok," said Payal stepping away from the open door, "I'll get him."

As she walked away from the door Anita's dad gently pried his hand from her grip. He put a hand on her shoulder and spoke quietly so only she could hear him.

"I am here beta. Don't worry, he won't get near you. You don't even have to talk to that man again if you don't want to. I will do the talking."

Anita merely nodded, unable to take her eyes from Khush who looked directly at her too. *Mind games* she thought to herself, *even at this stage he's still playing mind games with me. Don't let him win this one. Head up, shoulders back and be confident…or at least pretend you are.*

She straightened herself up and breathed deeply. He hadn't said a word. Just stood there staring. Anita wasn't going to let him rattle her anymore. From the corner of her eye she saw her dad smile.

"Anita, Vinod, will you come in?" Khush's dad had walked up to the front door and held out an open arm inviting them into his home.

Anita looked past him at Khush, who had disappeared quickly.

"No thank you Akash," said Anita's dad shaking his other hand politely, "we will stay here. It will be better for us. Thank you for the offer."

"It's ok," said Akash nodding in understanding, "Anita, I don't know what to say."

Anita looked at Khush's dad. He seemed smaller than she recalled. Older. She realised that she had only seen him a few times since the funeral and that he had been sullen on those

312

occasions too. His fiery temperament seemed to have been fizzled out, now there was just a sad, old Indian man standing in front of her.

"Thank you," she said louder than she thought she was able to.

"Ok, I'll get Anand." Khush's dad turned to walk back into the house when Khush appeared at the end of the hallway again.

"He's here dad," he said bringing forward Anand who looked tired. Khush's voice didn't sound like his own. It sounded alien to Anita, much quieter and more unsure than his normal voice. Not cold. Anita realised that he'd been affected by everything too. But she forced herself not to feel sorry for him.

"Mum," squealed Anand as he saw his mother standing at the door. He ran straight into her arms and squeezed tight.

"Anand. Oh I'm so happy to see you!" said Anita kneeling down and kissing her son over and over again all over his face, "Are you ok?"

"He's fine," Khush snapped, the edge back in his voice again.

"Khush, inside. Now." Khush's dad said sternly looking at his son and frowning.

Without a word, Khush turned on his heels and walked away.

"Thank you for doing this Akash," Anita's dad said shaking Khush's dad's hand and nodding.

Nodding, Khush's dad quietly said, "Anita, again, I know it is between you and Khush, but I would like to say that I love my grandson. I know I should not ask this of you now, but I need to. Please do not take away Anand from us. We would still like to be in his life. I know Khush would too."

"I wouldn't do that to Anand, or to you all. You will still see your grandson grow up," Anita replied standing up.

313

Anita looked at her father-in-law, a man she had once despised, and felt pity; this man in front of her had stripped himself of his pride and anger and had just pleaded with her. She wasn't so spiteful that she would keep Anand from him. He nodded, a small smile trying to contain his tears.

"Please tell Khush that Anita and Anand will be staying with us. He can have the house. She will be gone by this evening." Anita's dad said shaking Akash's hand again.

Ruffling his grandson's hair and giving him a quick hug, Akash turned to Anand, "be good to your mummy ok? See you soon beta."

"Bye, bapa. See you soon," said Anand following his mum to the car.

Getting in the car and shutting the door, Anita felt something less than relief and comfort. Waves of fear, shame and regret washed over her too. There was still a long way to go and Anita was petrified of what was to come, but this was the beginning of her next chapter. Her eyes stung with tears, and she looked at the house seeing Khush standing at the window looking out at them, a blank expression on his face.

"Wave to your dad," she said to Anand through tears.

Epilogue: One Year Later

The sound of the letterbox clattering made Anita jump. She ran to the front door scooping up letters, leaflets and a thick envelope she had been waiting to arrive for weeks. She threw the rest on the counter in the kitchen and held the envelope in her hands, breathing heavy. She turned it around carefully as if whatever was inside would be broken if she didn't handle it with care. It didn't look life changing, just a simple white indiscreet card envelope with her name on the front.

Mrs Anita Govind.

She smiled and ripped open the envelope.

"Is that what I think it is?"

Anita jumped. She had thought she was alone and the sound of a deep voice entering the kitchen had surprised her.

"This? Yes, it is," she said smiling and waving the envelope in front of her dad.

"Have you opened it yet?"

"No, well I have but I haven't looked at the papers yet."

"Want to be on your own beta?" he asked.

"Not at all, actually I may wait until mum is here before I open it."

"She'll be here in a minute. She is just doing her prayers."

Anita and her father sat in silence for the next few minutes, each looking at the envelope and then at one another.

"Mum," Anand's voice broke the silence and the electric energy Anita could feel build.

"Yes Anand?" she said swivelling the chair to face her son.

He had grown tall in the past year. His hair had grown thicker and curlier, just like his father's, and his face become more angled and featured. Anita couldn't deny it, her son was the miniature version of Khush.

"Can I have a snack please?"

"Sure," said Anita pointing to the fridge, "apples in the fridge, pears and oranges too. If you want a banana there's some on the side."

"Fruit?" Anand said looking sulkily at his granddad, "got anything else?"

"Nope. Fruit it is for now. If you want something else, you can wait until lunchtime."

Anand, defeated and knowing it, walked over the counter and grabbed a banana. He looked at his grandad and pushed his bottom lip out.

"Bapa…"

"Sorry beta," said Anita's dad laughing, "your mum has said fruit only. I have to stick with what she said otherwise I won't be allowed my snack either."

Anita laughed as Anand's head bobbed; he was trying to roll his eyes at his grandad and not laugh at the same time. He failed at both.

"Ah mum!" he groaned.

"Can you do me a favour too, please?" Anita added.

"Mmm?"

"Can you go get your aajima please? See if she is finished with her prayers?"

"Ok," said Anand and spinning around he almost knocked over Anita's mum who was walking into the kitchen.

"Oops," said Anand arms outstretched, "sorry aajima."

"It's ok beta," said Anita's mum ruffling his hair, "what did you need me for Anita?"

"It's arrived." Anita said pointing to the white envelope on the tabletop.

Her mum's eyes widened, and she smiled.

"Good news?" she asked her hands together as if in prayer.

"She hasn't opened it yet she was waiting for you too." Anita's dad responded.

"I am here now. Open it then."

Anita reached nervously for the envelope. She knew what was inside, and knew what it would say, but she still felt apprehensive. It had been almost a year since she had filed for divorce, and only a handful of months since her and Khush had gone through the mediators on custody over Anand, their joint possessions and the house she no longer lived in. To Anita's surprise everything had gone as she had wanted it to; the house would change to just in Khush's name and he would buy her out, she gained some of the possessions in the house that were important to her including most of Anand's things, and they would have joint custody of their son, with Anand spending two weekends a month with Khush and one evening a week with him too. This suited both of them and made life easier for Anand too. All she had needed was for Khush to finally sign the papers.

These papers.

She leafed through the documents and stopped at the most important one; the one that legally and officially ended her marriage to Khush. The one that released her from his tyrannical hold, that freed her from his controlling mind games and his hateful words. As she read the words, she felt a weightlessness envelope her and felt the shackles fall away from her heart and mind. This significant piece of paper allowed Anita to be freed, to be confident again, to find the time and space to find herself again too. She had finally done it.

She was divorced.

Anita sat in silence and her parents mirrored her silence with their own. She blinked. Blinked again. Hoping that she wasn't dreaming, that she wasn't going to be woken up and still be in her bed next to the man who had spent years of her life breaking her down to nothing.

"Anita?" her mum broke the silence and bringing Anita back to reality.

"It's done." Anita said and then she wept.

Later that evening, Anita looked around the table at her loved ones; her parents so strong and pure in their love for her; her sister and Ash both passionate and together, a force to be reckoned with; Jitesh a kind and loving man who saw through the façade she had once tried to shield herself with; and Reena a dear friend, who had shown Anita in more ways than one, that there was life beyond the pain she had suffered. Anita was happy and she felt fulfilled. These were the people who had helped her through the crisis and sheltered her and comforted her and Anand through the hard days. And there had been many. But they had all persisted and eventually Anita had broken free and she knew that without this family in front of her, she would never have been able to.

The evening was spent laughing, eating, drinking and celebrating Anita's divorce. As the night went on her parents were the first to retire to bed, the celebrating had led to her dad telling and retelling drunken stories about his time as a 'naughty little boy', climbing trees and stealing mangos from the neighbours. Stories Anita and Henna had heard a thousand times and would normally resist and voice their boredom with. Tonight however, they allowed it, smiling at the glistening eyes of their father and his slurred words, and laughing at their mother's rosy cheeks and high-pitched giggles.

Henna and Ash were next to leave. They left hugging and kissing Anita, telling her how proud they were of her and what she had managed to achieve. Anita grinned as a tipsy Henna proudly announced the next stage was to get Anita a man that would be everything that Khush failed to be. Saying

God's name for a different reason. Ash had rolled his eyes and led Henna away smiling and saying that she would regret all the wine the next day when she had to get up for work.

Reena and Jitesh stayed with Anita as she cleared up the kitchen. Filling the dishwasher that she had persuaded her parents to finally buy, with empty wine glasses and plates. They sat as a three for some time, eventually opting for soft drinks, talking about life and Anita's hopes for the future. An hour later, they were watching TV in the living room and Anita yawned.

"Think that's our cue to leave," Reena said standing up and stretching her long legs.

"Agreed," said Jitesh doing the same, "want a lift home Reena?"

"Yeah thanks," Reena said grabbing her coat, "saves me getting a taxi home or getting him to pick me up."

"Yeah, I don't think he'd like that!" said Anita laughing.

Reena had been seeing her new man for almost six months and they were totally smitten with one another. Anita loved seeing Reena happy and was secretly pleased the match-up between her and Jitesh hadn't worked.

As they walked out of the house, Reena ahead and walking in a not so straight line to Jitesh's car, Jitesh turned to Anita. They hugged and Anita closed her eyes and smiled.

"Anita," he said still holding on to the hug.

"Mmm," said Anita pulling away and looking at his face. Her sight was a little blurry from the wine, and her head felt faint, but she could still see the hints of green in his hazel-coloured eyes. He looked nervous.

"Can I ask you something? I've been wanting to ask it for a long time, but today seems the best time to ask."

"Sure" said Anita.

"Do...I was thinking maybe...and it's ok if not...but...do you want to go out for a meal or something with me?"

Anita smiled, Jitesh was anxiously shifting his weight from one foot to the other.

"You mean like a date?"

"Yeah, just me and you. I like you, but I don't want you to think that-"

Anita leaned in and pressed her lips against his, stopping him from speaking further. The kiss tasted sweet, a mixture of wine from her lips and juice from his. She felt his body tense for an instant then relax against hers as he kissed her back.

She pulled away from him and smiled, "I thought you'd never ask."

Acknowledgements

I would like to thank many people for the help and advice given on this book. My thanks are not just for those who became my test readers and editors but for those who were able to provide me with anecdotes from people who have been through the trials and heartache the character in my book, Anita, goes through.

Thank you to my amazing sister, Jyoti, my beautiful friends Nisha, Dina and Catherine whom without advice and notes, I would not have been able to make a character like Anita real.

I would also like to thank my mother-in-law Sandi, who was one of the first to read this- I will forever be grateful for your help in editing out any mistakes I made whilst blindly throwing my words onto the page.

Thank you to an amazing artist and friend, Anisha Chauhan, who seamlessly painted and created my book cover; such talent should not go unnoticed.

Finally, I would like to thank anyone who reads this and makes even the slightest connection with Anita's plight- you are all amazing, strong and brave. There has been an awful lot I have learned writing this book, but the most poignant thing is that I am one of the lucky few.

I love you all.

About the Author

Maaya Brooker is a teacher of English and Media, happily married and mother of a beautiful daughter, living in Milton Keynes, in the UK. She spends a lot of her time reading thrillers and crime books, so writing this one was a step outside of her comfort zone, but the stories she read in her research and experienced through people she spoke to, called out to her to write this book.

Maaya Brooker has also written a spooky horror Children's book based on her daughter called The Danger Kids: The Haunted House and Other Stories.

You can contact Maaya on the following social media:

Twitter @maayabrooker

Instagram @maayabrooker

Facebook https://www.facebook.com/maaya.brooker

Printed in Great Britain
by Amazon

41567277R00178